CREEP

CReeP

EIREANN CORRIGAN

Scholastic Press

New York

Library of Congress Cataloging-in-Publication Data available

ISBN 978-1-338-09508-1

10 9 8 7 6 5 4 3 2 1   19 20 21 22 23

Printed in the U.S.A.   23

First edition, October 2019

Book design by Christopher Stengel

for Anne Glennon—
She knows why since she knows all.

CHAPTER ONE

People who don't live here, who have just heard of our town, know it for two reasons. Back in the 1980s, a man murdered his whole family, wrapped their bodies up in sleeping bags, and cut his own face out of every photo. He stopped the mail, called the high school to say the family was off on a trip, and then disappeared. He left the lights on throughout the house, some lamps shining through the windows. A month passed, and that provided the man with a head start, until the lights burned out one by one, and the neighbors finally called the police.

I'm less familiar with that story. After all, it happened

long before my time. But the house still stands, as unyielding as it looks in the black-and-white photos on Wikipedia. Someone bought it eventually, but they never decorate the yard with Christmas lights or place boxes of flowers in front of the windows. As if that's the compromise. They moved into that home, with all its ghosts, but decided to never celebrate living there.

Lots of people in Glennon Heights think the house should have been bulldozed. Maybe you can scrub blood off the floorboards, but people still died in those rooms. When you stand at the front walk and consider approaching, the fine hairs on the back of your neck might prickle. You might feel a static electricity crackle over you, carrying a current of fear.

I don't believe in ghosts the way most people imagine them. When I walk by that house, I don't envision floaty wisps shaped like people darting in and out of the attic windows. No invisible clammy hand clamps on my shoulder. I think it's more likely that when people feel really intense feelings— the worst kind of feelings—those feelings imprint the earth and the air. They don't dissipate even when we disappear. So it wouldn't matter if you knocked the house down where that family died. Those deaths would still create a permanent and painful haze on that property, in our town.

Besides, if we intend to go around knocking houses to the ground, we can't stop with that one. There is, after all, another house that put Glennon Heights on the map. Another place of nightmares. And now, after everything that's happened, I get the same cold ball in my belly when I walk past it. The Donahue house. The Sentry's house. What happened there stamped the air with fear and put a family to ruin as much as if they were sitting at their dining room table, eating supper as the bulldozers plowed through.

CHAPTER TWO

I'm pretty much an expert on the Sentry. As Janie Donahue's closest friend, I can speak with authority on the matter. From the morning the moving truck blocked her driveway until classes started six weeks later, Janie and I spent almost every minute together. You know how it is when you meet someone designed the same way as you? When she makes sense to you like no one else has ever made sense? That's the reassurance that meeting Janie Donahue gave me.

It's not like I didn't have friends before Janie. Glennon Heights is tiny enough that everyone has to get along. It's the kind of place where your mom makes you invite the entire class to your birthday party. But every year, in every grade, there's always one or two kids who just can't handle the rest of us. I can remember in kindergarten it was Raf Cruz because he hated loud noises so much he wore earmuffs year round. And now none of us would dare to mention the earmuffs. Raf is certainly not the same Raf, with his tousled hair and dirt bike expertise. Now our outsider is probably Julia Haber because she refuses to launder her yoga pants and picks her top lip until it bleeds.

It has never been me. I've always moved through school with a group of girls who dress like me and talk like me. We sleep over at each other's houses and text our outfits in the mornings. Sometimes the configurations change; Kaia, Allie, Brooke, and me evolved into Brooke, Allie, and me, and then adjusted to Allie, Kaia, Mirabelle, and me. With drama club and cross-country practice, we made room for Tyler and Nicholas. Liam and Micah. Eddie Roebuck. I could walk into the coffee shop and join a table. Whenever a teacher announced group work, my heart didn't sink. I didn't ever have to search desperately for someone to talk to.

But with Janie, it was another kind of talking. I never worried that what scrolled across her brain was different from the thoughts scrolling across her face. That first day, when the Donahues arrived, my mom said, "Olivia, you should stop over and introduce yourself." I did it to be kind, standing at the back door and calling out, "Yoo-hoo?" because it seemed like something a neighbor might say. As soon as the syllables floated up from my mouth, I heard my mistake. *Yoo-hoo* was an old person sound, the coo of a fat lady in an apron, the jolly neighbor.

Janie was unpacking boxes in the kitchen. She wore a bandanna on her hair and cut through the packing tape with an enormous carving knife. I could see the silver blade glinting in the light.

"Hello?" she called out.

"Hi. I'm Olivia. Danvers. From up the street."

Janie stood up and pushed the screen door open. I could tell she was about my age, maybe a year younger. She blew the hair out of her eyes and her face crinkled with questions.

"Do people talk like that here?" she asked.

"No. I was trying it out," I answered. She nodded like she absolutely understood and held the door open for me to come inside.

"Olivia Danvers, you've been promised to me," Janie proclaimed in a solemn voice while brandishing the knife. My eyes must have darted back to the door because she laughed, a quick bark that sounded almost angry. "Don't worry—you're not the first person my parental figures have ruthlessly used to get their way in the world. They're basically mercenaries climbing over the corpses of anyone who doesn't scurry out of their way."

"Janie, stop." A tiny woman with a blond pixie cut hovered

in the kitchen doorway. "Please excuse my charming daughter, Olivia. The realtor told us someone Janie's age lived nearby. Edward McGovern—I believe he knows your aunt? It's so kind of you to stop by."

Janie glowered for a second and I thought, *This was the worst idea, ever. Thanks, Mom. Thanks, Janie's mom. Thanks, moms everywhere for insinuating yourselves into the social lives of your teenagers.*

Janie's smile broke through into a fit of giggles. "I'm sorry—sometimes I like to scare my mom and make her think I'm more like my brother, Ben, than my sister, Lucy. They're twins, but she's a valedictorian and he's a sociopath."

"Janie! Honestly!" Her mom shook her head. "I told you to stop calling your sister a valedictorian."

"She would have been." Janie leaned forward and revealed the first of five thousand secrets we'd share. "In our old town. Now she has to start from scratch and she's pretty much frothing at the mouth."

"What about you?"

Janie smiled in a small way, as if making a compromise with herself before she spoke. "Freshman year is a great time for me to move. I don't have to switch high schools like the twins." This bright version of her voice sounded more like her mom's. "Besides, we get to live in these digs." She gestured all around her. "Back in Northampton, we were not a mansion-dwelling family."

For the first time, I let myself look around and actually take the house in. My whole life, I'd lived four doors down and had never ventured past the front door. Sixteen Olcott Place was the kind of home you assumed would shelter someone famous. Or magical. A majestic Victorian with bay windows and a rounded turret, its three stories stacked up like the layers of a wedding cake. It was white, with gray slate shingles and shutters painted deep green. None of the other homes nearby matched its grandeur, and my dad said that made it vulgar—like a guest who'd shown up overdressed for a party. But what did he know? He measured homes by the amount of time it would take to mow the lawn.

The house did not have marble columns or those statues of lions poised on either side of the stone steps. But it could have. You wouldn't have wondered, *Hey, what are these disproportionately fancy lions doing here?* They would have fit right in.

I'd been trying to look around surreptitiously. I hadn't wanted to seem so easily impressed. When Janie called it a mansion, she gave me permission to openly stare. While the kitchen was all white marble and sleek silver, the rest could have been rooms in a church, with vaulted ceilings and the smell of furniture polish. So much wood everywhere— paneling on the walls and thin bands of darker wood edging the ceiling. The heavy sliding door that separated the kitchen from the dining room made me realize how lovely a plank of wood could be, with its deep chestnut color and the swirling pattern of its grain. Behind me, the windows stood taller than I could reach, the center one filtering sunlight through stained glass.

I could see a winding staircase with a thick, tawny bannister snaking toward the upper floors. In the living room, the fireplace yawned, flanked by two more soaring windows. Floor-to-ceiling bookcases stood in one corner; I hoped fervently that leaning back against one might trigger a mechanism that would swivel you into a secret chamber behind the wall. All the furniture looked small in the rooms, but I felt gratified to see the pieces shrouded in white sheets in the tradition of haunted castles and Scooby-Doo cartoons. Unpacked boxes and crates sat waiting all over the place, but the spaces still seemed empty.

I liked Janie the minute I met her. I liked the honest way she spoke and how she made me wonder what she'd say next. Some people, kids I've known forever, have no idea how tense they make me. Janie set me at ease.

But the truth is that even if she hadn't, I probably would've faked it, at least that first day or week. All those times I'd walked by the house, making up stories in my head, 16 Olcott had become a little bit my own.

Now I'd made it inside.

CHAPTER THREE

Before the Donahues moved to Glennon Heights, before they agreed to buy the house in the first place, the Langsoms lived there. And even before the Langsoms officially put the house on the market, I knew they were moving.

My mom and my aunt Jillian had taken over the screened-in porch for one of their Sangria Saturdays. Sangria is basically juice and booze and every time they mix up a pitcher, Aunt Jillian ends up staying in the guest room. That day was particularly rowdy because Aunt Jillian had expected to get the listing for 16 Olcott Place. She and my mom had gone to high school with Dr. and Mrs. Langsom. Mrs. Langsom had been Helena Davenport back then and she'd practically lived at my grandparents' house growing up.

Aunt Jillian works for House Max Realtors though, and the Langsoms listed elsewhere.

"Harrington's," Aunt Jillian sniffed.

"Well, it's a lovely property." My mom sat back on the glider.

"We list lovely properties."

My mom sat up to say, "I didn't mean—"

"This is Glennon Heights. Lots of lovely properties."

"And lots of them are listed with Harrington's, Jill. I wouldn't take it personally."

Aunt Jillian takes most things personally. She probably took the Langsoms getting married in the first place personally. Dr. Langsom was handsome—broad shouldered and soap star faced. He was a surgeon of some kind. Mrs. Langsom was glamorous and tan and always laughing about how much her three boys eat or how much laundry they generate.

The youngest Langsom, Thatcher, was a senior and cute in a smug, my-parents-send-me-to-water-polo-camp way. It shocked me to imagine the Langsoms moving with Thatcher about to graduate.

I tried to keep my voice bored, like it pained me to participate in the conversation. "How come they're moving anyway?"

But Mom and Aunt Jillian just went on as if I'd never even

asked the question—Aunt Jillian pouting and my mother trying to comfort her, but also trying to remind her that she
maybe didn't count as the entire reason the earth spun or the
Langsoms made real estate decisions.

I hate Sangria Saturdays. For one, I can't have friends
over if Aunt Jillian is stumbling around the screened porch.
My mom doesn't say that—she claims that she needs time
with her friends just like I do and that too many guests at
once makes the house feel chaotic. I want to say, well, yeah,
when one of those guests is drunk, it gets a little chaotic.
Instead I just think it. I don't point out that my mom doesn't
really have friends; she has her sister.

Once Mom got a little weepy herself and apologized to
me—solemnly and sincerely—for the absence of a sister in
my life. "Your father was always so adamant about only having one child, but I should have pressed harder . . ." I shut
that conversation down pretty quickly, but later by myself,
I lay in my loft bed and imagined another bunk below. I
would be the quiet, more practical sister just like my mom.
My sister would be funny and glamorous and would always
have a story to tell. Growing up with her would exhaust me,
though. Overshadow me.

Janie had a sister and a brother, but because Lucy and Ben
were twins, it was different.

"Even when they despise each other, it's a sealed bubble,"

Janie told me. It was still in the early days, just after she'd moved in. "It's still just a hatred between the two of them."

I didn't ask why they hated each other right then. I didn't want Janie to stop talking. She said, "People describe our family in terms of them: the twins and their little sister. I don't exist unless in relation to them."

"But you and Lucy are *sisters*." I pronounced the word like my mom does, as if it were sacred.

"Lucy doesn't work like that. She's basically a human hard drive." But then Janie's voice softened. "Not always. But growing up beside Ben ruined her life. You can't really blame her for refusing to engage."

"How did it ruin her life?"

Janie fidgeted. She picked at a peeling bit of paint on the back porch where we sat. "They're just polar opposites," she said finally. "Lucy doesn't understand the point of not being perfect. You'll see—she needs to rank the highest, run the fastest. But even that's not enough. On top of that, you're required to genuinely like her. Just wait—she hasn't launched her charm offensive on you yet. She'll learn your favorite bands; she'll offer to help with your homework. She'll do whatever it takes to make sure you like her more."

"More than what?"

"More than me."

"That's crazy."

But didn't I also have it in my head that I needed to hide Janie away somehow, like if she met anyone else, she'd disappear? As soon as she'd heard we were friends, Mom had offered a sleepover at our house. "Invite a bunch of the girls," she said. "Introduce Janie to the gang!" But I didn't. I knew it was the right thing to do, the kind of thing you were supposed to do, but it felt like that might ruin something—break some kind of secret spell that Janie and I had cast over each other.

Four days after the Donahues moved in, we did venture out to the coffee shop and I texted Kaia and Brooke to meet us. It was fine for the most part. Except Brooke got hypercompetitive once she heard Janie swam and Kaia did her thing when she makes really shocking comments to prove she's edgier than everyone else. We spent an hour at the corner table and I spent most of it wondering why my friends were my friends. How had I survived all these years?

They liked Janie. Of course they liked Janie. But her new address seemed to intrigue them more.

"I can't believe you live in the Langsom house," Kaia said as she basically buttered her bagel with envy.

"Have you found out any deep, dark secrets about *Thatcher Langsom*?" Brooke giggled and hid her face behind her large latte. Her eyebrows wriggled over her mug.

On cue, Kaia gasped dramatically. "Brooke!"

"Who's Thatcher Langsom?" Janie asked.

"He's hot. He's a senior. He's hot. He plays lacrosse. That doesn't matter, because he's still hot."

Janie asked, "What's wrong with lacrosse?"

I tried to be helpful. "Lax bros are what's wrong with lacrosse."

"Ben plays lacrosse," Janie admitted. Then she explained to the others, "Ben's my older brother. He's also a senior."

Kaia's eyes widened as she looked past us to the café counter. She started shaking her head frantically.

"What?" Brooke turned to look behind her.

"Don't!" Kaia hushed her. "Just stop!"

"What's going . . ." Her voice trailed off and she, like me, noticed the issue. "Whoa."

"I don't get it." We had lost poor Janie, who kept looking around Slave to the Grind for the source of all our drama.

"Thatcher Langsom—that's him," I told her. "Behind the counter."

Brooke howled with laughter and I kicked her under the table. Janie craned her head to see. "Don't stare," Kaia scolded.

"What's the big deal?"

"He must work here now."

"Well, I doubt he heard us."

"It's not that—"

"Then what? Why is that funny?" Janie sounded exasperated. I sank down farther in the red vinyl seats, trying to escape the disaster. She'd probably ask her parents to move again.

Just as I opened my mouth to smooth things over, Brooke explained, "The Langsoms don't work at coffee shops." But Thatcher stood there, clear as day, taking a new shift, his white apron signaling surrender to the town gossips.

"What does that even mean?" Janie asked.

"It just confirms a lot," Brooke announced imperiously. She couldn't stop herself. "We thought they were moving out of town. I mean, that's the only way it made sense. It's the Langsom house, whether or not you live there. The Langsom family built it generations ago. So when they put it on the market, it was just weird, especially during Thatcher's last year of high school. I mean, who moves right before their kid's graduation?"

"My family, for one," Janie said with an edge in her voice. "It's not ideal, but we're making it work."

"Yeah, you're making it work in a landmark home. And why? Why did you move here from—?"

"Northampton. And there were lots of reasons." The edge sounded sharper.

"Janie's dad was transferred—" I added, but she cut me off.

"There were lots of reasons."

I felt desperate to move on from the conversation. "Stuff like that happens," I said. "And we don't know—maybe Dr. Langsom got transferred too."

We were careening off-road somehow, into dangerous territory. But Brooke seemed determined to keep us skidding. "Clearly he didn't," she said. "Because Thatcher's still here. Only now, he's washing our mugs and mopping floors, which is seriously un-Langsom-like behavior. I mean, where is he living?"

"Maybe he's going to finish out the year on his own," Kaia offered. "His parents moved but he wanted to stay on."

"So what? He took a job to pay rent?" Brooke shook her head. "No, something else is going on. And luckily for Janie, whatever happened to the Langsoms gave her family a chance to swoop in and move here."

"Yeah. Lucky me," Janie said coldly.

Brooke bristled. "What does that mean?"

"It means why does it matter? Maybe they just felt like moving. Maybe that kid just feels like working at a coffee shop. Why do you all care so much?"

"You don't really understand the Langsoms," I tried to explain.

"They're a little snobby," Kaia offered.

Janie looked directly at me. "That's not what you said before. You said they were nice."

"Well, yeah, but kind of aloof, you know? Like they're kind to us little people. That type of thing."

"I didn't know money mattered so much around here."

"It doesn't!" Kaia and I practically leapt to say it at the same time.

"I mean, not really," I added. I turned back to see Thatcher smiling at the middle-aged woman at the register, handing back change that she promptly sank into the tip jar. The coins made a cheerful clanging noise as they landed. "The Langsoms sort of symbolize something in Glennon Heights."

"Well, he's a person," Janie said. "Not a symbol."

"Maybe you should go say hi," Brooke suggested. "Tell him who you are. Maybe he wants to come over and see his old bedroom."

To my complete relief, Janie laughed. She said, "I'll wait and let him wonder who I am a bit. Besides, I don't want to make my approach from a table of you goons." We all laughed then, pretending she was entirely joking. I told myself that I only imagined the way Brooke and Kaia rolled their eyes at each other. Just like Janie probably told herself that she'd eventually get used to us all; we couldn't be as shallow as we seemed.

And Thatcher Langsom?

His face remained as blank as his apron. I had no clue what Thatcher Langsom was thinking at all.

////////

After the listing went up with Harrington's, Aunt Jillian had made it her mission to get the scoop on the Langsoms' move. Days later she was back in our kitchen, reporting on the results of her sleuthing.

It hadn't taken much digging for her to discover Dr. Langsom hadn't been transferred; in fact, he wasn't allowed to practice medicine anymore. No one would say definitively why.

Aunt Jillian pursued various theories. First she assumed he'd been arrested for drunk driving, but then she worked out this whole story involving a missing prescription pad. Whatever he did, it was bad enough for them to revoke his license, instead of just suspending it.

"That poor woman," Aunt Jillian kept saying, in a way that made it absolutely clear she didn't feel sorry for Helena Langsom at all. "She was probably so embarrassed she couldn't come to me with the listing." My mom nodded in the way that usually calmed her sister down. "As if I would ever judge her situation!"

According to Aunt Jillian's sources, the Langsoms had planned for Thatcher to attend boarding school for his last year, just in case the story broke in the news. But Thatcher didn't want to leave, especially when he was about to captain the lacrosse team and college recruiters were circling. So they moved into a two-bedroom apartment on the other side of town.

"That's temporary," Aunt Jillian reassured my mom, as if it should matter to either of them where their former friend lived with her disgraced husband and deflated son. "He's still hoping the board reverses their decision, but he is absolutely deluded. Textbook denial—those surgeons, they all think they're infallible. And Helena's staying with him, even after all this."

"Well, Jill, you just don't pack it in the moment life gets hard," my mom murmured. I forced my eyes to stay on the pages of the book I'd been pretending had my full attention.

That night turned out to be one of the hottest of the summer. It was humid and stuffy in the house, so I went and sat on our front steps, thinking about my mom and wondering when her life had gotten hard and if it had stayed that way. Fireflies blinked across the lawns. Up and down our street, some porch lights shone, collecting halos of moths around them. Sixteen Olcott sat dark. I tried to imagine Dr. and Mrs. Langsom screaming at each other. Or Thatcher lying on his bed, holding a pillow over his head to block out the sounds.

I stared at the house—and it almost felt like the house was staring back.

It knew what had happened.

I could only guess.

CHAPTER FOUR

Like criminals on the run or a family whisked away by witness protection, the Langsoms had moved from 16 Olcott Place in the dead of night. Maybe they packed up all their possessions into brown cardboard boxes during the days and scheduled the movers to come long after dark. As the neighborhood slept, the movers skulked up and down the porch steps—somehow hauling out four generations of furniture and the wardrobes and belongings of a family of five without a loud grunt of exertion or the heart-stopping rattle of good china. Maybe Dr. Langsom slipped the driver a fifty-dollar bill and asked him to wait until he turned the corner before flicking on his headlights. They might have dressed in all black, the Langsoms and the movers, so that they looked like a band of night prowlers. They might have worn ski masks to camouflage themselves more thoroughly in the darkness.

Whatever they did, none of us saw it.

////////

We found out they'd left from the mailman, who wondered aloud when the new folks would be moving in. "Been on this route for forty years," he told my dad. "Strange to see that house in particular change hands."

We didn't know then who would be moving in, just that the house had been listed low, according to Aunt Jillian, and it sold fast. There wasn't an open house or anything—my mom had planned to go just to look around. By the time the realtor came by to hammer a sign into the lawn, it already read *SOLD*.

"Why do they need a sign, then?" I'd asked Aunt Jillian. We were walking my dog, Toby. Or rather, I was walking Toby and Aunt Jillian was capitalizing on the excuse to take a closer look at the Harrington's sign.

"It's a feather in his cap. Although a property that well maintained, priced to move, you'd have to be half-dead to botch that sale." She jabbed her finger at the sign. Ned McGovern's cheesy mug grinned at us from the swinging, wooden panel.

"Smug idiot," Aunt Jillian muttered. With the sign slightly moving, it looked like Ned was winking.

"You still hang out with him?" I asked Aunt Jillian, without being entirely sure she would answer. They had dated a little when he'd separated from his wife. It hadn't gone well.

"Ned McGovern? You remember that whole episode?" she asked. I looked straight at her in response. "Yeah, I guess that one would be hard to forget, huh? No. And that's okay." She turned away from the sign and tugged at Toby's leash in my hand. "Let's walk to the park."

I glanced sideways at Aunt Jillian. "You okay?"

She sighed. "Yeah. That was a hard time. But you know, Olivia, we were both adults, making adult decisions. I knew what I was getting into. Maybe I shouldn't have gotten into it. But I did."

"He's still married?" I knew he'd gotten back together with his wife. We sometimes saw them at church, sitting third row, with two little boys who drove toy cars all over Ned's shoulders.

"Yep. And I switched agencies. So we don't see each other. We don't talk. If Ned McGovern wrecks anything now, it sure won't be because of me." She looked at the house then. "And anyway—that place has a history, and part of me feels relieved that I don't have to deal with it. The less you tell the new owners, the better. That's always true."

"What do you mean?" I asked.

But she just shook her head and walked away.

//////////

That day I kept turning it over in my mind—the strange way that friendships sometimes work. I passed the four houses that stood between our home and the Langsom house. Which was no longer the Langsom house. Where my mom's best friend growing up recently lived, except that by the time she lived at that address, they were no longer best friends. I thought of the way I had felt so close to Kaia Gillespie in the second grade, how people pronounced our names LivandKai so frequently together it became its own name, to which we both answered. And we were still friends, but the rhythm of Brooke and Kaia sounded much more familiar lately. And that summer I'd hardly spoken to Allie Hodges, even though I used to go up with the Hodges to their lake house every Labor Day weekend, for years.

That's the ebb and flow I was thinking about when I followed Aunt Jillian up the street. My friendship with Janie Donahue did not ebb and flow and lap softly like lake water against the shore.

With Janie, friendship was more like the ocean, sometimes with crashing waves and an unexpected undertow.

///////////

Here is a comprehensive list of facts I learned about Janie Donahue in the last week of July and the first week of our friendship:

Her real-life laugh sounded like a fake laugh; she actually said, "Ha-ha-ha-ha."

She used to be pigeon-toed when she was little, and still had to wear specially molded inserts in her shoes, which meant she did not wear open-toed shoes, even flip-flops in the summertime.

Even though the pigeon-toed thing gave me pause, because people who walk like that tend to run faster than average, Janie didn't run cross-country, or even track. She wouldn't compete with me for a spot on the team. Her sister, Lucy, was the runner. Janie was into diving.

She could not remember a sequence of numbers to save her life, so we decided early on that we'd share a locker at school and I would remember the combo for both of us.

Janie hated the Beatles, and when I asked, "Who hates the Beatles?" it turned out she had this theory that a person either loves the Rolling Stones or the Beatles and whichever is the case reveals his or her whole personality.

That theory was probably her dad's, but she claimed it as her own.

I used to think I liked the Beatles fine, but sitting up in Janie's freshly painted and still empty room, with the milk crates that held her father's record collection between us, and listening to Mick Jagger's gravelly voice singing, "She's my little rock and roll," I stopped being so sure.

"I mean, okay," I told her. "But I still don't hate the Beatles. I don't see how anyone hates the Beatles." Throughout most of elementary school, our vacation bible school chorus had sung "Let it Be." No anthem of youth or anything, but a perfectly fine sentiment for a song.

"But it doesn't make you move in your seat," Janie pointed out. "Who would you rather dance to?"

"Well, you wouldn't sing this song at vacation bible school, that's for sure."

We abandoned records to unpack the rest of her stuff. Between us, we maneuvered a rolled-up rug to the center of the room and unfurled it. Janie was apparently really into chevron. "You think you'll try to stay in touch with anyone?" I asked. But what I meant was *Is there space for me?* Janie FaceTimed a lot with her old friends. Her phone would chime with texts. Back then, in the first weeks, she'd read them to herself so it felt like I existed on only one strand of her social life. She was also living another version, one that didn't include me.

"It feels like I'm in orbit," she told me. "You know, like in space? It's self-centered and everything, but it's hard to believe life is still going on like normal without me there. Like someone else will use the locker I would have used and after a week or two, it won't even seem strange that I'm not at lunch. Everything will just seal up again. Without FaceTime, it would feel even weirder—like when we left home, home evaporated."

"Would that be better or worse?" I asked. As I opened boxes, I handed over piles of clothes and Janie filled her closet with them. Janie's closet was worth moving to a new state for. It had built-in drawers and a small ladder that led up to the attic.

She shrugged. "I don't know. Maybe easier." She shut one drawer, then another, and looked past me at the shambles of bedding and boxes in the room. "My dad says I have four years here and that I need to make the most of them."

The Donahues talked a lot about college and the future and potential. I figured that out in the first few days, when Mrs. Donahue asked me about my courses and if most kids in Glennon Heights took the ACT or the SAT, which I didn't know because I am not some kind of prodigy like Lucy apparently is. Janie generally assumed the twins would be headed back to Massachusetts when it was time to go away to school. "At least Lucy will. She'll apply early to Smith."

"Will Ben apply there too?"

Janie snorted with laughter. "He wishes. Smith is all girls and that's probably why Lucy's so set on it—he can't follow her there. He might take a year off first anyway."

Ben still had not said a single word to me, even though I'd spent most of my waking hours at the house since the Donahues had first moved in. Occasionally, we'd see him in the kitchen and he'd grunt, but I honestly couldn't tell if he was making a minimal effort to acknowledge us or if they were accidental noises. I couldn't imagine Ben taking a gap year and volunteering in Honduras or building houses for

Habitat for Humanity. At that point, I could not picture him interacting with other people at all.

"What will he do?" I asked.

"He'll probably be on parole or something." Janie shrugged and laughed.

"I plan to go to college in your new closet."

"It's dope, right?"

"Are you kidding? It's entirely possible that we can climb that ladder and find ourselves in a magical realm."

"I'm thinking that once I get done with my room, I'll start taking over the attic before Lucy and Ben even realize it's open space." The attic extended the full length of the house. It was hot and creaky, but the beamed ceilings made it look like the inside of a Viking ship.

"I can basically run cross-country up there."

Janie grinned. "I'll ask to install a pool for Christmas."

I knew she was joking, but it was the kind of joke that pried open a window to talk about a topic I'd studiously avoided since the coffee shop debacle. I didn't know how Janie would take it, so instead of wading in, I just dove.

"Can I ask you a question? What does your dad do?"

"You mean, are we rich?"

"It's a really nice house."

"It's my mom's dream house." Janie looked around. "Maybe she's having a midlife crisis or something, but she found the listing online and just went crazy. She had to have it."

I tried to wrap my head around uprooting a whole family, making the kids switch schools, and moving to a new state after finding a house online. It was a beautiful house, but still. "Wait—are you serious? Aren't you so angry?"

"We had to move anyway." I waited for the rest of the explanation, but it didn't come. Instead, after a few beats of silence, Janie said, "But no, we're not rich. My dad's a consultant, so he can work from anywhere, really. And my mom's a nurse. I mean, I don't think we're hurting, but back in our old house, Lucy and I had to share a room. Now she gets a turret and I have that closet."

"But that doesn't just happen, right? Maybe they won the lottery. They just don't want to tell you in case it ruins your work ethic." I didn't want to believe Janie would lie but she wasn't making a whole lot of sense either. So maybe she was just wrong. Maybe it was Janie who was so trusting, believing her parents despite any logical explanation to the contrary. "Did somebody you know die recently?" I asked her. "Maybe it's an inheritance? Maybe your mom was caring for a really wealthy patient, who had no family of her own—"

"Seriously, all anyone seems to care about around here is money." Which was the last thing I wanted Janie to think, of course. I'd just gotten wrapped up in the mystery. Taking a step back, seeing it from her side, I felt instantly sorry.

"We don't— It really doesn't matter to anyone. I just wondered and figured it was better to ask."

Janie looked away and bit her lip and for a second it seemed like she had something else to tell me. Then she nodded. "It is better. I'd rather you ask. But if other people are wondering, Olivia, there's no story. It's my mom's dream house. She does a lot for us. We weren't going to stand between her and something that would make her so happy. At least I wouldn't anyway."

Because I didn't want to annoy her with more questions, I didn't ask Janie who would stand between her mom and 16 Olcott. None of it made a whole lot of sense, but it wasn't mine to make sense of. I tried to find a way back to the easy jokes we'd been sharing a few minutes before.

"So does that mean there's no budget for an attic pool?"

Janie looked grateful then, and lobbed a chevron throw pillow in my general direction. "Hey, I have four more years to get my room just right. Let's get out of here. There has to be a town pool or something, right? Can we go on our own? Or do we have to invite the catty coffee shop crew?"

I felt relieved that we'd escaped the tension I created by nosing around the Donahues' personal business. How could I have insisted we call Brooke and Kaia after that? Or anyone else who I couldn't guarantee would steer clear of the wrong questions? It was like I was some kind of ambassador between Janie Donahue and the gossiping forces of our small town.

Janie changed into a no-nonsense Speedo and a pair of denim cutoffs and strapped a pair of goggles onto her head.

Kaia would have asked her, "That's what you're wearing?" so I stopped the question at my lips. We detoured at my house on the way so I could change. "Hurry—I can already smell the chlorine," Janie insisted, so I took the steps two at a time and left her out on the front stoop. I chose a bikini and threw on a clean pair of running shorts, but tucked a silk sarong in my backpack along with sunscreen and two bottles of water.

I came banging out of the front door to find Janie staring at her own new home. "Jeez, it's really enormous, isn't it?"

I nodded toward my house. "In comparison."

"I didn't mean that," she rushed to say. "When we pulled up in the car the other day, for once we all went silent at the same time. My mom and dad had done a walk-through but it was the first time Lucy, Ben, and I had seen it." She shrugged like she was attempting to shake off a spell. "I live there now."

"Yeah, you do, you snob." She snapped her towel at me and we laughed halfway to the pool, riding our bikes with our towels around our necks. "No locks?" Janie asked when I guided her to the bike rack.

"No locks."

"I feel like Ben might end up stealing a lot of bikes," she joked. Or at least I thought she was joking.

I signed us in with the lifeguard and scanned the pool and the chaises for anyone we might know. Or rather, anyone I might know. In the back corner, close to the snack stand, Natalie Kaye and Nicole Brody hovered over their phones together. I recognized a few sophomores and juniors and saw a lot of younger kids—sixth and seventh graders, and a cabal of their moms holding court in front of the cabanas. And then there were a few couples, maybe home from college, stretched out and sunbathing.

My mom called the pool "one of the jewels of Glennon Heights" and it shone that way in the bright sun. My dad referred to it as "our obscene taxes at work" and maybe it was that too, but in the summertime it functioned as a social hub of our town just like the coffee shop and Tewksbury Park. It didn't matter if you went to vacation bible school or Hebrew school or CCD, you still had a family pass to the pool. Everyone gathered there, like we were cave people circling around the water hole.

I stood by an empty chaise, shimmied out of my shorts, and tied the sarong around my waist in one quick moment. Janie noticed and nodded her approval. "That's really pretty."

"Thanks."

"But we are going to swim, right? You do swim?"

"Not like I run."

"Meaning?"

I smiled. "Not fast."

Janie stepped out of her shorts and kicked them over to the chaise. "I swim really fast." And then she sprang from the deep end and dove in, cutting neatly into the surface of the water.

She didn't come up for air until she reached the far end of the pool. I hadn't realized how muscular she was, but as her arms cut rhythmically through the water, she became the sort of athlete I wished I could transform myself into: deliberate and powerful and absolutely in control.

She strode to the diving board purposefully, with her brow set in concentration, her gaze fixed at some point at the end of the board. She took four or five unwavering steps across, executed a quick two-part hop, then bounced off the board in spectacular fashion.

I had never seen someone dive like that in real life. She sprang up; her body coiled and she tucked her thighs into her arms, making a tight rotation in the air before slicing into the water.

The upperclassmen who had been lounging poolside sat up as Janie arrowed through the water in a blur of tan limbs and black Speedo. One senior boy even sauntered over to stand next to me and watch from the edge. He was tall and lanky with longer reddish hair tucked behind his ears. I recognized him, but didn't know his name. "Is that your friend?" he asked.

By that time, I'd ceased to breathe and was concentrating on Janie so I didn't have to look up at his face. Janie's legs kicked underwater while I managed to look at his feet. They had freckles and fine red hair sprouted from the tops of his toes.

"She go to Glennon Heights?"

"She does now."

"Nice." As if she heard him underwater, Janie headed straight for us. She broke through the surface and reached for the tiled edge, stretching her arms and shaking her wet hair out of her eyes. Lanky ginger nodded down at her; I could see his shadow moving on the stucco.

"Yeah?" Janie asked, as if he had made a whole statement I had somehow missed.

The lifeguard's whistle shrilly interjected. "No diving," he intoned.

Janie swung around and looked up. "There's a diving board."

"No diving like that."

Lanky ginger rolled his eyes. "Calm down, officer." His lips curved into the tiniest of smiles and he told Janie, "See you around." Then he headed back to his friends. I noticed how openly Janie watched him go.

"Who is that?" she asked.

"I don't know. A senior. Can we talk about that amazing thing you just did?"

"He must swim."

"I mean, I guess. You know you basically have a superpower."

"Should we go over?"

"No, we should not. They're seniors. All of them."

"Yeah, exactly. They're Ben and Lucy's age, not so much older than us."

I just looked down and shook my head. Janie could have gone over to them, no problem. They would have congratulated and complimented, and she would have pretended that she didn't how extraordinary she was, falling through the air like that. I would have stood there counting down the seconds until I could skulk away.

But Janie didn't press. "Okay. Are you going to swim?"

I laughed. "Those are my choices?"

That night we shut the pool down. I even stopped checking to see who was looking at us and just enjoyed slipping back and forth between the warm water and the cooler air. Janie snuck in dives any time the lifeguard looked the other way. Each time people craned their necks to see her and once a mom at the shallow end of the pool even clapped. Every so often, we took breaks to lean our backs against the side of the pool and talk.

"I feel like me again," she confessed, kicking her legs in front of her. "It helps to know that I can move to a whole other state but this"—she nodded at the pool—"will still feel like home."

"We can come back tomorrow."

"First thing in the morning?" Janie asked hopefully.

"It opens at eight, but that's really early. That's twelve hours." My fingers might still be pruned in twelve hours.

"Usually, I dive before school—every day."

"How about this? We get up early and run here and then you can swim."

"We can both swim, and by the end of the summer we will

be the most ripped girls in the freshman class. We'll be iron women."

I laughed at the idea of Janie and I strutting through the high school, intimidating upperclassmen with our well-defined calves. "I hope we have classes together. If we're in the same homeroom, that means we'll share gym and lunch too."

The lifeguard blew his whistle and called out, "Closing in five minutes!" But he said it with an inflection of respect in his voice. He'd noticed Janie too.

"Thanks." Janie nodded at him and boosted herself out in one strong motion. I climbed the ladder like the normal, un-bionic woman I am. "I have to get my parents to get a membership here too. What's the school pool like?"

I toweled off my hair and bit my lip, trying to remember. We'd taken a tour during orientation last May. "It's got water . . ."

"Boards?"

I shook my head.

My legs ached as we cycled home. I rode ahead and pointed out the houses of our classmates as we whizzed by. The sun was setting so we rode under a canopy of pink clouds. I remember thinking how lovely our town looked, how Janie couldn't possibly feel homesick on a night like this.

When we reached Janie's house, we walked our bikes around back and found her whole family on the patio. "Olivia!" Janie's mom called out my name as if I were the guest of honor at a party. Mrs. Donahue sat on a white wooden glider, beside Lucy. The two of them were shucking a pile of corn that sat between them. "You are right on time. We were just settling down for a late supper. Gavin, this is Olivia Danvers, from a few doors down."

I hadn't officially met Mr. Donahue before. Every time I'd seen him at the house, he'd had his cell phone pressed to his ear. Usually, he was gesticulating wildly with the other hand.

"Hello there, Olivia. Thanks for making Jane feel so welcome." He smiled broadly. "You want a burger? We'll put some more on." He nodded to Ben, who stood over the grill.

I expected Ben to glower, but he just smiled like any other teenage boy. And because he was a teenage boy and I was tragically socially inept, I found it impossible to make eye contact. Instead I murmured, "I like burgers."

"We were at the pool. It was heaven." Janie sat down and sighed dramatically. "And we're starving. Right, Liv? Aren't you starving?" Maybe she hadn't heard me. Or maybe she was throwing me a lifeline—a chance to participate in the conversation like an actual well-adjusted member of society.

"Yes," I managed. "I'm really hungry." And then, since that bit was so successful: "We swam a lot."

"Where did you all go?" Lucy sounded almost envious.

Janie stretched her arms. "There's a town pool."

"Cedar Ridge. Anyone can join. You can use our guest passes," I offered. "If you want to check it out."

"It's not bad. And Liv is gonna take me to school to see about meeting the swim coach." She turned to me. "Maybe tomorrow?"

Mrs. Donahue gathered the corn husks into a small metal trash can. "Liv is very kind to act as our concierge but we can all go to the high school together. I want to make sure your transcripts have arrived."

"We can introduce ourselves to the college counselors." Lucy looked eager.

"Not me." Ben piled the burgers on a plate. But before I'd figured out how to respond, he turned and flashed a killer smile. "No offense, Livvie. Just not ready to even consider school yet."

"No, I get it," I said. And I must have blushed. No one called me Livvie. For a second, I imagined that Janie's older brother had bestowed a nickname on me. Then I reminded myself that he'd probably just gotten my name wrong.

"Yeah, we get it." Lucy rolled her eyes at me. "You are far too cool to care about anything."

"Lucy, enough please," Mrs. Donahue warned. "Janie, Olivia—go wash up and bring the salads in from the kitchen."

When we stepped back outside, my hands smelled like honeysuckle soap, the sun had set completely, and someone had lit candles around the deck. We set down the bowls on the table and Ben and Lucy scooted over to make room for us to pull over another chair. My stomach, a living creature I'd basically abandoned since breakfast, almost leapt at the sight of the cheeseburgers piled high in the center of the table.

"It looks delicious, thank you," I said.

"We're not a praying-at-the-table kind of family—" Ben, Lucy, and Janie smirked at each other and I got the sense that Mr. Donahue always gave this same speech when guests joined them for supper.

"But we practice gratitude," said Mrs. Donahue.

"That's right. We like to speak about something we feel thankful for before eating. Ben—do you want to start us off?"

Ben cleared his throat dramatically. He sounded grown-up, like an actual man. "I'm really thankful that we finally have Wi-Fi."

"Very profound," Lucy said. "But I agree with you. Thank you, Comcast." And then quickly, before her mom had a chance to get annoyed, she added, "Thank you for new challenges." There was an edge to her voice, so I wasn't sure if she was being a little sarcastic.

"I am grateful for my spirited, adaptable, and generous children," Mrs. Donahue announced. "And for Olivia."

"Me too." Janie smiled at me. "I am grateful for Olivia."

"Wonderful." Mr. Donahue smiled grandly around the table. "And I am thankful for my beautiful wife. And her potato salad." The Donahue kids groaned and Janie told me, "He always says the same thing. About his wife."

Ben said, "We don't always have potato salad."

Janie pointed out, "Liv didn't go yet." All the hands that had just reached out for the food on the table hung momentarily in midair. Janie turned to me. "You go," she urged.

"I'm grateful for our neighborhood." It didn't come out right. "And for you, for joining it." That was closer to what I meant. Had I been totally honest, had it been acceptable for me to speak completely sincerely in that moment, I might have said, "Thank you for allowing me to feel like I belong." That's how I felt so I just smiled and looked around the table and hoped that at least Janie understood that.

"Hey, Lucy," Janie said. "Liv runs cross-country."

"Mom said that. I run too. What's your best time?"

"I don't know yet." I felt stupid admitting it. "I haven't run a full course."

"She's only going to be a freshman," Ben explained.

"I know that," Lucy said, and then asked him, "do you know that?"

"Lucy—" There went Mrs. Donahue again, with the warning bells ringing in her voice.

Lucy took a visible breath as if to remind herself to stay calm. "I might actually not run." Hands passing plates around the table paused. "I'm still thinking about it. I just really need to focus on academics. Once my schedule's finalized, then I can figure out the rest."

"Running helps keep you disciplined," Mr. Donahue said.

Mrs. Donahue rushed in to finish his thought. "There's

plenty of time. We're all still settling in. We'll see what the guidance counselor has to say and go from there."

I wanted the Donahues to go back to talking about gratitude and potato salad. I wanted to have answers about something, to speak with authority. So I said, "They might already have sent your schedules." I looked around at Janie, Ben, and Lucy. "At least an early version. They sent mine to the house. It came last week."

Lucy set down her fork. "Did something come from school?" She looked at her mother first and then her father. "Did you check?"

Mr. Donahue coughed. "You know I've just been piling mail on that little marble table in the front hall. I don't think I saw anything from the school. A lot from the township— bills probably. I'm going to go through them all tomorrow."

"Well, Gav, school stuff would come from the township." Mrs. Donahue spoke slowly, pointing out what she clearly felt was obvious. "Thank you, Olivia. We'll look out for that."

"It would just be preliminary." I hadn't meant to stress Lucy out further.

Lucy stood up, pushing her chair out from behind her, and flounced inside. Almost a full minute later, we heard a shriek. "They're here, I think. These are them."

"The suspense—I die," Ben muttered.

Lucy came barreling back onto the deck, clutching a thick packet of envelopes, catalogs, and advertisements in her hands.

"They're addressed to us, Dad," she said, dumping the rest of the pile in the center of the table. "I don't know why you would have thought they were bills." She handed Ben a thick envelope with a typed address. "Unless you're already racking up fines." He shrugged, took the envelope, and set it next to his plate.

Janie grabbed her schedule and immediately tore into it. "Do you remember yours?" she asked me frantically.

"Sort of." I looked up, trying to picture the printed grid in my mind. We looked at Janie's together. "I think we have history together. And gym. That's good because then we'll have the same lunch and homeroom." I looked closer. "I have Ms. Montrose for geometry too—she's great. She gives a lot of extra help. Even if we're not in the same class, we can do the homework together."

I looked up to make sure I hadn't broken a Donahue honor code or something with that suggestion. Mr. and Mrs. Donahue were just staring across the table at Lucy, who was barely breathing. Mrs. Donahue spoke up. "Well, Lucy? What do you think?"

The silence stretched on and the only sound I heard was Ben chewing. Lucy looked up at her parents. "It happens to be ideal." She stamped the last word on the sentence like a gold star of approval and beamed at the rest of us sitting at the table. "They've placed me in Differential Math, which is actually a step beyond the AP curriculum. I am completely up for that challenge. I've got AP Econ and AP Physics and then

Honors Latin and a Shakespeare elective to round that out. It looks like they accepted my art credits so I have room if I want to add AP Comp Sci."

"Or you could take an art class for fun," Mrs. Donahue suggested. "Or sign up for a study hall to ease your homework load a bit."

Lucy continued as if Mrs. Donahue hadn't spoken. "Liv, do you know any of these teachers? Have you heard of them?" She slid the schedule to me and reached for Ben's. "Don't you care?" He said nothing but reached for a second cheeseburger.

Lucy sighed dramatically. She sliced open Ben's envelope with her immaculately manicured fingernail. "We have Latin together. But that's good news, because you're better in Latin."

"What is this?" Janie had been sorting out the rest of the mail, and now she held up a white, square envelope, addressed in careful block lettering and without a stamp or postmark marring its pristine blankness. She flipped it to me. Before passing it back, I noticed it felt heavy and formal, like a wedding invitation.

Only one line of black ink marched across the letter.

The Residents of 16 Olcott Place.

Janie was the one who opened it.

CHAPTER FIVE

She slid out a thick card, and as she read it, her expression transformed from curiosity to confusion and then to distress. This time when Janie asked, "What is this?" there was a different edge to her voice: fear. She dropped the card onto the table, facedown.

"What on earth?" Mrs. Donahue asked, reaching for the card.

"No—don't," Janie said.

Lucy moved faster than her mom and snatched it up. She read it quickly and bit her lip. She zeroed in on Ben immediately. "You're really sick, you know that?" She practically pelted him with the envelope.

Ben looked baffled. "Okay, crazy lady."

"No, you have legitimate problems."

"Ben didn't write that," Janie whispered. "Come on. You can't think—"

"She can't think what?" Ben asked. "What are you two even going on about?" He examined the envelope intently.

"Exactly," Mrs. Donahue said. "Girls, what's happening here?"

Lucy slid the white card into the center of the table. Candlelight illuminated it so that the paper glowed behind the stark black writing. The contrast made it easy to read:

I am the Sentry of Glennon Heights. Long ago, I claimed 16 Olcott Place as levy for my guardianship. The walls will not tolerate your trespass. The ceilings will bleed and the windows will shatter. If you do not cease your intrusion, the rooms will soon smell of corpses.

I scanned the paper quickly, believing I must have misread something. But the words stayed the same, even as the family around the table began dissolving into accusations and bewilderment.

"He has to ruin everything!" Lucy said.

"You're a lunatic. I'm sitting here, just enjoying a cheeseburger."

Janie sprang into the role of peacemaker between her two siblings. "Maybe you meant it as a joke. But, Ben, it's not funny."

Mr. Donahue had picked up the card. He held it close to his face and seemed to be inspecting it.

"Gavin, what are you doing?" Mrs. Donahue cried out. "They might need to dust it for prints."

"Dust *what* for prints? Who? Come off it, Lindsay. Ben, straight talk now, did you do this?"

"Straight talk, Dad—no." Ben rolled his eyes at me. I felt my cheeks flush; he counted me as his ally. But I caught myself and remembered that I was Janie's ally.

Mr. Donahue tossed the card back into the center of the table. "He says he didn't do it."

"Well then." Lucy's voice dripped with sarcasm.

"And really, it's a harmless prank."

"I'd hardly call it harmless, Gavin."

"Probably just some locals having some fun at our expense."

I shifted uncomfortably in my seat.

Janie patted my hand. "Dad doesn't mean you, Liv."

"I can't imagine anyone who would do that—" I started to say.

"But somebody did." Lucy's clipped tone made it clear that she hadn't entirely ruled me out as the guilty party.

Mrs. Donahue cleared her throat. She'd been clutching her napkin in one hand. When she set it down, it looked like a flower that had been picked and then crushed. "Kids, why don't you clear the table, please? Your father and I need a few minutes." She looked down at me. "Please excuse us, Olivia."

I just about leapt out of my seat, trying to pile up as many plates as possible. Janie worked next to me while Ben and Lucy both stayed at the table, staring each other down until their father said, "Lucy and Ben—does your mother need to issue you a formal invitation?" Then their chairs scraped on the deck and they each picked up a salad bowl, grudgingly.

As I scurried to the door, I heard Mrs. Donahue scold Janie's dad. "Not everyone speaks your particular language of sarcasm, Gavin. They've had quite the shock."

"Somehow I think they'll survive. Unless their mother keeps treating them like they're three years old."

"Excuse me?"

"You heard me."

The only thing more uncomfortable than hearing my parents fight was hearing someone else's parents fight. And yet I drifted toward the kitchen window, straining to hear their voices over the clatter of Janie and Lucy doing dishes.

"I beg your pardon for taking this matter seriously. Are you going to call the police or shall I?"

"Do you even hear yourself?"

"I will call the nonemergency line."

"Wonderful. Because I think even in Michigan, they experience very few postal emergencies."

"Did you not read the same letter I did? This is a very threatening letter."

"A *prank* letter. You're the adult, Lindsay. It's your job to dial it down, not rile the situation up."

"I consider protecting my children the first component of my job, thank you—"

A hand clamped down on my upper arm and I gasped out loud. Ben leaned in and asked me in a stage whisper, "Are you entertained?" He was disappointed in me, I could tell.

"I'm sorry. I just—"

"You couldn't look away from the train wreck."

"I've survived similar train wrecks."

"I doubt it. Why don't you go help dry?"

"Of course." I couldn't get the words out fast enough. As I moved toward the sink though, the unmistakable sound of glass breaking silenced all of us. The Donahue kids paused, then Lucy spoke. "It's just not a party until . . ."

"We should have made more of an effort to carry the plates inside," Ben added. For a split second a look of understanding passed between Ben and Lucy. "Lucy, I didn't write that. I wouldn't— Okay, possibly I would have, during my younger, more reckless phase. But I didn't. I swear to you.

Janiebear?" He reached to put an arm around Janie. "I swear."

"Makes sense," Lucy said, sighing. "You wouldn't have put the effort into disguising your handwriting." The three of them stood in a line at the sink. Lucy rested her head on Ben's shoulder and Ben squeezed Janie in his arm. Standing behind the three Donahue siblings, I keenly felt my only-child status. Only the sensation of being an unwelcome guest overshadowed that.

The voices outside rose in volume, and Janie, Lucy, and Ben busied themselves again. They didn't seem particularly shocked or concerned, but they stayed focused on the task at hand, as if all it took to return to a normal evening was a filled dishwasher. Not even Janie turned around to speak to me. I backed into the living room and texted my mom quickly: *I think you should come and get me.*

I saw the familiar ellipses blink on the phone's screen: my mother thinking. And then: *Everything ok?*

As soon as I involved my mom, it would be a Thing. I knew that. She didn't like drama, of any sort. And already my mom had questioned if Janie and I were spending too much time together. "You're practically joined at the hip," she'd told me just that morning. "Sweetheart, you're lucky to have so many friends. Don't get carried away with the shiny new thing."

In minutes, my mother would arrive at the Donahues' doorstop and see the tarnish on our shiny new neighbors. I didn't want to give her any more reason to side-eye Janie. So trying to downplay how weird the whole situation was, I ended up writing and rewriting my reply. Mom must have freaked out because she wrote another message: *Janie? What's up?* Those dots blinked, expectantly.

We could use your perspective. I realized that indicated absolutely nothing, but figured Janie and I could explain it more easily in person. If I wrote *The new family just got a death threat*, my mom would definitely consider it unwelcome drama.

In the kitchen, Janie and Lucy sat at the table and Ben sat on the steps leading up to the floors above. Earlier, when she'd toured me through some of the house, Mrs. Donahue had told me that the kitchen staircase had been used by servants back in the day. That's why it had been built so narrow.

"Because the servants were small?" I'd asked stupidly.

"No." She'd laughed. "Because it didn't matter if they were comfortable." I had thought living in a house with back passages and secret ladders was so cool. Waiting for my mom, I reassessed the charm of all those dark corners and secret nooks. I'd felt so self-conscious and intrusive—it hadn't occurred to me to be afraid. But as I remembered the letter's deliberate words, my heart pounded. I fought the urge to sprint out of the dimly lit house and run home.

From his perch on the steps, Ben looked up at all of us and said, "Guys, what if it's true?"

"I'd say the house smells like Pine-Sol rather than corpses," Lucy said dryly.

"Come on—you know what I mean. What if someone feels like we're invading his space? What if the people who used to live here are crazy?"

"You mean the people who MOVED AWAY?" Lucy asked, but Ben didn't get it. "They moved away, Ben. That letter wasn't even stamped." Janie and I glanced at each other. "What?" I shook my head—I don't know why—out of some sense of loyalty to the Langsoms, I suppose. But Lucy demanded, "Right now, one of you, spit it out."

"There's no way—" I started to say.

"They didn't move away," Janie told her sister. "It sounds like maybe they were going to lose the house. That's probably why we could afford it."

"So where are they?" Lucy looked incredulous.

I shrugged. "An apartment maybe? In town."

"Well, then all this makes sense. I mean, not really—that note is still insane, but at least it's understandably insane." Lucy rubbed her temples. "Someone should tell Mom and Dad."

"Yeah," Ben said. "And someone should maybe apologize for randomly accusing her own brother—"

"Not randomly." Lucy shook her head. "I think I have some credit banked. No apologies for years."

Ben just shook his head.

"I don't think one of the Langsoms would do this." I

forced myself to speak up. "I know they wouldn't." I looked to Janie, hoping she'd back me up, but what could she say? She didn't know Thatcher Langsom. I mean, *I* didn't know Thatcher Langsom. But I said, "It's just not their way." My voice shrank. "It seems like you're making assumptions. You can't be certain."

Janie said, "We can't be certain of anything."

I wondered if she meant me.

The doorbell rang then. All the Donahue kids looked so terrified that I felt awful for not telling them my mom was headed over. Janie opened the door and relief washed over her face.

"Mrs. Danvers, hi." She turned to face Ben and Lucy. "Guys, this is Olivia's mom."

"Are we going to insist that Mrs. Danvers provide a hand-writing sample?" Ben suggested. But then he stood up to shake my mom's hand. "Nice to meet you."

"Now what exactly is going on? Olivia, you want to fill me in?" My mom looked so expectant and so clueless. Why had I involved her in this? I prayed that whoever had written the letter wasn't watching the house right at that moment, fancy black pen in hand, adding my mother to some kind of list of doom.

"Well, there's a situation." I looked around the room, wish-ing one of the Donahue kids would interrupt me to explain.

"I gathered." Mom clasped her hands together. "Are your

parents home?" On cue, Mr. and Mrs. Donahue came in from the back deck, speaking softly into each other's ears. They looked like an anniversary card, not *Divorce Court* guest stars.

"Hi there," Mom said before I could introduce her. "I'm Melinda Danvers, from up the street."

"Olivia's mom, hello! I'm sorry—we weren't expecting you. We were just all clearing the table and washing up."

"Thank you for dinner, Mrs. Donahue," I said automatically.

"You're very welcome, Olivia. I'm sorry that our family discussion got a bit heated."

I could tell my mom's antennae were up. I stepped in.

"I texted my mom and asked her to come over. I thought it might help to talk to her." Everyone stared at me. "About the letter."

"Oh, you're a dear." Janie's mom turned to her dad. "She's a dear." Then she said to my mom, "We're so grateful that the girls have connected. Truly. You've raised such a wonderful young lady. Right, Gavin?" Mr. Donahue nodded.

Mrs. Donahue gazed down at the white card in her hand, as if she had just noticed it there. She shoved it hastily back into its envelope. "I'm sure it's nothing."

"What's nothing? Has Olivia done something?"

"No." My denial came swift and certain. "Mom, no, I didn't do anything." I wanted to bolt all over again, feeling the heat of Lucy's suspicion in particular. It reddened my face.

"Absolutely not. We seem to be the recipients of a sick joke. But no one believes that Olivia, or any of the children, are responsible." Mrs. Donahue's steely gaze traveled across the room, stopping at each of us, silently reiterating her point.

"Oh dear." That's what my mother said, but she shot me a look that indicated that what she regretted most was that I had roped her into this exchange. "Oh dear," she said again. I thought that she might just keep repeating it, until someone said something else, something that made sense.

"Actually, do you have a minute, Melinda? May I just show you?" Mrs. Donahue took my mother by the arm and steered her into the dining room. They closed the French doors behind them so I could only hear bits and pieces: the lack of stamp, the debate about calling the police.

"All right." Janie's dad gave two quick claps. "Family meeting. On the sofa." I froze, not sure if he meant me as well, but Mr. Donahue signaled for me to take a spot on the couch. He said, "Just while Mom talks things over with Mrs. Danvers."

Janie scooted over to make room for me. Her dad sort of nodded to himself and then launched into a pep talk. "So we can all agree that tonight got a little weird. And we're all tired and maybe emotions ran higher than usual. Moving is stressful; it's the second-most stressful time in a person's life."

"What's the first?" Lucy asked immediately.

"Getting married, actually." He half laughed and then, realizing none of his children were laughing along, abruptly cut it short. "But my point is, let's rein in our imaginations a bit. Right? It's like a crank call on paper. Some weirdo. Some creep. Nothing for you all to worry about. Your mom and I will figure out the next steps and we'll keep you posted." Mr. Donahue grinned broadly. "Does that sound like a plan?"

He nodded and then we all nodded because it was apparent he wouldn't stop nodding unless we started. "Great." One more nod, this last one in the direction of the dining room. "I have a couple of questions for your mom myself, Olivia."

As soon as he shut the doors behind him, Lucy exhaled loudly and Janie said, "That does *not* sound like much of a plan."

"Well, I have a plan." Ben stood up and cracked his back. The sound made me think of footsteps creaking across a floor or a door, splintering. "Right?" He directed that question straight to Lucy.

"That's right." She nodded again, but this was a nod of actual agreement. "We have a plan."

"Which is?" Janie prompted.

Lucy and Ben stared at each other. She said, "If it's just that some weirdo decided to write a letter, then we find him."

"Exactly," Ben said. "We find the creep."

CHAPTER SIX

We had crossed only one lawn before my mother started in on me.

"I don't want you spending so much time at the Langsom house," she said, speaking a lot more slowly than she walked. Every word piled up like another brick between Janie and me.

"You mean the Donahue house?"

"You know what I mean. Janie is welcome to visit us, and I have no problem with you bringing her to the pool, but let's give her family a chance to settle in. I'm sure it doesn't help to have another teenager lying around when you're busy getting a house like that up and running."

"Mom—you're being ridiculous."

"Am I? When was the last time you needed me to come get you at a friend's house?"

"Never. But I was scared. And I sure as heck won't do it again, since you're effectively punishing me because I reached out to you for help." I had her then. I knew it. She knew it. Now it was just a matter of seeing how long we would pretend otherwise.

"Liv, I don't expect you to fully understand—"

"Good! Because I don't. It's not Janie's fault some crazy person put a note in her family's mailbox."

"That is the least of the problems in that household, Olivia." My mom lowered her voice to a whisper, even though we'd reached our own yard and there was no way the Donahues could hear us. "You just don't know. You can't always see the rot beneath the surface."

She held the screen door open for me so I had to follow her inside, even though most of me wanted to stay out on the back steps and keep a close watch on 16 Olcott. I compromised, collapsing on the overstuffed couch on the screened-in porch and looking toward the looming peaks of the house's roof.

Rot seemed like a strong word. When their dad had included me in the Donahue family meeting, I'd liked being counted as one of them. Already, I relished the busyness of their house, the pounding feet running up and down the stairs. I even enjoyed the sniping at the supper table. It was too quiet in my house. We rarely discussed anything that mattered at our kitchen table. Mostly we talked numbers: my latest times, the amount of miles on one of Dad's cars, how much Mom had spent on the cut of meat that sat steaming in front of us. It had weirded me out to witness Mr. and Mrs. Donahue fighting—but at least they spoke to each other. I couldn't remember the last time my parents had mattered enough to each other to argue.

//////////

The next morning I came down to run and found Jillian sitting at the kitchen island, my mom emptying the dishwasher, and my dad reading the paper. "You can't just forbid her from going over there," Jillian was saying. I hung back on the stairs and silently cheered her on.

"Of course I can. I'm the mother. Part of my job is to forbid."

"You are the mother of a teenager, and forbidding her will immediately drive her away. You might as well start paying that family rent."

I heard the paper rustle and my father sigh. "I don't even understand the problem."

"It was just a gut feeling, Brad. I can't explain it." Both Dad and Aunt Jillian raised their voices in objection. "I know, I know. But I trust my instincts. He's smarmy, that Donahue guy. It felt like he was trying to sell me something. He just seemed off somehow. The whole thing was peculiar. The letter for one, but it was all so melodramatic. She wanted to call the police about an anonymous note in the mailbox."

"To be fair, it sounded like a bizarre note," Jillian pointed out.

"Yes, but to fall to pieces like that? And he kept asking me if this was that kind of neighborhood? I wanted to ask, *What* kind of neighborhood?"

"I'm telling you—this is not the parental hill to die on." I heard my dad fold his paper. "Speaking of paying rent—are you going to start writing checks, Jill? Are we your official residence now?"

"You got a room for me, Brad?" They were teasing each other, but in the way my aunt and my dad always teased each other, with an underlying edge.

"The two of you—enough." My mother's attention had shifted from the Donahues' problems to our own problems. And at that moment, our family's problems were much less intriguing to me. I stood up and stomped down the last few steps. When I breezed through the kitchen, they were busying themselves, acting as if they hadn't been talking about Janie's family like a bunch of seventh-grade girls at a slumber party.

"You going for a run?" Aunt Jillian asked too brightly.

"Yep." As if the shorts and sneakers weren't self-explanatory.

"And then what?" My aunt asked the question, but it was my mom who was obviously waiting for the answer.

"I don't know." I drank my water, closed the fridge door, and stared at my mom.

"If you go to Janie's house—" she started, then paused. The room felt swollen, as if we were all holding our breath. "If you go to Janie's house, please make sure your phone is on. I'd like you to check in."

"Can I ping you?" *Ping* meant I didn't have to write anything really, just the word *Ping*. *Ping* meant I was alive and well and didn't need my mom to rescue me.

"Sure." My mom and dad exchanged a look—a kind look, like they were running on the same team and she had just posted an awesome time.

"Okay," I said. And then, "I love you." I said it to everyone in general. Right then I did love them all. My dad didn't offer to time me and that was also okay. I took a few deep breaths. I shook myself loose.

Then I ran.

Pounding through the neighborhood, I rehashed everything I knew about the Donahues, every unexpected facet I'd seen of each of them, every question I had filed away for later. Hard as it was to admit, my mom wasn't entirely wrong—Mr. Donahue tried hard at everything, and his trying wore a veneer of someone who hoped to distract the world. At my mom's annual company party, her boss always hired a magician to circulate around the tables, possibly to entertain us kids. But the magician always worked so frantically and failed so often that you spent most of the time eating your food really enthusiastically, hoping he wouldn't approach. Mr. Donahue reminded me of that.

Until she sat across from her husband at dinner, Mrs. Donahue had seemed more sincere. Or maybe she had more effective camouflage. I thought of Mrs. Donahue's chore charts and systems and the careful way she spoke to her children and wondered if she ever relinquished her relentless self-control. If my mom could have been more patient, they might have been friends with each other.

Lucy was mean and bitter and pretty high-strung. She scared me because she didn't appear to be scared of anything. I knew that Janie had predicted she'd lay it on thick and pretend to like me, and sometimes Lucy did that. I recognized that, but mostly I knew Lucy didn't like anyone and was one breath from saying that at any given moment.

I ran harder, faster, and admitted to myself that what Ben thought of me mattered more than it should have. Like the night before, cracking jokes clearly meant to make Janie or Lucy shriek in outrage, he looked at me. He noticed me there.

But something had happened with Ben, back in Northampton. You could tell. His parents treated him so gingerly, like a delicate flower or a live grenade.

And then there was Janie. Shrouded in mystery, basically

a mermaid. How she'd text on her phone when she thought I wasn't looking but never wanted to talk about her last school. It felt like I knew Janie, but I didn't understand Janie. So I kept running—through the stitch in my side and the pain in my chest. I ran past the aching in my legs.

When I ran past the park, I spotted Janie in the visitors' dugout as if I'd conjured her. I veered off course and slowed to a jog. She sat slumped on the bench. She'd pulled back her dark hair in a braid, the lighter strands glinting in the sun.

"Don't stop on my account," she said when I got to her. "I'm just sitting."

"I need to stop." I heard the wheeze in my voice. "What are you doing here?"

Janie looked around. "I'm at the park."

"Yeah, I just—" I caught myself before I said it aloud, before I said, *It's my park.*

But Janie heard it anyway. "You don't have to show me around everywhere."

"It's just a place I come to a lot."

"Yeah, but you don't own it."

"Whoa." I almost asked, *Where did that come from?* But I knew where it had come from. It came from me acting ridiculously possessive about a park.

Janie stopped herself too. "I'm sorry," she said. "It's just—eventually I need to not feel like a guest here, you know? At the park, at the pool, in my own house."

I sat down beside her and propped my legs against the chain-link fence. "Were you scared? Could you sleep?"

"Yeah, I slept." Janie watched me stretch. "What did your mom say?"

I searched for something that wouldn't make Janie feel worse. "She thinks it's a dumb joke. Probably kids."

"We're kids."

"Well, she doesn't think *we* did it."

"Right. But would you ever do something like that?"

"Of course not."

"See? I don't think it's kids."

"So you think someone is obsessed with your family's new house and has watched over it for generations? Really? Somebody's just giving you guys a hard time. I'm sorry. It sucks and you don't deserve this. Nobody deserves this." I stood up. "Listen, I have to grab a shower. Then do you want to go to the pool? Maybe ask your mom to go and sign your family up. Then it will feel like your place too, you know? Or let's ask Lucy to go up to the high school—"

"I have to get back." Janie spoke in a flat voice that I hadn't yet heard. "Mom wants us to all stay in. She has an appointment with the realtor."

"Janie, are you okay?"

"Have you ever felt like there's something you can't outrun?" She looked up at me and at first it looked like she would cry any second. But instead she started giggling, a little maniacally at first and then sounding like her old self, or at least the self I'd known for about five whole days.

"I'm sorry," she said. "Look at you"—she gestured to my sneakers, my gym clothes—"you're training to outrun everyone." Janie laughed harder and I tried to laugh with her, but really it didn't seem so funny to me. It seemed like a strange question for anyone to ask, let alone a fourteen-year-old girl, and I got the uncomfortable feeling that my mom might be on to something.

Maybe there was something wrong at the Donahue house after all.

But that didn't stop me from heading there immediately after showering. I texted Janie and asked, *Do you need anything?* She wrote back, *You mean like weapons?* So that clued me in on what to expect from the afternoon. She wrote, *Come right in,* but it still felt weird to just barge into the house, so I went around to the back door and lightly rapped on it, hoping she was in the kitchen. But instead Mr. Donahue answered; he was on his cell phone, so he just mouthed a greeting to me and pointed toward the stairway three times, which I took to mean the third floor.

All three Donahue siblings sat in the turret room. Lucy sat on the bed, with her legs tucked beneath her and an iPad on her lap. Janie perched on a fuzzy stool in front of what looked like an old-fashioned vanity. And Ben sat sprawled on a fur beanbag.

If Janie's room was a kaleidoscope of cheerful colors and busy prints, Lucy's looked like the stark canvas of an unapologetic perfectionist. Her bed, bookshelves, chair, rugs—all of it shone pristinely white. I worried about sitting down. I had grabbed a blueberry muffin on my way out the door and maybe a stray crumb had stuck to my leg. Because of its rounded walls, the turret room was smaller than most bedrooms. Lucy had piled in so many white pillows, gauzy blankets, and fuzzy rugs, it felt like we were tucked inside a roll of paper towels. We were cramped but not exactly uncomfortable. Everything was so soft and plush.

"Welcome to our Center of Operations." Ben sat up straighter in his seat and I could hear the beans resettle in the bag.

Lucy pointed to the foot of her bed. "Take a seat."

"Your room is really glamorous," I said, sitting delicately on the white quilt.

"She means ridiculous," Ben corrected. "How many polar bears had to die for your ice princess palace?"

Janie swiveled toward me on the stool. "We've been organizing a plan of attack?" Her voice lilted like she was asking a question and her gaze shifted to Lucy, as if seeking confirmation. Janie seemed younger sitting in the room with her older brother and sister. But maybe that happened with all families.

"Do you have the note?" I asked. Three heads shook in response.

"Mom still has it," Janie reported. "She brought it to the realtor."

"Why?" I asked, and got three shrugs in return.

Lucy looked bored. "I basically know it by heart."

Janie told me, "We're putting together a list of suspects."

"Okay." Before I could stop myself, I looked at Lucy's screen. It was as blank as the rest of the room.

"You're not a suspect," Janie assured me.

Ben looked up at me. "We didn't agree on that." I didn't think he was serious.

"If I were to write a threatening note, I'd address it only to you." The words just spilled out of my mouth.

"Oh no, Olivia's getting sassy!" Ben crowed. I saw a look pass between Lucy and Janie.

"Sorry," I said quickly. "So I'm not a suspect. Who is?"

"You tell us." Lucy picked up her stylus.

Janie added, "We figure you know all the neighbors. Is there anyone you can think of? Maybe someone who's a little . . . off?"

"No! I mean, I can't think of anyone."

"Well, that's ridiculous. Every neighborhood has weirdos." Ben slapped the ground beside his chair. "Do you remember Mr. Cuddy? How he'd never want anyone to park in front of his house?"

"He'd threaten to tow people," Janie explained.

Lucy added, "Like our grandparents on Christmas morning."

"He was a little high-strung."

"He was insane."

"There's nobody really like that." I thought harder. "My dad says Mr. Park gets angry when people let dandelions grow." Janie looked quizzical. "They spread. One year he tried to organize all the dads to go to Home Depot together and get the same lawn treatment so that everyone's yards matched. But that didn't really get off the ground."

"The letter didn't really address landscaping," Ben pointed out.

"Right."

"What about the lady on the corner? The yellow house?"

"Miss Abbot?"

"I don't know her name. She look likes Anna Wintour, but older."

I watched Lucy carefully write out the name of the sweet older lady who never failed to compliment me on my first day of school outfit every September. "Miss Abbot would never send hate mail," I said.

"She's always peering out her windows. Or sitting on her patio. Watching."

"She smokes cigarettes."

"So?"

"That's why she spends a lot of time on the patio."

"So why is she looking out the windows?"

"Because that's why you have windows—to see through them."

"It's creepy. Is she married? Kids? Grandkids?"

"You know this is what happened in Salem, right?"

Lucy rolled her eyes. "We grew up in Massachusetts," she reminded me. "We know all about Salem."

"Well, then you know they accused single women living on their own, who didn't have family to protect them. Mostly because the judges wanted their land."

"We have plenty of land," Lucy replied.

"We even have a turret," Ben added, pointing at the ceiling.

"You can't just go accusing little old ladies who've lived here forever!"

"That is the whole point of this exercise." Lucy raised her voice to match my own, held up her hand, and made a face to Janie, as if to say, *I told you so.* "You saw the note. It's not like we made it up. Somebody had to have written it. The note talked about 'waiting generations.' Apparently Miss Abbot has lived here for generations."

"She smokes."

"You've said that."

"Did the note smell like cigarettes? At all?"

Lucy sighed. "I didn't smell it."

"It didn't." We all glanced at Ben. "Don't look at me like I'm a crazy person." He shifted uncomfortably in the beanbag. "I was using all my senses. It just smelled like paper, maybe a little earthy, like wet cardboard."

"We're not eliminating her," Lucy decided. "But let's move on for now."

The silence stretched out until Janie spoke up. "Okay, you can't get defensive, Liv." Long pause. "There's someone else we should consider. Other people." I waited. Seconds ticked by. Janie took a deep breath and said, "I don't know them that well, but from what I do know . . ." She trailed off.

I looked around the room, incredulous. "Are you talking about my parents?"

"What? No! I'm talking about Brooke or Kaia. I'm not try- ing to criticize, but Brooke especially seems to enjoy stirring things up."

"Could you please stop apologizing and just own an opinion?" Lucy threw her stylus and it left a long, squiggly line next to Brooke's misspelled name. She turned to me. "Apparently, your friends are not the most welcoming crowd. Maybe they're mad you ditched them for Janie? Or they're just testing her or something before she gets to join your pseudo cool girl group? Maybe this is hazing?"

It might have made me disloyal, but I wasn't angry. I understood how Lucy had arrived at the thought. But it didn't feel right.

"It's too polished," I told them. "Even if they were working at it, they would have oversold it, I think. And they would have typed it rather than risk me recognizing the handwriting."

"That's excellent analysis," Ben said, and I tried not to let the compliment matter to me. "But we're all ignoring the obvious: the people who used to live here. Either the Langsom kids or their parents, whoever's more emotionally eroded over the whole move."

"Dr. Langsom sort of lost it, professionally." As soon as I offered that tidbit up, I regretted sharing anything I'd overheard during Sangria Saturdays.

Lucy leaned in. "What does that mean?"

"I don't know exactly."

"Well, is he mental?" Ben asked. "Could he have done this?"

"I don't know."

Lucy wrote the name *Langsom* down, then neatly indented and added *Dr. Langsom*. "I sort of pictured a kid."

"Well, yeah," Ben said. "You pictured me."

She talked on as if her brother hadn't spoken. "I mean, he's a surgeon, right? Aren't you vetted before you're allowed to cut people open?"

"Right," Janie said. "He was vetted and they decided he couldn't handle operating anymore. Right, Liv?"

"I guess so. I don't know details."

"Can you find them out?"

"I can try."

Lucy nodded. "Olivia, you take the doctor. I'll see what I can dig up about Mrs. Langsom. There are three kids, right?"

"Yeah." I thought of Thatcher behind the coffee shop counter. And his brothers, both slightly older, equally attractive, alternate versions of him.

"But the older ones are in college, right? They don't care. Ben, you need some friends anyway. Cozy up to Thatcher. He's in our grade."

"How is that going to work? We just bought their foreclosed house."

"Figure it out. If he wrote the letter, he'd want to keep you close just to stay connected with the house."

"What about me?" Janie asked, and I glimpsed how she must have looked as a little kid, running frantically to catch up with the twins.

"Miss Abbot."

"What?" she groaned. "That's not even a real assignment. We ruled her out."

"No, we moved on. Go on over and introduce yourself. See if she has a lot of stationery around. Maybe she's a stretch, but if she's peering out the window as much as you say, maybe she saw something. You never know." Lucy jotted down a bunch of notes. "It goes without saying that we only report to each other." Ben and Janie nodded. "Right?" Lucy added, possibly for my benefit only.

"Of course," I answered immediately and waited for Lucy to say something else, like maybe *I believe in you* or *Go team* or something inspirational to break up the family huddle. Instead she just reached over to her lacquered bedside table and grabbed a set of earbuds. She plugged them into the iPad and turned over on her side with her back to us. We were dismissed.

Janie stood up. "Pool?"

"Sure." I turned around to see Ben still sitting there, watching Lucy watch Netflix. He didn't look up when we left. Janie must have turned to see me look toward Ben. "Just us, okay?" she asked.

"Of course. I mean, who else?"

She didn't even bother to answer.

I followed Janie down the hall to her room. "You don't actually have to ask your mom or anyone about Dr. Langsom," she said, after shutting her bedroom door.

"But we all decided—"

"It just helps steer Lucy away from an anxiety attack."

"I don't understand." Eager Janie who meekly sat listening to her older siblings had vanished. This Janie stood in front of me and looked as fearless as she did climbing onto a diving board.

"She just needs to feel like she's in control. Otherwise it stresses her out. There's nothing to do about all this. It's a scary note. Nobody shoved an animal carcass through the mail slot."

Hearing Janie dismiss our plans felt oddly deflating. I had bought into the whole secret agent vibe. It was exciting to join forces on something. I tried to find my footing again, to figure out what was real, what was less real. I reminded her, "It's normal to be a little freaked out, though."

She sighed. "Yeah. I am a little freaked out. But there's no sense in alienating everyone in Glennon Heights over it." She rummaged through her closet and calmly packed a small tote with a towel and a change of clothes. "On the other hand, it does feel weird to think it could be anyone. It makes you dissect the people around you and try to imagine someone else's motive. I almost can't help it," Janie confessed. "It's like a puzzle I need to put together. You know what I mean?"

I nodded. I knew exactly what she meant. After all, even before we played detective with Lucy and Ben, I had spent most of my morning run considering possible suspects.

But my list had been shorter and composed exclusively of Janie and her family.

CHAPTER SEVEN

Three days later, I was at the Donahue house when the second letter arrived.

It came through the mail slot. Whether it arrived with the rest of the mail or someone slipped it in afterward, we couldn't tell. Janie and I found it lying on top of the rest, the same square of heavy white paper.

Of course, we knew what it was instantly. Janie saw it first, on our way down the stairs. My mom had offered to take us shopping for school supplies, so we might have been running. At least we were bounding fast enough that when

Janie stopped so abruptly at the landing between the first and second floors, I crashed into her.

"Look," she said.

We just stood there for a few seconds, staring down. Then Janie took the rest of the steps two at a time. Just as she was bending down to pick the letter up, I yelled, "Wait!" and whipped my phone out to take a picture.

"What are you doing?" Janie asked.

"Maybe for the police?"

"Should I not touch it?"

I shook my head, not to mean *No* but to mean *Why should I decide?*

Janie looked around the house, maybe hoping that her mom or sister would swoop in and take over. But it was just her and me. The white envelope on the floor seemed to dare us. We couldn't walk by it.

She crouched down and snatched it up in one quick motion. I opened the door and checked the front porch, just in case whoever delivered it had hidden outside, waiting. Instead I spotted my mom down the street, climbing into her car.

I held up my hand, waving at her before I had the chance to formulate a plan. So I switched gears and called out, "Five minutes!" I shut the door and stood with my back bracing it closed as if she might shoulder her way through.

"My mom's out there."

Janie blinked. "Like on the porch?"

"No. In her car." I realized what Janie meant. "She just went to her car. To drive us to the store. She didn't leave the note." I nodded to the envelope in her hand.

"Right." Janie looked as panicked as I felt. "I didn't mean that. Not really." She glanced down at the envelope.

"Maybe it's an apology."

"Maybe." But she didn't sound convinced. "I'm just going to open it right now." We both stared for a little while longer.

Then Janie tore open the letter. As soon as she read it, she sat back on the first step of the staircase behind her. It looked like the force of the letter's message pushed her backward, the way a poltergeist might shove someone out of the blue.

"Is it bad?" I asked, which was dumb. It was an anonymous letter, left in her mail slot by a person who had earlier claimed that soon her house would smell like dead bodies. I sank down next to her and Janie handed over the note. The envelope was addressed the same as before: *The Residents of 16 Olcott Place.* I slid out the card.

Heed my warnings. I am the Sentry. Blood
will seep from the ceiling of 16 Olcott Place.
Trespassers will be punished. Have you lifted
up the floorboards yet? Have you discovered what
the house is hiding?

Involuntarily, my eyes lifted to the ceiling. "No blood yet,"
Janie commented dully. I shoved the card back into the envelope, trying to be careful but also rushing to hide the awful
message as quickly as possible. The whole house looked eerie
now. Afternoon shadows threw wide swaths of darkness over
the living room. I heard creaking above us and even though I
knew it must be Ben or Lucy moving around upstairs, I fought
the urge to run.

"What should we do?" I asked.

She unzipped the front pocket of her knapsack and placed
the card inside. She patted it after closing it back up, like it
held a treasure she needed to keep safe. "We should go shopping for school supplies."

"We should find your mom or dad. Or Ben or Lucy." And
then, even though I knew it would only complicate matters, I
offered, "We could tell my mom, if you'd rather."

"Nope." Janie bent down to gather the rest of the mail and

placed the pile on the small marble table. She took a deep breath. "It's going to start everything back up again. I'll tell them when we get home."

So that's what we did. We rode in the car with my mom and Janie answered questions cheerfully, as if she hadn't just been threatened by some faceless sociopath. At Target, my mom went off to get groceries and Janie and I went to the school supply corner on our own. We filled our baskets with gel pens and academic planners. Janie put a tie-dyed lunch bag in with her stuff and I put it back.

"Everybody buys lunch," I explained.

"Is the food good?"

"It's all right," I told her, thinking that was a difference between Janie and me. Had I said the cafeteria was awful, she would have brought her lunch each day. She wouldn't have minded being the only one eating a meal from home.

First, she returned the bag to its shelf. Then, right after, she grabbed it and put it back in the basket. "Maybe we won't stay."

"What? Are you serious?"

"Olivia, we're getting death threats."

"They're not exactly death threats," I argued. Janie just stared at me. "Okay, fine. But you'd really leave? Where would you go?"

"Maybe back home." She meant Massachusetts, I knew. "Or to stay with my grandparents."

"Have you all discussed that?" Apparently, I hadn't been included in every Donahue family meeting.

But Janie shook her head. "I'm just guessing."

"Maybe you shouldn't tell them." I said it lightly, just a suggestion. "I mean, it's ninety-nine percent likely it's only a sick joke, right? So maybe the best thing to do is to ignore it."

"What if I pull up the floorboards and there's a dead body? What if this guy, this Sentry, breaks in at night?"

"The chances of that are—"

"Would you take that chance?" Janie demanded.

I held my hands up, trying to calm her. "Back at the house, you said you didn't want to start the drama back up again. That's all." We wandered down the aisles in silence. Finally, I said, "Janie, you have to know I'm on your side here. I'm just giving you my honest opinion."

"How about this? You sleep over tonight and see what you think tomorrow morning."

"Sleep over at your house?"

"Yeah. My house. Or the Langsom house. Or the Sentry's house. Whoever wants to claim it. You stay over and by tomorrow we decide if we should keep the second letter a secret."

My mouth dried up and my tongue felt too big for my face. "Well, I run first thing in the mornings, so—"

"So tomorrow, you'll run like a hundred yards farther. We

won't stay up all night, but it will still give us a chance to look around."

"For what? What do you expect to find?" All of a sudden, I envisioned a secret room, in which a monstrous man sat writing on good stationery.

"I just need you to help me look."

Truthfully, the prospect of it took the excitement away from back to school shopping. Especially because in the very next aisle, Target had already started displaying Halloween decorations. I gazed at the row of plastic and Styrofoam haunted houses. They were exclusively gray or neon green. They had skulls peeking through their windows and crows perched on the peaks of their roofs. They weren't even slightly realistic. What made the Langsom house so scary was its loveliness, once you understood the trouble masked by its pretty facade. And its size, once you realized how long you'd have to search through its darkest corners before feeling certain of your own safety.

I asked my mom about sleeping over at Janie's in the car ride home, with Janie sitting right there in the back seat. I knew I'd hear about that later; my mom's deepest fear isn't ghosts or intruders but being impolite. She wouldn't risk offending Janie by implying that I shouldn't stay the night. Instead Mom tried her best, saying, "You girls are welcome to stay at our place. Janie, I make awesome pancakes. Right, Olivia?" Her voice vibrated with unspoken aggravation.

"They *are* delicious."

"Oh, thank you," Janie said. "Maybe later in the week? I'm trying to get my room set up just right. Olivia said she'd help."

"Wonderful," Mom said. She didn't mean it. "Mr. Danvers and I would love to see you girls at our place too. You can help with Liv's room." She laughed but not really.

Once we got home, Janie stood in our living room while I grabbed my toothbrush and a change of clothes. Dad walked in just as Mom and I were negotiating terms.

"Ping me," Mom said.

"Of course."

"Don't *of course* me right now. We are going to have a discussion tomorrow."

"Yeah, I know." I looked from Mom to Janie. No contest. Mom would rebound; she wouldn't feel permanently disappointed in me. I couldn't count on that with Janie.

Janie followed me down the steps but she looked back up at the screen-in porch. "What's going on with your mom?" she whispered.

"The whole scene the other night—she doesn't really want me at your house."

Janie and I walked through backyards. As we passed the houses between our own, Janie and I gazed up at the kitchen windows, the back bedrooms. Who knew what the three families inside fought about? It didn't matter how many family meetings you sat in on. You didn't really know someone until you'd heard her parents hiss at each other like they regretted ever meeting.

From the back, Janie's house stood just as grand in size, but it lacked the eaves and the turret showcased in the front. It looked more institutional, like a tiny hospital or the dorm of a boarding school. Chokecherry trees lined the backyard, standing at attention like a formation of guards. In one spot though, right near the woodshed, a hole gaped in the row of shrubs. A wheelbarrow sat parked there, looking lonesome. The ground had been battened down a bit and we found a bunch of litter (two flattened soda cans, a cellophane wrapper, and an empty bag of chips) concentrated right in the gap.

I took out my phone and snapped some photos. "What are you doing?" Janie asked, and at first I didn't want to tell her. But I knelt right in the spot and noticed that it afforded me a clear view of the house's south windows. I also saw that the litter seemed to radiate out, except the cellophane, which hung caught on a nearby branch. "It looks like someone stands or sits here. A lot. Maybe the Sentry stands here. You know, watching."

Inside we worked systematically but quietly so that no one else in her family would notice us. We took pictures of the woods from each of the back windows to see which had the clearest view from the worn spot in the yard. We watched YouTube tutorials on finding hollow passages in walls. We tapped on wood panels and closely examined the staircases.

We tried to pry off the ornate carvings that snaked around the doorframes on the first floor. We felt behind all the mirrors in the bathrooms.

Nothing. In the living room, we stared at the enormous, floor-to-ceiling built-in bookshelf and then each other.

"Maybe?" Janie asked.

I nodded. "It would be cool." Up close, most of the books seemed old. The vast majority had leather covers. I didn't recognize any of them from our summer reading list or anything. There were hundreds. "Are these your books? You brought them?"

She shook her head. "No way. These were here."

So we started pulling them off the shelves. "Go slow." Janie reminded me. "In the video, it triggered some kind of mechanism. If it's old, it might be delicate." Kneeling, we got through the first two shelves from the bottom, then the third. Halfway through the fourth, Janie's dad came through the room, on his way to the kitchen. He was on his phone, so at first we thought maybe he wouldn't notice. He entered the room and we froze. I stretched my body as widely as possible, trying to hide the books piled on the floor. Janie stood up and peered at the middle shelves, as if she was searching for a particular title.

"I'm telling you to recheck the numbers," I heard him say. "No excuses." It looked like he would just keep walking, but then just as he reached the arched doorway, he stopped.

"Steve, hold on. You're cutting out. The reception in this place is awful." His roaming gaze seemed to settle on us. "Steve, just give me a second." He spun around, holding the phone to his chest. "What is this?" Same clipped tone, but this time directed at Janie and me.

"Jane Louise. I asked a question."

"We were just— I was going to reorganize some things. Do we want to keep these?"

Still squinting at us, he brought the phone back to his mouth. "Steve, one more minute. Please." And then to Janie, "You have a beautiful room. Go reorganize the shelves there. This is not your space."

"We were only trying to help, Mr. Donahue."

He glared at me. "This is definitely not your space."

My face burned.

"Dad!" Janie sounded outraged.

"I don't have time for this, Jane. I don't have the energy for this." He waved his free hand around the room. "Clean it up before your mother comes home from her meeting with McGovern."

"Ned McGovern?" I asked without thinking. Mr. Donahue looked at me in disbelief. I wished we had found a stupid trapdoor so I could have dropped through it. "It's just that I know him," I explained weakly.

"Well, that's perfect," Mr. Donahue declared. Then he pivoted, pulled the phone back up to his ear, and stormed out.

Janie looked down at me and shut her eyes, like she was trying to blot out reality. "I'm so sorry."

"What did I do?"

"He's just stressed out. And there's something going on about the realtor. He hates the realtor."

"Yeah, but also he seems to hate me."

"He doesn't, Liv. I'm so sorry. He just . . . he just hates everything right now, especially anything having to do with this town."

"Glennon Heights?" I didn't get it. No one hated Glennon Heights. That would have been like hating milk or Labor Day.

"It's not what they expected, I guess. And then that letter came." She buried her face in her hands. "God. The first letter, I mean. It's just a mess." For a second, I thought she might cry. Then Janie seemed to shake herself out of it. She tied her long, dark hair into a ponytail, then turned back to the floor-to-ceiling wall of books. She worked quickly as she spoke, carefully lifting each book up and then pressing against the wood. "Why don't you start putting the books on the lower shelves back in place?" We fell into a rhythm, with Janie standing above me. I didn't feel much like talking. It made it tense and awkward to stand so close and stay silent, all the while listening for footsteps coming back into the room. "He's not usually like that," Janie said. "He's just under so much pressure."

"What do you mean?" I spoke grudgingly and felt her take a deep breath in the space right above me.

"I don't know that we could truly afford this place." She sounded like she was going to say more, but stopped herself. Instead, she lifted a maroon leather-bound book, we heard a decisive click, and the wall opened up.

We stood there gaping at a tiny room, about three feet deep. It had a cement floor, like a cellar. Wooden planks lined the walls.

"What's over there, in the corner?" As I pointed to a shadowy figure, crouched in the corner, I saw my own finger tremble and felt a scream build in my throat. For a second I actually believed it was a person sitting hunched over.

Janie stepped forward and kicked it.

"Janie!" I gasped.

"It's a sleeping bag." But it wasn't the nylon kind that you wanted with you on a camping trip. This was army green, thick canvas. When Janie kicked it, a plume of dust rose like smoke.

"Janie, this is really creepy. Someone's been sleeping in here."

"Not recently." Janie rubbed her nose and sniffled. "All this dust—I bet it's been sitting here rolled up for ages." She picked it up with both hands and held it toward me. Before I could stop her, she buried her face in the flannel lining. "Smells old." Wrinkling her nose, Janie dug into the sleeping bag's folds. "Look—this was jammed in the corner." She held up a spiral-bound paperback book: *My Scouting Journal.* On its cover, an eagle held an American flag in each talon.

"Is there a name inside?"

Janie shook her head. "Just initials: TM. And look—" She showed me the places where pages had been torn out. Between the few pages left, someone had neatly folded old Hershey wrappers. "Hey—*T* for *Thatcher*, maybe? What's his middle name? Are the Langsom brothers Boy Scouts?"

"I think we need to ask if their grandfather was a Boy Scout. This stuff looks vintage."

"Yeah. Maybe if you were old enough to keep watch over a house for decades and develop an unhealthy attachment to it, you might have collected similar camping equipment." Janie bit her lip. "Hold on a second—close me in."

"What?" I watched her back into the little room. "No way. Come back out."

"Just do it. You know how to open the door if you need to." I still hesitated. "Come on, Liv. It's not like we found an actual dead body."

"Yet."

"Do it."

So I shut the door. "Are you happy now?" I called to her.

"I wouldn't say *happy*. I'd say *super freaked out*. I can't believe this."

"You can't believe what?" I asked, desperate to know. And of course right then, Mr. Donahue came back into the room.

"Just me," he said, looking around for Janie.

"Oh, Mr. Donahue." I turned to face him and pinned my

back against the bookcase. "You're right here in the room—hi." I bit my lip, seeing him slip his phone into his back pocket. Unfortunately, I had his undivided attention. "Janie took some books up to her room. We need them for school, for English class." I was a terrible liar. Nothing I said made any sense. "Every year, this teacher gives us the same project. It's a magazine. About books. So I told Janie and now we're starting early. To get on the right foot. With this teacher."

"Janie's really lucky you've been here to show her around."

"Yeah, you said that at dinner the other day," I said. I didn't add *before you were inexplicably mean to me.* "It's no problem."

"I need to apologize for lashing out at you, Olivia."

The laugh that emerged from me could only be described as maniacal. "Oh, it's fine. We shouldn't have been in the living room, touching books."

"Of course you should. I was being ridiculous. You should feel welcome anywhere in the house."

"Thanks, Mr. Donahue," I said, feeling buried in the rubble of a thousand worries.

He nodded, but didn't walk away like I hoped. He just kept gazing at me, as if he could pass secret messages with his eyes. He reminded me of Ben right at that moment.

"I'm sure Janie will be right down."

"Absolutely." He stared at me for another moment. "Again, my apologies." And then, finally, Janie's dad left the room.

"Is he gone?" Janie's voice rang out clearly as if she stood right next to me, unobstructed.

"Wait a sec." I moved toward the window, trying to get a better look outside. No sign of Mr. Donahue. "Yeah. He's gone." I heard a soft click, and then the bookshelf pivoted out and Janie emerged, a dusty ghost. "Could you hear everything clearly?"

"Completely," Janie said excitedly. "It's even crazier, though. Come see." She tugged at my hand.

"No way." I could barely take one step forward into the little room, let alone close myself up in it.

"You have to," Janie ordered. "You have to check this out." She put one arm around my shoulders and we stepped back in together. There was a metal handle inside, like you might find on an old chest of drawers. That's what Janie tugged on to close us in. I shut my eyes instinctively, as if I were diving underwater without goggles. It smelled musty.

"Do you see it? It's insane, right?" Janie asked. Her breath tickled my ear.

I blinked open my eyes. It took a second to get used to the almost pitch-black. Janie was a darker shadow beside me in the darkness. She pointed to a single sliver of light that glowed in the door. Cut into the wooden panels of the door and then presumably into the cover of a book was a tiny slit that lined up at just about eye level. Shadow Janie nodded at it and I stepped forward to look.

The peephole in front of us provided a clear line of vision to the Donahues' living room: the huge tufted sofa and the trunk they used as a coffee table. In the corner, I spied a slice of the front door. Then Janie spun me around and pointed me toward a second opening. This one afforded a perfect view of the dining room table. I could see the cornflower blue of Mrs. Donahue's tablecloth and the silver candlesticks positioned right in the center. I could see the crystal chandelier twinkling overhead. At first I thought it was swaying, but then I realized I was swaying. I felt sick and faint and threw myself against the door, trying to break free.

"Whoa, whoa, what are you doing?" Janie asked. She pulled me back to the door and reached in the corner to flip some kind of switch. "You have to be careful." The narrow opening widened and I shouldered my way out.

"Yeah, Janie. We do have to be careful." My knees were still shaking. I clutched at the back of one of the living room chairs and propped myself up. "That's really messed up. Someone's been sitting in there, watching you guys."

"No! I don't think so. Calm down, Liv. No one ever really sits in here since Mom set up the TV in the family room. And we eat in the kitchen or on the deck; we haven't used the dining room once since we moved here." She pointed through the arched doorway at the chandelier. "We positioned the table beneath the light because that's what you do. I'm sure as long as that thing's been hanging, whoever's lived here put their dining room table there."

"It's still really scary. Oh"—I'd thought of something else—"the chocolate wrappers. Whoever hid in there probably got hungry, watching someone else's family dinner. So they ate the chocolate." For some reason, that was the worst part for me, imagining someone hiding and eating candy like they were sitting in a movie theater.

But Janie just kind of shrugged. "At least we know the Sentry isn't a cannibal."

How can she make jokes? I thought.

"We have to tell your parents about the second letter."

"Well, we can't now. The mail hasn't come yet. And you just lied to my dad."

"So what do you want to do?" I asked, half-fearful of what she might say.

Janie smiled at me like this was the greatest adventure she'd ever embarked on. She walked to the window and pointed across the street, at the yellow house on the corner. Miss Abbot's house.

"I think it's time you introduced me to some neighbors," she said.

CHAPTER EIGHT

"The box needs to look official." Janie stood at the doors of her pantry, perusing its contents. "We can't use just any old cardboard box."

"I still don't understand the plan here, Janie," I said. But she didn't answer me. She only dug more frantically through the kitchenware and emerged triumphantly with a black milk crate.

"This is perfect." I waited for an explanation that Janie didn't offer. Instead, she moved a step stool over to the refrigerator and climbed up, reaching into the top cupboard above the freezer. Just as she brought out an enormous, warehouse package of chocolate candy, Ben breezed in through the back door.

"Put back the chocolate."

"I need it."

"I'm telling Mom."

Janie sighed dramatically and stared balefully down at him. "Please. It's for investigative purposes."

Ben rolled his eyes at me. "How much are my parents paying you to mind my sister? Aren't you supposed to help steer her toward normal?"

"I thought they were paying me to talk to you." As soon as I spoke, I wanted to clap my hand over my own mouth. Why did every word I uttered to Ben sound like a dare?

Ben looked startled for a second and then he grinned. I went warm everywhere, thinking to myself, *I surprised him.* But then he glanced up at Janie and seemed momentarily abashed, as if he were the one caught raiding the sweets. He reached his hand up. At first, I thought he was raising his hand to speak, but then, wordlessly, Janie placed a pack of peanut butter cups in his hand. At least he was forgiven.

"Speaking of investigations," he said, "consider me officially cozied to our boy Thatcher Langsom."

"Seriously?" Janie asked.

"You move fast," I muttered.

Ben raised one eyebrow at me and I felt it as a zap in my throat. He leaned against the counter. "Oh yeah. We're basically bros now."

"Does he know where you live?" Janie asked.

"Yep."

"Well, don't you think that's going to work against us? I mean, the whole point was to trick him into confiding in you."

"Only if there was something to confess. He's a pretty chill dude—not someone who's going to get worked up enough to write a letter in his own blood."

"It was ink."

"You know what I mean. Besides I don't get the feeling there's a deluge of new families moving into Glennon Heights in any given year. We're sort of conspicuous."

I remembered Thatcher at the coffee shop. "Does he seem sad? About having to move?"

"Kind of lost, I guess. Mostly stressed out about college—he talked about needing a scholarship and how he would have planned differently. You know—had he known that life would go to pieces. He did tell me that there were all these secret hiding places built into the house." Janie and I exchanged a look. "But when I asked him to come over and show me, he said it'd be too bizarre to come over so soon."

"Well, of course, Ben." I heard the groan in Janie's voice. "Way to work that empathy muscle."

"That's not the muscle I'm famous for." Ben knocked against the granite top, as if he'd just remembered something. "Speaking of muscles, I saw you running this morning, Livvie." All of a sudden, my chest felt like I'd just started my tenth mile. "You have really good form."

My chest might have broken open and maybe a cartoon bird flew out, singing a cheesy musical theater tune. Or I just nodded dumbly and remembered to say, "Thank you."

Ben pointed up at Janie. "Put that candy back." He ambled out of the room and I stood there, trying to stop myself from staring at his retreating back, trying to avoid looking up to Janie's disappointed face.

But she wouldn't have it. She snorted derisively. "You must be joking."

"What do we need chocolate for?"

"You have no idea."

"Are we enticing Miss Abbot to speak with our stash of Snickers bars?"

"Listen, Olivia: You don't need my brother and my brother definitely doesn't need you."

"Are you going to fill me in on the candy plan or not?" I managed to make eye contact with Janie's knees.

"I'm asking you; I am pretty much begging you—"

"We were just talking about running."

"He doesn't care about running. I'm asking you this one thing." She sighed and passed the box of candy bars down to me. "I just don't want to see you get hurt. I don't want to see *anyone* get hurt."

"Of course." And then I said, because I never wanted to revisit the conversation again, "Besides, he's your brother. That would be too weird."

"Right. Way too weird. Thank you." I held the step stool as Janie climbed down. Then she unboxed the packs of chocolate and lined them precisely into the milk crate like they were gold bars and she was executing a proper heist. She nodded and smiled in a small way, the kind of smile that forgave me, but only grudgingly.

"Let's go chase a different kind of weirdness," she said.

Minutes later, we stood on Miss Abbot's well-tended front porch. Before my finger could connect with the doorbell, the front door swung open, and Miss Abbot stood there, studying us.

"Yes?" It sounded like she was scolding us, as if we'd interrupted some quiet reverie.

That's when the Janie Donahue charm factory sprang into action. "Good morning, ma'am! How are you today? Would you like to support the Glennon Heights diving team by purchasing some delicious chocolate?" Janie gestured to the assortment of candy with a flourish.

But Miss Abbot pretty much ignored Janie and inspected me carefully. "Olivia Danvers, is that you? Since when are you diving?"

"Well . . ." I completely blanked. I made a terrible spy.

"Every morning, I see you charging around the neighborhood like you're auditioning for a remake of *Chariots of Fire*." She lowered her eyeglasses and peered at me even more closely. Miss Abbot's eyes were chlorinated pools, sparkling in the sunlight. "Tell me, are you under the mistaken assumption that you are swimming laps instead?"

Janie laughed gamely. "Of course not! Olivia just volunteered to accompany me around the neighborhood. I'm still just getting acclimated on account of our just moving here, right across the street. We're neighbors." Janie made a big show of balancing the milk crate on one knee and reaching out to shake Miss Abbot's hand. "Pleased to meet you. I'm Jane Louise Donahue."

"Well, it's lovely to meet you, Jane Louise." Somewhat suddenly, Janie practically threw herself down on the bricks, fumbling her crate of chocolate as she tumbled.

"Oh dear." Miss Abbot shook her head in dismay and her silver hair swayed at the temples. "Why don't you girls come in and cool off with a glass of iced tea?"

"Thank you!" Janie exclaimed and mouthed *See?* to me once Miss Abbot turned her back. "It's so kind of you. This August heat takes some getting used to."

"They don't have August where you're from?"

Janie laughed nervously. "It's just really humid here."

Miss Abbot led us through her front parlor and into her

sitting room. I suppose it was technically a living room, but fancier, with its velvet furniture and embroidered pillows. It seemed like a room that would insist on a more formal name. "Please have a seat, girls."

I moved to sit down, but Janie took a detour to an oak desk in the corner as soon as Miss Abbot was out of the room. She kept one eye on the kitchen while thumbing through the small piles of papers. I realized she was checking for white stationery.

"What a lovely home, Miss Abbot," I croaked out while Janie opened drawers and shook her head at me: *Nothing.* We heard soft footsteps approach from the kitchen and rushed to take our places on the velvet sofa.

It was impossible to slouch in Miss Abbot's home. I looked across at Janie and she looked as stiff and on display as I felt. When Miss Abbot returned with a tray of glasses and graham crackers, we sat up even straighter. The ice clinked as she set down the tray. An orange cat, one I'd thought might be stuffed, leapt off the far end of the sofa in response.

"Poor Horatio," Miss Abbot murmured. "We've disturbed your beauty sleep."

"He's a handsome cat," Janie offered. "Is he your only one?"

Miss Abbot sipped her iced tea. "Well, I keep the other forty in the freezer."

My eyes snapped open and met Janie's widened gaze. "Miss Abbot?"

"Oh, I'm teasing, dear. Horatio's my one familiar. But that's what society has come to expect from a woman my age, isn't it? Too many cats. Maybe not enough sense."

"Oh no, you probably know every little thing that goes on in this neighborhood." I knew where Janie was headed, but she spoke to Miss Abbot like she was a child we might baby-sit. When she patted her hand and said, "I bet you don't miss a beat," I cringed despite every effort to keep my face still.

"Of course I don't, dear," Miss Abbot answered. The iced tea sweat in its glass but suddenly the room felt chilly. "So you two are fund-raising this morning?"

"Yes. We're selling chocolate door-to-door."

"You should be careful. I question the wisdom of sending young girls to doorsteps asking for money. After all, not everyone is harmless." There was the slightest edge running under Miss Abbot's words. I swallowed and told myself that I was officially paranoid. This was sweet Miss Abbot, after all—not some neighborhood menace making sly threats.

Janie sat back in her seat then and gazed directly at her. My heart sank. Even after only a week, I knew that look. It was the staring-down-the-high-dive look. We wouldn't be collecting a few dollars and making a quick exit anytime soon. Miss Abbot reached over and broke off a piece of graham cracker into her hand. She chewed slowly, savoring the moment with a tiny smile on her lips. She seemed pleased to have scored a formidable opponent.

Janie went on. "Glennon Heights seems so picturesque, though. It's hard to imagine anything happening here."

"Well, you should be careful about painting us with such broad strokes, Jane Louise. After all, one man killed his entire family not too far from where we sit."

I couldn't believe I was hearing this out loud. Miss Abbot was speaking about the Unspeakable. Hardly anyone in Glennon Heights ever mentioned the VonHolt murders. On significant anniversary years, news magazines made the rounds. Occasionally, some tabloid took a picture that we'd later see splashed across *Dateline* or *48 Hours*. I'd first learned about the case from one of those programs.

Janie listened closely as Miss Abbot described the initial discovery of the bodies and the manhunt that followed. I'd forgotten that she'd taught at the high school back then. Two of the VonHolt children had been in her classes, she told us. "The oldest, the daughter, had a real vibrancy to her. A bit too clever for her own good. She was a B-minus student who considered herself a solid A student." Miss Abbot crossed her feet at the ankles and bit down on another cracker. "Not that she deserved to be shot."

"Of course not," Janie said. "Ma'am, this might sound crazy, but is there any link between my house and the VonHolts? Did the families know each other?"

"The Langsom house? Oh, I don't think so. Not intimately. It's a small town, after all. We all feel like we know each other, but that's what the VonHolt case taught us. That maybe we don't really know our neighbors at all."

"But you knew the Langsoms?"

"Well, of course. Everyone knows the Langsoms." Miss Abbot looked over to me. "At one time, the Danvers and the Langsoms were quite close."

Janie swiveled to me.

"No, I'm sorry—that's actually not true." I laughed, embarrassed at having to correct Miss Abbot. "My mom and Mrs. Langsom knew each other back in high school. But by the time my parents moved into the neighborhood, they'd grown apart."

Miss Abbot sipped from her glass. "Oh no, dear. I meant your father." She shrugged and returned to bemoaning the downfall of the Langsom name. "In any case, it was a terrible thing, seeing an established family like that packing up and moving in the night like some band of thieves. After all they've done for this town, they deserved better. You know, they used to host tours." Miss Abbot nodded to herself, remembering. "Dr. Langsom's great-grandfather—he was before even my time—amassed some of his fortune bootlegging through the 1920s. He built the house with hidden cellars and passages to store and move his product. Apparently, he shipped to the city on canoes, right up the Belvidere River. Although perhaps that bit of history is a tad too resonant, with all the gossip about Dr. Langsom's . . . indulgences." Miss

Abbot clucked her tongue. "But when the doctor was a boy, the family hosted haunted houses every Halloween. I think they took a certain amount of pride in their renegade ancestry."

Across the room, the orange cat stretched on a sill. Through the window, I could see the grand facade of 16 Olcott Place. We all sat silently for a moment, and I pictured the old-fashioned ghosts and vampires floating through the yard, parading up the porch steps with pillowcases of candy slung over their shoulders.

"Well," Miss Abbot spoke suddenly, "I'll take one pack of peanut M&M's, please." She stood up and reached for the leather coin purse that rested on top of the TV stand.

It took a moment for Janie to jump to attention. "Right! Of course. Thank you so much for supporting our team." She dug through the candy, handing over a yellow packet. Miss Abbot took it and gazed steadily at her, still waiting.

"How much, dear?"

"Yes." Janie nodded. "I mean, that will be one dollar."

Miss Abbot unfolded a bill from her purse. "Those are slim profit margins. You divers should have the economics club advise you. Especially if they're having you girls traipse around town, knocking on doors"—she paused and stared meaningfully at both of us—"randomly?"

She knew. Of course she knew. She knew everything.

Just when I thought she would simply take the dollar and

slink away, Janie asked, "Ma'am, you're pretty much an expert on Glennon Heights, right?"

"I've learned to be cautious about calling myself an expert in anything . . . but I've lived here long enough to know the scenery pretty well." Miss Abbot moved to the door and reached for the knob. Janie's eyes darted to mine. *Last chance*, I tried to tell her. *You might as well ask.*

Janie nodded. "Miss Abbot, have you ever noticed anyone taking an unusual interest in my home? I know it's a landmark and all, but maybe someone has seemed preoccupied in a way that was creepy? You know, like inappropriate? Maybe mentally unsound?"

"Oh dear." Miss Abbot grimaced. "You're talking about the Sentry, aren't you?"

I felt myself go absolutely still. My neck prickled like when you're playing hide-and-seek—that moment right before you're found. Miss Abbot stood, still blocking the front door. Janie jutted her chin out, as if to say, *We can take her.* And I reminded myself that it was crazy to consider physically overpowering a seventy-year-old woman in her own home. Besides I wasn't sure if we could take her. We'd underestimated Miss Abbot all along.

She nodded kindly at us. "You must have received a letter." She reached for the door. At first I had a nightmarish vision of Miss Abbot flicking the bolt and locking us forever in her home: two dolls enclosed in glass domes. But that was silly; that was nuts. That was Janie's influence, along with this week of increasingly exposed secrets. Miss Abbot only held open the screen and ushered us out.

Janie had halted in her tracks. I wrenched her forward. Nuts or not, I was done with feeling like a mouse struggling under Horatio's paw. We needed to scamper off. Still caught, Janie stared at Miss Abbot in amazement. "You know about the letter?"

"Well, yes, dear." Miss Abbot smiled. Not menacingly, really. More like she'd read our every thought and had been disappointed. The screen door slammed and our sweet, elderly neighbor retreated into the shadows of her darkened hallway. We could barely see her as she spoke. "And you mean *letters*. The Langsoms received several."

CHAPTER NINE

We managed to walk calmly across the street back to Janie's house, quickening our pace once we reached her yard. As soon as we got inside, we sprinted straight up to her third-floor bedroom.

Once there, Janie paced the length of her room, occasionally flicking open the curtains to peek out at Miss Abbot's yellow house.

"I vote we come completely clean and tell your parents about the second note immediately."

"That serves no purpose."

"Are we going to tell them about Miss Abbot?"

"That she's oddly intimidating and harbors strong opinions about school fund-raisers?"

I tried to lower the drama barometer. "Nope. That she's an elder in the neighborhood whose help we sought out." Second attempt: "Janie, sit down a sec. That was really tense and stressful, okay? I get that. But we gathered some information, which was our goal. And really we only discovered good news."

She leveled her gaze at me as if to say, *Liv, please.* But she sat down, clutching a pillow to her chest. "How is it good news?"

"Because it's not personal." I raised my hands to fend off her arguments before she voiced them. "It feels that way, sure. But if the Sentry started with the Langsoms, then the obsession really does focus on the house. Nobody's angry that you moved here. Nobody's attacking you or your family." Janie's hands relaxed their grip on her pillow just a bit. "But listen, there's bad news too. It makes it creepier that the Langsoms also got letters. Whoever is sending them probably won't stop anytime soon. If you ignore them, who knows what they'll try next? We need to talk to your parents. We'll show them the second note."

"You're a really good friend." Janie's voice sounded small, muffled against the pillow.

I was trying to be. Or that's what I told myself a short time later, as I sat beside Janie in the dining room waiting for the latest Donahue family meeting to come to session. The whole crew had assembled: Ben and Lucy both looked bored, scrolling through their phones. Mrs. Donahue kept smoothing out the stitching on the tablecloth and glancing up at the doorway, where her husband stood with his eyes fixed on the kitchen TV.

I kept my face still and peaceful. On my lap, I held Janie's backpack. I watched her eyes dart around the room and settle on the bag periodically. Each time, she looked pleadingly at me, as if I could call the whole thing off even if I wanted to. The two of us sat with our backs to the bookshelves. I reminded myself that we'd just checked the secret hideaway—there was no possible way an intruder hid there, peeking out from the darkness, listening to what we were about to announce.

"Gavin?" Mrs. Donahue's tone sounded sharp.

"Yes! I hear you." Mr. Donahue ran his hands through his hair, leaving the sides sticking up like two silver wings. "You all understand the concept of working at home, correct? That it involves actually working?" At least he turned around, though. His angry glower swung around the room, like a spotlight into which none of us wanted to step.

"Daddy, I'm sorry. I'm so sorry." Janie sounded miserable.

Mr. Donahue visibly softened. For a second, he actually looked like a kind man, a good dad. "Aww, Jane. I'm the one who's sorry. Your old man's just feeling the pressure a little.

Everything is fine. At least on my end. What's with the family meeting, guys? What's going on?"

Ben stretched and shrugged. "Well, it's not my meeting. That's for sure."

Lucy rolled her eyes. "Maybe your parole officer called the meeting."

"I don't have a parole officer," he muttered in a softer voice. "I have a court-appointed legal advocate."

"That's enough." Mrs. Donahue rested her head in her hands.

I'd been waiting for Janie to give a signal. The longer we stalled, the more it seemed likely that the Donahue family would completely unravel. As much as I wanted to learn more about Ben Donahue's legal advocate and what necessitated that role, it was time to move things along. I unzipped the front pocket of her backpack and tried to pass Janie the envelope under the table.

Ben noticed and immediately swung his eyes up to mine. "Sorry," I whispered, without being sure exactly what I was apologizing for.

"This came today." Janie placed the letter in the middle of the dining room table. "It's just like the other one." Mrs. Donahue gasped. Janie rushed to keep talking. "I don't know why I kept it from you. It's another scary message. We picked it up—" Janie looked toward me and corrected herself.

"I mean, I picked it up and just didn't feel like dealing with it. Olivia tried to get me to tell you right away."

"You didn't feel like dealing with it?" Lucy sounded unnerved. "Who are you—Ben?"

"Give me that." Mrs. Donahue reached out for the card and whipped it out of the envelope.

"Careful. It's evidence," Mr. Donahue said. But Mrs. Donahue was too busy reading.

"Gavin, it's terrible. It's sickening."

Ben leaned forward to read the message but his mom snatched the card up and held it closer to her chest. "No. I will not have my children reading this filth any longer."

"Mom, Janie's been carrying it around like an invitation to the prom." Ben held his hand out, but Mrs. Donahue shook her head.

"Absolutely not."

Lucy looked at her mother and then me. "Can you just paraphrase?"

"I said no."

"Gory like the last one?" Ben asked me. I nodded. "Blood in the walls?" I lowered my eyes to my lap.

"Gavin, we need to call the police."

"Let's just think on it. There's no rush . . ."

"Now," Lucy finished his sentence. "There's no rush *now*, hours after the evidence arrived." She glared at Janie and me.

"What were the two of you thinking, holding on to that? And not telling anyone?"

Janie pushed on. "We also talked to Miss Abbot, who lives in the yellow house on the corner lot. She's kind of like the town Wikipedia. She knows everything."

"Gavin, we need to call the police," Mrs. Donahue repeated.

"For instance," Janie continued, "she knows that the Langsoms received letters from the Sentry too."

Mrs. Donahue stopped ignoring us then. Mr. Donahue stopped ignoring Mrs. Donahue. Even Ben started paying attention.

"How many letters?" Lucy asked.

"She said several."

"Why were you talking to this woman about the Sentry?" Mrs. Donahue asked.

Janie's eyes darted to me and I rushed to fill in the silence. "Janie stopped by Miss Abbot's house with me. She likes when people from the neighborhood visit and somehow we got to talking about the letters. Janie and I were nervous because the new note had arrived. I thought maybe—"

Mr. Donahue interrupted. "Janie, this is a family matter. We talked about being discreet about these letters."

"I hardly think that's the priority, Gavin," Mrs. Donahue said.

A cloud passed over Mr. Donahue's face. But he said only, "We discussed this."

Mrs. Donahue clutched the second card closely, reading it again. "That woman told you the Langsoms received letters?"

Janie nodded. "Several."

And I added, hoping to placate her dad, "She mentioned it pretty matter-of-factly. Like it was common knowledge in the neighborhood."

"But it wasn't, right?" Ben asked me. "You didn't know about it."

"Yeah, but I'm fourteen. And it turns out we didn't know a lot about the Langsoms. No one even knew they were moving."

"It just seems strange that Ned wouldn't have mentioned these letters." Mrs. Donahue tapped the corner of the envelope on her pursed lips.

"Yeah, it seems strange. It seems like nondisclosure. And it seems like good ol' Ned didn't want to interfere with his own huge commission." Janie's dad stood up and began pacing around the room.

"It's pretty clear that we should call the police—"

"Stop." Mr. Donahue slammed his fist against the ornate doorframe arching between the living room and dining rooms. "We're not calling the police. Not before I go down to see McGovern and find out what he has to say. And believe me, I'm going to record the whole conversation. Because if he admits to knowing about these letters ahead of time—this campaign of terror—well, then he will see himself named in a lawsuit. Along with the Langsoms and the mortgage company and anyone else involved in this deception." He held out his hand, waiting. Mrs. Donahue seemed to look pleadingly at him even as she placed the envelope in his hand. "That's all there is to it, Lindsay."

He tucked the envelope into his jacket. It seemed to me like there was a lot more to it, actually. He hadn't even taken the time to read this latest note in the so-called campaign of terror. He didn't want the police involved but had already planned out a possible lawsuit.

Janie stood up. "See, this is what I worried about." Her dad didn't even turn around, though. He headed out the front door and let it slam behind him.

Mrs. Donahue bit her lip, watching him go. "Everything's going to be fine. You'll see. There's got to be a perfectly reasonable expectation. A silly prank or one of those quaint small-town traditions." She trailed off and then said more to herself than to us, "I should give Ned a call and just let him know your dad's on the warpath."

Ben watched her wander out of the room, his brow furrowed. "Sure, because when your husband sets off in a homicidal rage, you definitely don't want your realtor to get the wrong impression of where your loyalty lies."

"Shut up," Lucy snapped.

Janie and I tried to retreat back to her room then, to lose

ourselves watching videos about kittens in bathtubs and baby goats bouncing on trampolines—anything that wasn't the Sentry. But after only about ten videos, Lucy summoned us back down to the dining room. It seemed she and Ben had stayed there the whole time, conferencing.

It became immediately clear that I was going to be the subject of a cross-examination.

Lucy started by asking me, "What's Ned McGovern like?"

"What?" I saw Aunt Jillian's face in my mind. "Why?"

Ben leaned back. "Is he single? Dreamy?" He must have seen the look of dread drift across my face. "Uh-oh." He slammed all four legs of his chair back onto the floor with a thud.

"He's not single." And then because all three Donahue siblings were still staring at me: "I don't think he's dreamy." Then I sat frozen, unable to move past using the word *dreamy* in front of Ben Donahue. "He's married, but there are rumors . . ."

"Aha!" Ben punched into the air. "I told you, Lucy," he crowed.

"It's just so not the point right now."

"You don't think so? Why do you think Dad charged off to go talk to him? I bet it's less about the possibility that he's the Sentry and more about how often he's been texting Mom."

"You don't know that's who's been texting her."

"Okay, we literally just moved to this town, so thankfully there aren't a ton of candidates. Yet. And you heard how she just said his name: *Ned.*" Ben breathed out the name and managed to make its one syllable sound obscene. "We've been down this road before." Maybe he was reminding his sisters. He might have been explaining it to me.

"I was surprised," I offered tentatively, aware that I was stepping across a minefield. "Your dad didn't seem so interested in what the note actually said. He didn't even look at it."

"I guess when you've read one piece of hate mail, you've read them all," Ben said.

"Yeah, I guess," I muttered.

"You guess what, Olivia? There's obviously something you want to say." Lucy folded her arms across her chest, daring me to speak up.

But there was nothing. What could I say? We didn't really have family meetings in my house, but I never imagined that the parents would simply wander away from them, leaving the kids to worry about the anonymous letters left in their mailbox. Was I supposed to confess that it seemed to me that Mr. Donahue had a rage problem, right after the Donahue kids confessed that their mom might have a flirting problem? Should I have spelled it out for them? That clearly their dad was financially overburdened? That maybe he regretted taking on the expense of their mom's dream house, especially if Mrs. Donahue was getting too close with the guy who brokered the deal for that dream house?

I stared at the grained wood of the dining room table and wished I could just disappear right into the wall.

Janie spoke up then, in the same uncertain voice she always used around her family. "What's going on?"

"You know how we had our suspect list?" Lucy answered her, but kept her eyes fixed on me. "Olivia thinks the order's off. She thinks our own dad should be at the top. That he's writing hate letters to his own family."

"I didn't say that." I rushed to defend myself, but really all I meant was, I didn't say that out loud.

While I was still searching to find the right words to tell Janie and Ben and even Lucy, a police car pulled into their driveway.

Even from the dining room, we could all see that it was Mr. Donahue hunched over in the back seat, looking defeated as he stared up at the house.

CHAPTER TEN

"Mom!" Ben bellowed. "You need to get down here, right away!"

The rest of us stood frozen and wordless as we watched one of the police officers climb out of the car. It looked like his partner was on the radio. Then the partner leaned back, speaking to Mr. Donahue. The first cop slammed his door and peered at the front door through aviator sunglasses. I recognized him as the school outreach officer. He'd taught me everything I knew about not abusing prescription drugs and not soliciting online predators.

As if snapping out of a trance, Lucy sprang into action

and said, "I'll go get her." She darted out of the room and squeezed Ben's arm as she passed. Janie, still silent, reached for me. She nodded toward the bookshelf, and before I even had the chance to react, she had triggered the mechanism to the hidden hollow. She snaked one arm around my waist; together we stepped back into the darkness.

We shoved the door closed and crouched down, taking turns pressing our faces up to each of the spyholes. They were small openings that framed only bits and pieces of the chaotic scene unfolding. The books muffled the shouting so we didn't hear Mrs. Donahue until she actually entered the room. "What has he done?" she asked. And then: "What was he thinking?" When the doorbell toned, we felt the vibrations in the walls.

"You have to answer the door for the police." That was Lucy.

"Just give me a minute." Mrs. Donahue's profile moved in and out of view. "I cannot believe this is happening." We watched her tuck errant strands of hair behind her ears and smooth her pants with her hands. Her eyes narrowed critically and I realized she was probably checking her reflection in the mirror above the fireplace.

"Mom!" That was Ben again. I felt relieved that we couldn't see him, as if that made our hiding and spying somehow forgivable. The doorbell rang and shook the walls again.

"That's it," we heard Lucy bark. "I'm answering the door right this minute."

For the next few minutes, we heard only muffled voices, punctuated by Mrs. Donahue's occasional exclamation, like "You can't just keep him." Lucy's voice permeated the mumbling and then we heard hushing. Moments later two sets of footsteps stomped up the front staircase—Ben and Lucy banished from the scene by their mother.

"Ma'am, I realize your family has just moved to Glennon Heights and we want you to feel welcome." The officer's voice was stern and forceful. It cut right through our muffled hiding place. "But this is a quiet town with good people. It's not the kind of place where conflict gets resolved with violence."

"Of course, officer. My husband has been under an inordinate amount of stress."

"Moving is stressful."

"One of the most stressful times in a human being's life." Another deep voice chimed in. Maybe Sunglasses Cop visited office buildings, lecturing on the dangers of real estate.

"This is not who we are." Janie's mom sounded shaky.

"Hope not." One of the officers coughed. "Ma'am, has your husband always had a temper?"

"No. Certainly not."

"Do you feel safe in your home, ma'am?"

"I'm sorry? Absolutely not. I mean, I do. I absolutely feel safe. I am not—there is no—"

"You understand we have to ask."

"This has all been a complete misunderstanding." I

glimpsed a flash of blue uniform and realized one of the police officers had stepped closer to Janie's mom.

"Well, between us, Mrs. Donahue, your husband wouldn't be the first to misunderstand Ned McGovern." Next to me, Janie caught her breath.

"McGovern's friendly with many of the ladies in town. I'm sure it's part of the territory, selling homes and whatnot. But I could understand how a husband might misinterpret his . . . intentions."

From our perspective, only the rigid lines of Mrs. Donahue's stiffened back were visible. We could not see her face. But we heard her tell the police officers in a carefully steady voice, "You've been very kind and helpful. Thank you." Janie and I heard shuffling. "Will I have to pick up my husband at the station? Should I—I don't know—do I call an attorney?"

"Mr. McGovern declined to press charges," one of the officers said. Mrs. Donahue exhaled loudly. Beside me, Janie's released breath echoed her mom's relief. "We just wanted to give your husband some time to cool down—"

"And make sure things were okay with you. Make sure you knew you could tell us if you felt unsafe."

"That's very thoughtful, thank you."

"So you're sure, then? Anything else we need to know?"

Janie and I leaned forward, our foreheads pressing against the thin wood. Would she tell them? Would Mrs. Donahue mention the letters?

"No. There's nothing. This whole episode is out of character for us. I apologize for the trouble, officers."

In our hiding place, we exhaled. Janie chewed her lip and glowered at the light shining into the shadows. She held up two fingers. "Two lies."

In the dining room, Sunglasses Cop nodded to Janie's mom. "All right then. I'm going to go have a word with Mr. Donahue. We'll be right in." He edged out of view and we heard the front door open and close. Maybe if I were a good friend, my sense of bravery would have kicked in. I'd push my way out from behind the bookcase and demand that Mrs. Donahue tell the police all about the letters. *This has gone on long enough*, I'd say. *Can't you see what it's doing to Janie?* But instead I sat like a fellow statue at her side, ready to collect the pieces if she fell apart.

We heard her dad before we saw him framed in the peephole. He blustered through the door, asking, "Well, are you going to charge him with anything? Does McGovern get to sit in the back of a squad car in his own driveway?"

"Gavin." Mrs. Donahue sounded outraged. We couldn't see her, but I imagined she was giving the police her patented apologetic look.

"It's just like we said, Mr. Donahue." Sunglasses Cop kept his voice even, like he was trying to calm a room full of seventh graders. "I apologize for taking more of your time; we only wanted a chance to check in with your wife about how the move was going."

"That's terrific." Mr. Donahue's tone made me wonder if the police ever wrote tickets for sarcasm. "And I imagine she told you about those ridiculous letters."

"Pardon me? What letters?"

After a long stretch of tense silence and some frantic clarification, Sunglasses Cop and his partner stepped outside for some kind of cop conference while Mr. Donahue followed his wife into the dining room. Janie and I crowded against that side of the hideout, listening. Her parents hissed loudly at each other, as if intending to keep their voices down. Instead they sounded like two tangled snakes, fighting to get free of each other. "Well, how was I supposed to know?"

"I don't know, Gav. You told me you wanted it kept in the family, so I did as you asked. Maybe you could have trusted me."

"Wrong day to talk to me about trust. Or keeping it in the family."

"For goodness' sake, nothing happened."

"Nothing's happened *yet*. Where are you going now?"

"They're going to be here for a while. I thought I'd bring out a pitcher of lemonade."

Janie and I heard his clomping footsteps and the distant clatter of ice cubes colliding with glass. "Go, go, go," I whispered and pushed her forward. We took turns fumbling with the mechanism, frantically trying to spring open the secret door.

"Just grab some cookies or something." That was Janie's mom, in the kitchen. "Maybe that bowl of fruit."

"This is for you, you know, just to keep this happy housewife sham going strong. And that ship has sailed." Mr. Donahue's tone softened. I could barely hear him. "Tell me again that nothing happened."

"Gavin. Nothing happened." She said it like she meant it. I was so caught up eavesdropping on the Donahue marriage that I didn't notice that Janie had finally sprung open the door.

"Liv, let's go!" Janie urged, and I practically crashed into the dining room table. "Close it up behind you." I shut the bookcase and we ran, hunched over, toward the front stairs. I glanced back to make sure the shelf looked like an ordinary bookshelf again . . . and that's when I saw him.

Ben sat in an armchair in the family room, silent and watching. My eyes followed the sight line between him and the hideaway—a clear and unobstructed view. He raised his eyebrows at me and nodded slowly. Outside, the two officers conferred on the Donahues' front lawn. It seemed like pretty soon, we would all have a lot of explaining to do.

Janie and I went upstairs to give Lucy a heads-up. "Dad told the police about the letters," Janie said.

She had been lounging, but in her unique Lucy way, which meant doing leg lifts with an organic chemistry book splayed open on the bed. She sprang up as soon as Janie spoke. "What do you mean? Why? I thought—"

"He thought your mom had already told them."

"Why were the cops interviewing them separately?"

"I don't know, Judge Judy," Janie said. "We should go downstairs, though."

"They wanted to make sure your dad wasn't abusing your mom." Again my explanation did not calm the situation. Lucy muttered a vocabulary list of swear words and threw her hair into a businesslike bun.

"Yeah—we should go down. Olivia, maybe you have someplace else to be? I'm sure this is entertaining and all, but Janie can call you after and tell you about it then. I think it's safe to say your sleepover's canceled."

I felt torn—on one hand, I didn't relish the emotional tornado. But I didn't think it was fair to step out of the storm and leave Janie on her own. Besides, my adrenaline was still pumping. I felt like a fox in the night, either hunted or hunting. I couldn't imagine just slinking back home and watching from my back porch.

"Olivia stays," Janie announced firmly. "She's been here the whole time. And she's the one who got Miss Abbot to talk. The police will want to hear from her."

Lucy spun around then and pinned me in the doorframe.

"Fine, then. But let's be clear: None of this is material for freshmen gossip." She spit out the words and gestured around with one arm, while blocking me with the other.

"I would never—"

"But you probably would, and you know what? Ordinarily, I might even understand. But I'm about to start my senior year in a new school, and that already sucks hard enough. I don't want to walk down the halls and wonder what everyone's whispering about."

"Yeah, of course. I get it." And I did get it. In that moment, Lucy at least seemed human.

She nodded and led the way back downstairs. "We should get Ben."

"He's in the family room," I said. Janie shot me a questioning look. "Just sitting there."

"Cops make him nervous," Lucy said.

"Lucy—" Janie's voice carried a warning.

"You wanted her here. She's probably going to find out everything."

Before any more useful information emerged, we heard a soft knock at the front door. Sunglasses Cop didn't wait for an answer but simply opened the door.

Mrs. Donahue rushed over, drying her hands on her shirt. "Come in. We were just putting together some refreshments."

"That's not necessary," Other Cop said, without smiling.

"But very kind of you," said Sunglasses. I had seen this

routine on *Law & Order.* "Is there a comfortable place where we can all chat?"

Mr. Donahue wore the same unyielding face as Other Cop. "I'm going to ask again—do I need to call an attorney? To protect my family?"

Sunglasses Cop held his hands up. "We're all trying to protect your family, Mr. Donahue. It's just a conversation. Is everyone home right now?" Janie's mom and dad exchanged apprehensive eye contact.

"Yes." Janie's dad stood up straighter. He smiled reassuringly at the girls: his daughters, his wife, even me. "Let's all go into the family room." He motioned for us to come down the steps. "We're still unpacking of course, but there are plenty of places to sit." Lucy dutifully took the bowl of fruit from him and we all paraded into the family room, where Ben stood in front of the armchair, looking as if he occasionally, actually worried about something. Mr. Donahue had transformed into a levelheaded patriarch. "You've met my wife. Thank you so much for the assistance this afternoon." He strode over to stand beside Ben. "This is Benjamin, my son. My daughters Lucy and Jane. And Olivia is also here—a neighbor friend of the girls. Olivia, honey, I apologize—I've gone blank on your last name?"

"Danvers." My voice sounded impossibly small, so I said it again more loudly, like a teacher was taking attendance. "Olivia Danvers."

"Danvers, huh?" Sunglasses Copy said.

"Yes, my dad owns the tire shop right off Landing Lane."

"Fine mechanic, your father. Don't tell anyone, but when our guys at the station can't handle an issue with a vehicle, we take it to your old man. He's a master." Sunglasses Cop grinned widely, all white teeth and rapport.

"Thank you."

"Should we send Olivia home?" Mrs. Donahue asked. I stood back up right in the middle of sitting down. Everyone turned to look at me. "After all, we don't have permission from her parents. I wouldn't want my child questioned without me there—"

"Again, we're not questioning anyone. We're just here to help." The policeman turned to me. "Olivia, what do you say? Do you think you might be able to add something to the conversation?"

I looked to Janie, who nodded at me. "Yeah. I'm happy to help."

"Okay, then." I sat back down and prepared to talk about the letters again. Mrs. Donahue handed them over and the officers read them carefully, grimacing.

"Have you all read the letters?" Sunglasses Cop asked.

Nods all around. I didn't think that was technically true and hoped we wouldn't be quizzed on them.

"Have you had many visitors to the house?"

"Movers," Mrs. Donahue answered. "A few neighbors

have dropped by to welcome us." Mrs. Donahue stopped and brought her hand to her mouth.

"What is it?" Other Cop asked.

"Well, people have brought muffins, cake, zucchini. We've been eating that food, but if it's this Sentry person . . ."

"You all seem fine," Other Cop observed.

Sunglasses cleared his throat. "But it can't hurt to be careful from now on. No unpackaged, unsealed food. Just save it for us to check out. So which neighbors dropped off food?"

"I made a list." Mrs. Donahue rushed to retrieve it.

"Really?" Lucy asked. "You made a list of suspects?"

Mrs. Donahue called back from the kitchen. "Of course not. I made a list for thank-you notes." Mr. Donahue exhaled deeply as his wife came back in. "Here you go."

"Great." Sunglasses jotted down the names in his notebook. "Anyone else?"

"Olivia." Lucy tilted her head in my direction. "And Olivia's mother."

"Of course," Mrs. Donahue said. "Olivia's been a wonderful friend to Janie. And when we received the first note, we did ask her mother for advice."

"That's great." Sunglasses smiled encouragingly. "You've already made some connections in the neighborhood. Somebody might see something, and it always helps if your neighbors are also staying vigilant. Otherwise do you get the feeling you're being watched? Other than just the general curiosity since you're a new family in a relatively small town?" The Donahues all sort of shrugged off that question. "Any strange phone calls? Hang-ups?" Heads shook all around.

"We have awful reception here," Lucy announced sourly. "Calls drop all the time."

Mrs. Donahue flashed a desperate smile in her direction. "That's not really what the officer's asking about, honey." She looked apologetic, explaining, "Sometimes the charms of this old house get lost on the teenaged members of our family."

"Yes. I always forget to find terrible reception and anonymous letters delightful," Lucy remarked.

Other Cop continued, "These letters? They were placed in the mailbox—"

"Mail slot," Mr. Donahue corrected.

"But without a stamp." The two officers glanced at each other. "You didn't speak to your mail carrier?"

"We just found out about the second note today. And the first . . . Well, I suppose we wanted to believe it was an anomaly. Just a freak thing." Mrs. Donahue smiled nervously.

"Right. Well, we'll check in down at the post office. Tampering with the mail is a federal issue, but we'll ask Al—you're on his route, I'm sure—to keep an eye out."

"So it seems like the plan is to keep a lot of eyes out," Mr. Donahue muttered.

Sunglasses held his hands up again, keeping the peace. "Listen, it's too late to dust either envelope for prints. They've passed through too many hands." Lucy glared at Janie and me pointedly. "Honestly, best-case scenario? We get another letter. We're going to set up some plastic covering on the floor right by the door. If it arrives, you leave it right where it is." His eyes swept the room, making contact with each of us. "And then you call us."

"It would seem like the best-case scenario is that we don't get another letter," Mr. Donahue argued.

"Well, then won't you just worry every time the mail comes? Won't you always be waiting?" The room fell silent as we all imagined that option.

"Will you speak to this Miss Abbot?" Mrs. Donahue asked. "She told the girls these letters actually began before we moved into the residence."

"Grace Abbot? What did she say?"

Janie knocked my knee with her own. My turn. "Miss Abbot mentioned the Langsoms had also received some letters from the Sentry."

Sunglasses sighed and rubbed his temples.

"Exactly!" Mr. Donahue practically leapt out of his seat. "You see? That should have been disclosed like any other issue with the house. These people, the Langsoms, they put my family at risk. And Ned McGovern served as their accomplice."

"Did the Langsoms ever report this?" Mrs. Donahue asked in a calmer tone.

The two officers shifted in their seats. "No, ma'am. We'll stop by and speak to Miss Abbot."

"Why not go right to the source and speak to the Langsoms? Frankly, I want them put on notice—"

"We'll discuss that with our chief, sir." Sunglasses seemed to be thinking hard about something and then he wrote in his little book. "Aside from these letters, how has the move gone?" He paused to look in his notebook. "Lucy?"

"It's great. Other than this, it's great."

"But you're seventeen, right? It must have been a shock to move away from your friends so close to graduation."

Lucy cocked her head and directly met his eyes. When she spoke, any trace of her early frustration and sarcasm had evaporated. "Glennon Heights has a phenomenal school system, so this move provides a lot of academic opportunities. And I make friends easily, so I'm not worried about connecting with my classmates."

Wow, I thought. *She's really good.*

"What about you, Ben?" Other Cop leaned forward in his seat. "Do you make friends easily?"

Mr. Donahue leaned forward as well. "What is this?"

"Nothing. I'm just asking Ben how it's going."

"It's going fine." Ben sounded weary.

"You miss your friends?"

"Sure."

"Any trouble back home?"

Everyone in the room sat very still.

Finally, Ben answered, "A little bit."

"A little bit. Care to elaborate?"

"Not really."

Mr. Donahue looked as if he was struggling to keep his voice steady. "Clearly, you ran my son's name when you stepped outside. Why don't you tell us what came up?"

"Well, I'm sure you know. Initial charges of assault, for one. That seemed noteworthy. Do the folks at our local high school know about these charges?"

"He wasn't found guilty of any of the charges."

"You pled out, from what I understand." Other Cop pulled out his own little book. "To harassment of this other student?" Ben nodded. "That's still some kind of trouble. I mean, I don't know about you, Officer Wycoff, but I certainly never had to plead to harassing a classmate back in my day. Is that why you all moved here?"

"No." Mr. Donahue spoke defiantly. "In this family, we don't run from our problems." Next to me, Janie fidgeted.

Other Cop was still focused on Ben. "You miss your crew back home? What would it take to get your parents to move back east?"

"Excuse me." Mrs. Donahue stood up. "What are you implying?"

"We don't really bother with implying. You'll know if we believe something."

"What Officer Coronado means is that we have to explore all avenues. You understand this, right? And so the first question we have to ask is, Who benefits if you all move out? The Langsoms sold their house. They're not looking back. And given your son's record for making poor choices, we'd be remiss if we didn't ask."

"I don't benefit from moving back home." Ben spoke flatly. "There's nothing there for me."

"Okay. And what's here?" Other Cop asked.

Ben met his eyes. I felt weirdly proud of him for that.

"A fresh start, sir," he said.

Other Cop gave the slightest nod to Sunglasses, as if Ben had passed some kind of test. "Good to know." He stood up. "Folks, we have the best possible plan in place. Officer Wycoff and I will follow up and have a few conversations around town. And you know what to do if another message shows up.

"We will get to the bottom of this. In the meantime, try not to panic. And don't go around town accusing people either. Mr. Donahue, we'd appreciate if you and Ned McGovern gave each other a wide berth for a while. Truth is, I'd like to see the men in this family take some cues from the ladies. Think things through a bit."

Janie's dad looked like he was thinking through the possible penalties for assaulting a police officer. He just stood there blinking slowly, obviously seething.

Thankfully, Janie's mom stepped in. "We appreciate all

your assistance today. I assure you, we are a law-abiding family. These past few months have challenged our sense of justice a bit. But it's clear you gentlemen are here to help." Behind her, Mr. Donahue snorted. She ignored him. "We all thank you."

Officer Wycoff said, "I'll stop back tomorrow morning with a plastic tarp so that we can sift through mail on a plastic surface." Then the two cops were out of the house, back in their car, and down Olcott Place.

"Family meeting," Mr. Donahue announced, but the rest of the family groaned in protest.

"No. No more family meetings." Ben's jaw was set. "I'm going out."

"Keep your phone on," Mr. Donahue said.

But Ben was already out the door.

CHAPTER ELEVEN

I'd decided the Donahues definitely didn't need me lurking around. They had conversations to avoid, resentments to build. And the texts from my mom were piling up, in various degrees of dramatic capitalization and punctuation, because she'd seen the cop car in the Donahues' driveway. If I didn't get home soon, she was going to come and get me—and I didn't want that.

I made plans with Janie to meet a bunch of people at the mall the next day and then ducked out.

I offered to switch sleepover locations, but Janie wouldn't come with me.

I was home all of three seconds before my mom breezed deliberately into the kitchen. "You want to tell me what's going on?"

"Not really."

She rummaged in the fridge and pulled out three apples. "Ordinarily, I'd respect that. But not when the police are involved. So why don't you start talking?"

It felt good to spill, actually. I sat on the stool, watching the cutting board fill up with translucent white slices. It made my mom mad to hear about the second note and to realize that we'd been in the back of her car, on the way to Target, keeping it a secret. She didn't say that but she sucked on two front teeth, the way she does when she's considering how much temper to lose. And she cut that particular slice of apple really hard. But then she laughed at the idea of Gavin Donahue running out to beat up Ned McGovern.

"I can't think of two men I'd rather see punch each other," Mom told me. "Oh gosh—the disdain dripping between the two of them." She snorted. "Someone should have sold tickets." She offered me an apple slice and then said, "It sounds like you think Mr. Donahue wrote those letters."

"I did." I felt better, admitting it out loud. "He's weird. And he's really stressed out about money. Maybe he regrets buying the house. I got suspicious when he wouldn't read the second note, like maybe he already knew what it said. But then I saw the way he got so defensive about his family."

Mom sighed. "I don't like the guy. And this whole episode certainly doesn't reassure me about you spending so much time over there. But it would shock me if someone wrote notes like that to their own kids—prank or not. It just goes against every instinct you have as a parent—to protect and shield your child."

"Yeah. That makes sense." I nodded, mildly surprised that my mom wasn't going ballistic and locking me in my room or something. Had she always been this reasonable?

No, she had not. "Your father has forbidden me from forbidding you to spend time over there. But I'm not thrilled, Olivia Lynn. You're lucky you headed right home, because if you had let one more text go unanswered . . ."

"You said yourself they were just letters."

"I said that about the one letter, before the police were involved." She reached over and tucked a strand of my hair behind my ear. "I'm really trying, Olivia. I know it's important to give you a little more freedom, a little more privacy. But this is all so strange. No more secrets, okay?"

I pictured the hidden room behind the Donahues' bookshelf and thought about Ben and everything I'd learned about him that afternoon. "Of course," I lied. "No more secrets."

//////////

The next day at the mall, it became glaringly obvious that my friendship with Janie fed off secrets. Kaia was back from band camp, Mirabelle's beach tan hadn't yet faded, and of course Brooke had commentary on everything, but so many topics lay off-limits. We relied on our shared fascination with Thatcher Langsom to propel us through the awkward silences. And the imminent beginning to our high school careers.

"I'm leaving my backpack at home," Brooke announced while browsing through the Kate Spade store where none of us could afford a bag, let alone a key chain. "No one uses backpacks."

"They do, though. I think they do," Mirabelle supposed. "You have to carry stuff."

"I'll bring a bag, like a tote or something, but backpacks seem so juvenile."

"My sister brings a backpack. Every day," Kaia offered.

Janie nodded. "Yeah, the last thing you want is to have a handle break or swing a tote onto your shoulder and accidently hit someone."

"Janie, will the twins drive to school?" I hadn't thought of that. Would they? And more importantly, would they take me too? For a brief second I had myself sitting in the passenger seat, looking over at Ben, as he steered into a space in the high school parking lot. But that was ridiculous. Lucy would ride shotgun. She'd probably fold me into the trunk.

But the dream dissolved. "Neither of them drives. I guess we'll ride the bus." Janie noticed our troubled faces. "What? Don't people ride the bus?"

"I mean, sometimes," I said. "Usually, my mom drives me,

though. She could take you too, and Ben and Lucy, if they wanted." I saw the look curl between Mirabelle and Brooke. The only thing more awkward than a senior riding the bus was a pile of kids climbing out of some mom's minivan. "Or we could ride bikes." As soon as I said it, I could tell by their faces: Bikes counted as worse.

"Doesn't the bus come right to the corner?" We had migrated, en masse, to shop for cosmetics. Janie trailed her finger along the rows of magenta lip glosses. "My parents won't want me to ride a bike right now. Paranoid." She grinned at me and then realized her mistake. "They're just really protective," she told the rest. "Last year I fell and got a concussion."

"The worst," Kaia agreed. I almost snickered, thinking, *Yep, right up there with anonymous death threats.* Kaia said, "Brooke, I think you need a backpack for gym class."

"I'm not taking gym." And because she was Brooke, we didn't even question her. For a second I wished I could be someone that people didn't question so much. Or someone who didn't second-guess herself so often. If I could have been absolutely honest, in the middle of the makeup store, I would have told my friends how much I dreaded high school. I didn't want to be invisible again, to perch the lowest rung on the social totem and go through the work of climbing, climbing, climbing just to rate as good enough or fast enough or smart enough.

But before I made the grave social mistake of an epic

meltdown at Sephora, I snapped myself out of it. Janie could start over, knowing no one, without even a pool deep enough for her diving. I could certainly survive the town I'd grown up in. I didn't even need a blender to put my best face on. Even when Brooke asked, as we sauntered between stores, "Any Langsom news?" I didn't allow my eyes to flicker.

"What do you mean?" Mirabelle asked.

"Are they staying? Is Dr. Langsom in rehab? Does Thatcher need . . . comforting?" Brooke cackled. "Where is he staying?"

"There's this crawl space behind a wall in my dining room," Janie said, her face expressionless. "Thatcher and his mother live there now."

"Not Dr. Langsom?" I asked, even though I knew it was dangerous to goad her on the topic.

"I think he's in the chimney."

"You two are crazy." Mirabelle shook her head. But at least we all laughed and the moment moved forward.

//////////

We ended up going to dinner and a movie, so it was late when we got back to the Donahues'. Once again, I told Janie she could come sleep over at my house, but she opted out.

"I just feel like I need to be home," she said. Then she changed the subject and told me, "You know, your friends are okay." She laughed. "Even Brooke. I get her now. Sorry to be so judgey before."

"They can be a lot to deal with. But they're your friends now too," I told her.

"Not yet. That's okay." I watched her disappear into her house, making sure she wasn't snatched before making it through the door.

My house was quiet when I got home, my parents already asleep. When I heard the soft tapping on the screen door behind me, I assumed Janie had changed her mind and come over.

"Hold on," I whispered, worried more about waking my parents than hiding anything from them. By the time I reached the door, the tapping had stopped. I only saw the back of the person slipping away into the darkness.

It wasn't Janie.

Without thinking, I chased them. They were taller and decidedly masculine and for interminable seconds I watched the hooded figured skulk toward 16 Olcott. I could practically taste my halted breath.

"Stop," I hissed. And when the figure kept moving, I threatened more loudly, "Stop or I'll call the police."

Slowly, the figure turned. I gripped the deck railing, trying to gauge the distance between us. If he ran at me, could I get back to the screen door? If I screamed, would my dad hear over the hum of the air-conditioning?

"Please don't call the cops," the figure said, pulling off his hood. "We've already gone a few rounds today."

"Ben?" I said. His eyes gleamed a little, in Mr. Park's flood-lights. He raised his arms and hands, as if surrendering. "Are you nuts?" I couldn't be certain but it seemed like my heart was pounding even harder than before. "What are you doing?"

"I don't know." Ben's laugh scraped out of his throat like it was one step away from a sob. He held up two baseball mitts. "You wanna play catch?"

"What? Are you kidding?" The question escaped my lips before I considered a slicker way to play it.

"Listen, Livvie," he whispered. "Maybe you could keep your voice down? Someone might be watching." He giggled and then promptly shushed me again.

"Come inside," I said and then realized that if my mom came down and found Janie's older brother sitting in my family room, making Sentry jokes, ours would be the next house listed for sale in the neighborhood. "Never mind." I steered Ben back from the steps. "Let's go for a walk."

We moved slowly and he seemed to steady a little. "Sorry," he said a few times, then, "I don't know what I was thinking. I haven't been sleeping a lot. I tried to go to bed early tonight but . . . I'm just so tired I'm wired, you know?"

"I guess it was a hard day."

"I wanted to explain." He stopped walking and turned to me.

"You don't have anything to explain."

"Okay." We walked in silence for a little bit. He stopped again. "Where are we going?"

"I have a place." He nodded and kept going. I checked my phone, made sure my mom hadn't woken up and discovered me missing. No texts. I couldn't stop myself from asking, "What do you need to explain?"

"I thought maybe we could play catch."

"It's almost midnight."

"Is there some kind of town ordinance against playing catch in the middle of the night?"

"Probably. Yeah." We reached the park. "This is my place."

"This is a public park. I thought you meant like you had a fort in the woods or a vacant house."

"It's a baseball field. You've got two gloves. Sorry I don't have access to an abandoned stadium."

"Okay. Okay. I see it now. It's just that . . ."

"What? Just say it."

"The one place police usually patrol late at night is a public park. You know, because of unsavory characters."

"Glennon Heights isn't the kind of town that needs patrols."

"Even tonight? After meeting with us this afternoon? You don't think they might come by?"

"Nope. One of them will say, 'We should just swing by Olcott Place, check things out.'" It turns out my cop voice is sort of deep and doofus-like. "And then the other will say, 'No need, let's just think of more ways to be an absolute dorkwad.'"

Ben laughed, a full-bodied, belly-shaking laugh. "You're

pretty funny, Olivia Danvers." He reached toward me and handed me a glove.

A warmth spread across my chest. "Do you do this a lot?"

"Not a lot, really," Ben answered.

We were so close that it felt like if I concentrated really hard, the molecules of my body would reach out to the molecules of his body.

Finally I asked, "Are you going to tell me about it?"

Ben shook his head, then said, "Let's play catch."

He jogged out to second base and motioned with his gloved hand for me to take first.

"No pitching from the mound?" I asked mostly to have something to say.

He pointed to the place where the fence stopped and a white line differentiated the field from plain grass. "If we need to run, it's a clear shot," he instructed. "You're pretty fast."

"Just leave you behind to stumble around in the headlights of Officer Wycoff's squad car?"

Ben laughed ruefully. "It would probably go better for me if you weren't here."

"Yeah. Me too."

We started tossing the ball then. When I was little, I played rec softball and sort of hated it. In my first at bats, I really expected to hit the ball. I pictured nailing a line drive right past the pitcher or setting it to sail long into left field.

But then I'd get in the box and feel the weight of all those eyes on me. Even my teammates cheering me on made me uneasy. Mostly frozen, I hardly ever swung the bat. I certainly never connected. And eventually I couldn't even imagine hitting the ball.

Ben had brought a baseball in the front pocket of his hoodie. It felt better in my hand; it fit right. I liked winding up my body and unleashing the ball into the darkness, seeing it arc toward Ben, and then hearing the satisfying thwack of the leather of the ball meeting the leather of the glove.

"The fight I got into—it was over a girl," he said, lobbing the ball to me. "Her name was Andrea."

Thwack. I caught that one cleanly, easily. Then I threw the ball to him silently, as if passing back my turn to talk.

"We both enrolled in this conservation camp. This rich lady near us, some kind of heiress, died and they turned her whole estate into an environmental preserve. You signed up in the beginning of the fall and you cleared leaves and did some planting. We put up fencing and helped lay out the plans for footpaths. It was actually really cool."

The ball kept traveling back and forth. I didn't say a whole lot but figured every catch I made proved to him I was listening. "Anyway we got to be friends. Lots of Saturday mornings working the same projects. She had this stupid transistor radio—do you know what that is?"

"My dad has one in the garage." I threw the ball back, hoping he noticed the beauty of my form.

He did not. "Well, Andrea had this radio that clipped on to her belt. It looked ridiculous. Every time we went out, she had to put in new batteries—it was that old. It was a very Lloyd-Dobler-in-*Say-Anything* kind of accessory."

"That doesn't seem very environmentally sound." I shouldn't have said it out loud. The ball traveled back to me fast enough to sting my palm beneath the glove.

"It was cool. Because she didn't care that it wasn't. It got the worst stations. But she tried to dance to everything, no matter what came on. No matter what we were doing—raking, mulching—Andrea just bopped along." He had stopped, just standing there with the ball in his hand, remembering. Then he raised his arm to throw. "Anyway, I noticed her." The ball landed in my glove.

"I'm sure you did." I felt mean then and threw the ball hard.

I wanted to hear this and I didn't want to hear it at the same time.

The baseball cracked into his mitt. Ben stood still for a moment before curling his arm to throw again.

"So what happened?" I asked. "You came to my house. You want to tell me."

"I told her I loved her, okay?" He looked helplessly at me.

"I had these big feelings." He made the word sound like a disease. "So that demanded a big gesture, right?" I nodded. "So it was January and we were supposed to be there just checking on things. A little shoveling around the visitors' center."

So far I didn't see how the story ended in violence.

He went on. "There was this fort. Just a platform in the trees, really, overlooking a field. All the teen volunteers went there on breaks, to hang out after completing our assignments. So I made sure to get there early and stomped really carefully down in the snowy field and then I texted her. I told her to go up in the fort, that I'd left a surprise there for her."

"What was the surprise?"

"I'd spelled out *Andi, I love you.*"

"Whoa."

"Well, we agreed I needed a big gesture." But the ball came at me fast so I knew he felt a little embarrassed.

"Well, that qualifies. She didn't like it?" I tried to keep my voice neutral so that it didn't sound as if I meant *I cannot believe that moment didn't define her existence and make her whole life worth living.* Even though I sort of meant that.

"It didn't say that anymore when she saw it."

"I don't understand."

Ben sighed and stared up at the night sky as if searching for answers. "I told my friend Clayton. And he told some of his friends. One of whom happened to have a thing for Andi.

Anyway, this guy, Doug, waited there. And in between me writing the message and Andi getting there, he changed it."

"To what?"

He blinked a few times. "Maybe that's not important."

"Ben! How bad could it be?"

"Imagine the filthiest thing you could say about a girl. Then make it about a million times worse."

"Okay. I get the picture."

"She saw it and flipped out. I told her that wasn't what I'd written—but how could she believe me? Suddenly she was this girl stranded alone with a guy who'd written this awful message. She ran off, called her dad to pick her up—and her dad saw the writing too, and called the police."

"But how does writing something offensive count as assault?" I asked.

"No. Assault is what happened when I found out who'd changed what I'd written. But then Doug's mom lied and acted as his alibi. So it looked like I was both a sleazebag and a liar."

"Oh God."

"Yeah. You know the worst part? When I woke up that morning, I thought it was going to be this incredibly awesome day. I thought, *Today my whole life is going to change.*"

I put my glove down. "Didn't you explain to her what happened?"

"She wouldn't talk to me. It turned out Andi had always

liked Doug, for one thing. And then she read that and . . . I don't know. We had this meeting with the community service advisor—a conflict resolution session—and she said she felt betrayed. She said I had degraded her."

"Did you tell her what the original message said?"

"Well, that's beside the point." Ben took out his phone and looked at the time. "We really should go back before the sun comes up and the power-walkers start their neighborhood laps."

"You never told her what the message really said, did you?"

"It didn't matter. She wanted Doug. Even with his newly broken nose. You understand now why Janie and Lucy get so angry? It embarrassed our whole family." He held his hands up in surrender. "And listen—I freely admit to pummeling Doug Remo. But at least I'm pretty sure my sisters know I'm innocent of writing that message. My parents are a different story—they seem to think I'm capable of all kinds of terrible things."

"And it all goes on your permanent record?"

"It's on my record for two years actually. With good behavior, it gets expunged after that."

"Doesn't it bother you that she doesn't know the truth?" I asked him.

"I try not to think about it a lot. But I wanted you to understand. All that stuff you heard today." We had slowed down, maybe deliberately. Part of me never wanted to go home but the other part was so tired. I wanted to sink into my bed under the covers and go back to thinking of Ben as just a cute guy with a quick line—not someone flawed and afraid. Sometimes it was easier to feel barely noticed.

"I wasn't judging. It worried me." I clarified, "For you."

"You don't have to worry about me," Ben said. There were so many ways to interpret that sentence.

I stopped. "My house." I couldn't very well just amble up the front walk.

"Cut through the backyards and I'll stay on the sidewalk. If anyone's up, you went for a run."

I handed him back the glove I carried. "What's your cover story?"

"That I'm hoping to try out for baseball. Listen, I don't need to tell you not to tell—"

"No way." I tried to stay in the moment, but my eyes kept darting around, half expecting my mom to come charging outside.

"Do me a favor—when you get inside just flick a light on and off, so I know you're in safely."

"Does your parole officer know you're such a gentleman?"

He acted like he had seen that one coming. "Okay now." And then he nodded at my house as if to say, *Go on.*

I moved fast because it was like tearing off a Band-Aid— moving away from Ben after all that time and closeness. I didn't let myself look back longingly. Instead I kept myself focused on sneaking in unheard. Took off my shoes before stepping onto the wooden slats of the deck stairs, slid open the screen door, clicked off the TV, and climbed softly up the stairs. While I switched my bedroom light on and off, I thought of Ben keeping watch on the sidewalk below and remembered the letters and the reasons we all needed to be especially vigilant. I allowed myself one glimpse through my curtains and could barely make out Ben approaching his own home. He didn't turn and look either.

Maybe, right at that minute, I wasn't the only one watching. If the Sentry had seen us creep around the dark and silent streets, did it still count as a secret?

CHAPTER TWELVE

Whether they'd admit it or not, Mom and Dad had obviously coordinated with Aunt Jillian to keep me off Olcott Place for the next day, if not most of summer break's last week. It began with my dad poking his head into my room way too early. "Aren't you training?"

I'd been asleep all of three hours. "I think I'm sick."

"You've got to stay consistent."

"Maybe the flu."

"You don't look sick. How late did you stay up last night?"

I covered my head with my pillow. "Dad, I have four days left."

He seemed genuinely confused. "Well, that's exactly right. And if you sleep in too late, you'll be running at the hottest time of day."

"I'll run tonight."

"Jillian's coming to pick you up."

I sat straight up in bed. "Since when?"

"I don't know." He fiddled with the doorframe, as if examining it for flaws. Why did my dad always have to fix things? "She arranged it with your mom. She wants to take you school shopping."

"No one told me."

"I don't know, Olivia. Your aunt, who loves you very much, wishes to spend some time with you." And that is how I knew something was up: My father passed up a chance to express annoyance at Jillian. "Tell you what—go back to sleep for another hour. Go prop up the economy with your devoted aunt at ten. We'll fit in a run at night." He didn't normally let me run after dark. I squinted at him, looking for the angle. "I'll follow you in the car if I have to."

As soon as he shut the door, I burrowed back under my sheets and willed myself to sleep. But each time I closed my eyes, Ben materialized—all brooding and broken-spirited. I sat back up in bed. What the heck was that anyway? I checked my phone but I had no texts. All of a sudden a feeling of profound familial love swept over me. I needed a day without the

Donahues. Especially because I wasn't sure what, if anything, I could say to Janie about what had happened.

Nothing actually happened, I reminded myself, right then as I rolled out of bed and then later in the passenger seat next to Jillian. She had the air on full blast and I had goose bumps on my arms as we passed 16 Olcott.

"I'm glad we could do this," Jillian said as we turned off our street. "Thanks for making time for me."

"Are you kidding? This is awesome." I turned my head to face her. "I know Mom made you do it, though."

"Your mom doesn't make me do anything. I wanted to spend the day with you." Jillian kept her eyes on the road. "But yeah, the whole interviewed-by-the-police thing gave her an anxiety attack."

I laughed. "To her credit, she stayed really calm."

"Totally faking. You should have heard her on the phone with me. You would have thought that the Donahues had brought you with them to Guantanamo." She looked at me. "It is a lot, though, Liv. You kind of have to give her a pass."

Outside my passenger seat window, the well-maintained lawns of Glennon Heights blurred by. I figured I might as well get everything out in the open. "Did she tell you about Mrs. Donahue and Mr. McGovern?"

"Oh yes. She did pass along that tidbit of information."

"Is that okay?"

"Well, it doesn't sound like it was okay with Mr. Donahue. Listen—if the cops really had to pull him off Ned, then I don't care what your mom says, I like that guy a little more than I did before." I was relieved that it was sassy Aunt Jillian driving the car, grooving to bad eighties music and never using her blinker. I'd seen Mr. McGovern reduce her to a different Aunt Jillian, hollow-cheeked and red-eyed, and ensconced in our family room watching *The Bachelor* on demand.

"I don't know that the cops had to pull him off. I never told her that."

"Nope. I got that from Madeline Gorham, who still works as the receptionist at Harrington's. She said the agency opened a file on Ned, because the Langsom house is such a premier property and Mr. Donahue raised such a ruckus about Ned's *attentiveness*."

"I don't think anything really happened between him and Mrs. Donahue."

She glanced at me, surprised. "Well, look at you. Maybe you are ready for high school, Olivia. You're out of a booster seat and gossiping like a grown-up."

I don't know if it's from selling so many houses or just ardent consumerism but no one can cover square feet in a shopping mall like my aunt Jillian. My mom always tells her she has a good eye and it's true. Jillian can sift through an entire rack of clothing and pick out the piece that I expect to look least flattering on me and then, when I actually go to try it on, it makes me look amazing. "Do you even recognize your-self?" she asked me as I stood in the dressing room. "It's killer."

"Thanks, Aunt Jillian. Really."

"Well, we're not done. You can't just have one good outfit. That's showing everyone your potential and then refusing to live up to it."

"I'll just wear this every single day. They'll call it my sig-nature look."

"Yeah?" She grinned at me. "Who's *they*?"

"I don't know. Whoever it is who rules high school."

We strode through the mall, carrying all our packages. I felt like the lady from *Pretty Woman*, only less hookerish. "Here's the thing, sweets: You have to become the *they*. Judge the judgers, you know what I mean? Otherwise you'll spend the rest of your life waiting for permission to be yourself. Let your pure spirit attract others. Confidence draws in confi-dants." I love Aunt Jillian, but sometimes talking to her felt like downloading every self-help audiobook ever recorded. Still, somewhere in Northampton, that girl Andrea gardened with her transistor radio blaring beside her. That kind of con-fidence worked for her after all.

It was only when we stopped for lunch at the Sip and Sandwich that I realized I had my aunt's undivided attention. If I had enough confidence to ask, Jillian might be able to explain one of Miss Abbot's more mysterious remarks.

"I know Mom was friends with the Langsoms, but was

Dad? Not as adults. But before, when you were all in high school."

Jillian looked me strangely. "Where is this coming from?"

"Something someone said. About the Langsoms."

"We shouldn't talk about it."

"What? Mom and Mrs. Langsom were friends, right? Was Dad friends with Dr. Langsom?"

"No. Not really."

"So did Dad know Mrs. Langsom too?"

Jillian couldn't help herself. She snorted and said, "You could say that." Then she realized she was talking to me, not my mom, and tried to take it back. "Don't listen to me."

But it was out there. "Dad and Mrs. Langsom?" I asked. Aunt Jillian's mouth dropped open. "I knew it." And somehow I did.

The antennae of our fellow coffee shop clientele practically buzzed. Jillian leaned forward, her voice low and cautionary. "Olivia, this is totally different from discussing who's going together to the eighth-grade dance, or even Ned McGovern's misdeeds. This involves your mom and dad and you have no idea how hurtful it all was way back then. Way back, because we're talking years ago."

"Before or after I was born?" I don't know why that felt important, but it was.

Jillian glanced around furtively and our neighboring tables dutifully pretended not to listen. "It was before they got married. Listen, please trust me on this. You have to let this one go." She pushed aside her coffee and started gathering bags. "We should head out." And then she spoke more loudly. "I just love your vivid imagination." She looked around to make sure people heard her and then stood up.

We walked out together. Outside, in the mall, I asked, "If it happened so long ago, why was that necessary?"

"Because it's none of their business. Because this is Glennon Heights and sometimes the people we know and love so well act like jackals gnawing on the bones of our worst moments." I knew Jillian wasn't only talking about my parents then.

"Are you mad at me?" I asked once Jillian and I had gotten back in her car.

Seconds ticked by before she answered, "I just wish you'd consider what you're stirring up and how little it matters now." She reached over to wrap an arm around me. "I'm not mad. I'm mad at myself because I shouldn't have told you anything."

"You didn't."

"I confirmed. But that's all you get, Liv. Because really, it doesn't count for anything now. Some people would argue that it didn't count then. They both made a decision to work through it. Asking questions would really just hurt your mom. I know you don't want that."

"Of course not."

"Here's the thing about other people's relationships: They count as their own planets with just the two of them as occupants. Your orbits might cross but you can't really visit. You can't ever fully know what's going on." She looked over at me. "I promise you, it'll make more sense when you're older." She grimaced. "I hate saying that—it sounds so condescending, but maybe it's hard to understand without actually logging in time in a relationship."

Aunt Jillian and I rode in the car quietly for a while. Then, right as she pulled onto our street, she told me again, "Olivia, you have to let this one go."

And I nodded, because what else could I do?

//////////

After dinner, my dad and I got set to go for a night run.

"Night run?" My mom did not sound thrilled. "Brad, do you think that's a good idea? Given what's going on?"

"You mean with the Stalker?" Aunt Jillian asked.

"The Sentry," I corrected.

"Whatever it is, it doesn't seem like such a great time to test boundaries. Even before all this nonsense, we agreed no running at night."

"I completely agree," Dad said. "Which is why I'll be in the car, close behind, slowly following her."

"Really?" Jillian gave me a look. "I spent all this money to make you look cool and you're going to let your dad drive behind you while you jog?"

"Dad, you don't have to. As long as I don't do laps around the Langsom place, I can't see the Sentry having a problem with it."

"Right. Let's expect the guy writing anonymous letters about blood in the walls to rationalize like that." My mom rolled her eyes. "I also worry about you following her in the car, frankly. You read about these things all the time—parents who stop paying attention for a second and accidentally drive over their own children."

"Okay, now you have officially lost your mind," Jillian said. "I was on your side, Mel, but I cannot get behind the fear that Brad's going to run her over with his car."

"She's too fast for one thing." My dad beamed.

We were all having fun together. I don't know why I couldn't have just enjoyed those few minutes. But I had to pick at it, like an old scab I just noticed. "Miss Abbot says the Sentry began sending the letters a while ago, when the Langsoms still lived there. So whoever it is, he's not targeting the Donahues. He started with the Langsoms. But that sounds crazy too. Because how could you have any beef with the Langsoms? They're so nice to everyone."

I figured on getting a kick under the table from Jillian, but she just looked disappointed in me. She stood up and started to clear. When my mom said, "I'm sure someone has a reason," it didn't feel safe to make eye contact with anyone at the table. She said, "But that's life, right? If you haven't made anyone angry, you probably haven't really lived."

I stood up. "Should I do the dishes?"

Mom shook her head. "No, if you're going to run, run now."

I could still feel Jillian's eyes on me. "Thanks, Mom," I said, and I meant it. But I also meant *Sorry, Mom*. For bringing up the Langsoms, for trying to provoke some outpouring of hostility, for ruining the moment.

As I climbed the steps to my room, I heard Jillian half teasing my mom. "I bet you fifty bucks Grace Abbot's writing the letters."

"No way. I saw one, remember. Grace Abbot has much better handwriting."

"Oh God—she has that perfect penmanship. Do you remember? But this is totally the type of thing she would do just to stir stuff up around here."

"Jillian—she would not!" Then I heard the smile in my mom's voice. "Her letters would have been amazing. She would have included a quote from *Macbeth* or something."

"Yes! Exactly."

It occurred to me that Miss Abbot would have taught my mom and Jillian in high school. I spun right back down the stairs.

"Hey! Did you guys all go to school with the VonHolt kids?"

All three of them looked at me in horror.

Mom recovered first. "Olivia, what on earth has gotten into you?"

"I just wondered."

"Don't wonder about that story." Dad used his laying-down-the-law voice. "Go on and get ready. Let's get moving."

"Okay, but did you? It's not like it's some deep dark secret." I looked at Jillian.

"I'm just appalled that you thought we were that old," she responded. "Those kids were almost fifteen years ahead of us. Listen—did the latest Stalker letter include any Shakespearean references?"

"You're not helping, Jill." Mom sounded exasperated. "Olivia, we didn't go to school with the VonHolts. They were real people, though. Let's try not to wrap their tragedy into this whole mess. These letters—they're most likely just some-one's warped idea of a joke. Do you understand?"

I understood but I didn't agree. With my father trailing behind me in his SUV, I tried to focus. Earbuds in, course mapped out—my muscles felt good but my movements didn't. It felt like running through cough syrup. For one thing, I knew it must look ridiculous to have Dad follow, like some Secret Service agent protecting the president. If Ben happened to see, he would definitely think my parents had caught me sneaking back in the house and put me on complete lockdown.

Besides that, I couldn't figure out how to bypass the park. I didn't want to go back there yet and ruin it. If I ran past, it would just become a regular old park again and not the place where Ben told me his secrets. When I couldn't stop myself, I looked back at my dad, but he just kept waving me forward. I could read the impatience on his face—he didn't think I was on track for a good time either.

Make up time, not excuses. That's what Dad would have told me.

Janie had texted twice—once while I was shopping with Aunt Jillian and again right before dinner. And then she called, so whether I felt ready to face her or not, I'd have to call back when I got home.

I pushed myself into a sprint—feeling frustrated with myself. I forced myself to run faster only out of a desire to get it over with. My ears throbbed since I'd kept jacking up the volume of my music, listening so loudly I couldn't even hear my dad honking his horn.

I made it back to our porch steps and there, perched right at their foot, was a baseball glove, with the worn ball tucked inside. If you were strolling down the sidewalk and spotted it, you might not consider it out of place. You wouldn't understand because a game of catch is only a language on the planet I shared with Ben. And I didn't know if he left it as a greeting or a signal or what. But that's what I was focused on—the mitt in our front yard and figuring out what it meant.

My music was still blasting, so I didn't hear my dad coming up to me, didn't hear what he was saying to me. By the time I looked up, he stood between me and the house at 16 Olcott. The Langsom house. Or rather: the Donahue house. Or maybe: the Sentry's house.

Three police cars sat parked in front with their blue lights on, lighting up the late summer night.

CHAPTER THIRTEEN

I tried to run toward the house, but my legs were done and my dad wasn't having it anyway.

"Hold up. Hold up now. We'll find out what's happening. Okay, Liv? Let's just go inside for a minute."

Mom and Jillian stood in our front door, holding it open and beckoning me inside. I shook my head. Up and down Olcott Place, our neighbors poked their heads out and milled around their front yards. I saw Miss Abbot drag a lawn chair out of her garage, and in any other context, that would have been hilarious. I filed it away to tell Janie about later and then promptly started to feel shaky and weak. Two texts and a phone call and I hadn't responded all day. "How about you sit down?" Dad started to lower me to the curb and then thought better of it. He walked me back to the porch steps instead. "Over here. Melinda! Could you get us some water please?"

I kept thinking that I made it all happen. The way we used to say "Bloody Mary" three times in front of a mirror to see what we could conjure. Just mentioning the VonHolt name summoned whatever disaster had required half the Glennon Heights police force to come out. "I'm sure it's fine," Dad kept repeating as he rubbed circles on my back. Mom brought over a bottle of water.

"Why don't I go over?" she said. "Someone should. They just moved here; we probably know them best."

Dad sat next to me on the curb and we watched my mom walk toward the house.

Jillian charged out of the house. "Seriously? You're just going to let her go over there, Brad?"

"She knows what she's doing." He turned to me. "We'll wait for Mom inside." I opened my mouth to say no, but Dad held up his hand. "Liv. I'm not asking."

I grabbed Ben's baseball glove and carried it inside with me. If Dad or Jillian wondered, they didn't ask. I took it right up to my room and hid it in the space between the wall and my bed. I grabbed a fleece. I felt so cold. From my window, I had a clearer view of the Donahue house. It was just the same grand facade, but bathed in that blue light.

I went back downstairs and waited in view of the front door. I stared at the knob, waiting for it to turn. Eventually, both Jillian and my dad sat down with me.

When Mom finally came home, she walked into the house to find us sitting right there, leaning forward. "Hey, guys," she said, like she had just run out to the store and maybe could use a little help bringing in the groceries. "Everything's okay. They're shaken up, but no one's hurt. Everyone's accounted for." We must have looked incredulous. Mom explained, "Another letter from the Sentry arrived tonight."

My dad said what we were all thinking. "They got a letter? And it required three police cars? There wasn't some kind of violent incident?"

I stood up to look out the window. The squad cars had gone. It looked like every light in the Donahue house had been switched on.

"Well," Mom said, "it was a disturbing letter. And you know, I don't think the boys down at the station get a lot of calls to answer. They were very thorough."

"Our taxes at work." Dad stood up then, like he needed to test out his legs. "Come here for a second." His voice sounded gruffer than usual as he wrapped his arms around my mom. "I should have gone over instead. I don't know what we were thinking." When my mom stepped back, he pulled her in again. Jillian and I exchanged looks. They never acted like that.

"It was good that I was there. I helped calm down the kids. That let Gavin and Lindsay focus on the officers' questions."

"Did they see anything?"

Mom shook her head. "No, the whole family was out. They came home to find the letter with the rest of the mail . . ." She trailed off.

"On the tarp?" I asked.

"Yeah. The police had taped this plastic sheet under the mail slot. It caught everything that came through. They sent someone out specifically to handle the evidence. They're hoping, because this time they took such care, they'll get prints and figure this out."

"Did they still read it? What did it say?"

Mom hesitated. "Same kind of thing as before. Pretty disturbing."

"Can I go over and see Janie?" None of them answered. "One of you can walk me over if you have to. But the police wouldn't have left if it wasn't safe in the house."

"Oh, sweetheart, I know. And I'm sure Janie wants to see you too, but we need to give the Donahues some space tonight. It sounds like they have a lot to discuss."

"What do you mean? What else do they need to discuss?" The three adults looked at each other but not at me. "Are the Donahues going to move?"

"Nobody said that. But it was an eventful night. Why don't you just call her?"

Because then I wouldn't be able to look her in the eye. I wouldn't know if she was truly okay. And I wouldn't know if Ben had told her about last night. My eyes swung from my mom to my dad to my aunt Jillian. No one was going to budge.

When I first texted her, I just sent Janie a string of exclamation marks. She wrote back almost immediately *I know, right?*

U ok?

Can u come over?

Mom said no.

The three dots on my screen blinked. Janie was thinking. *Maybe later?*

I weighed the kind of trouble I could land myself in, sneaking out of the house. But I'd managed it just fine the night before. Wasn't my friendship with Janie worth the same kind of risk as my nothing with Ben?

Four houses down, she was staring at her phone, waiting for my answer. *Yeah,* I wrote. *Will text then.* Then I erased the text just in case. Every day I got sneakier. I showered and dressed in black leggings and a dark T-shirt. Nothing that screamed cat burglar, but it made me feel slick, like I could creep around unnoticed in the night.

By the time I got back downstairs, Jillian had left. "She said to tell you she'd give you a call tomorrow; apparently you're not done shopping." My mom hugged me. "Want to watch a movie?"

We ended up picking a romantic comedy and I dozed off

on the sofa before the people in it stopped stumbling around and figured out they loved each other.

I woke up curled up on the couch, snugly tucked under a blanket, the TV turned off. My parents had left the kitchen light on, leaving just enough illumination so that I wouldn't wake up scared. It stung how easy they made sneaking out for me. *Let her sleep*, Mom would have said. *She's had such a scare. She needs her rest.*

I checked my phone. 12:30 a.m. Just one text from Janie: *???????????*

Ten minutes, I replied.

Once I hit send, I'd committed myself. No backing out. I found my sneakers and stood at the bottom of the stairs, listening. My dad snored loudly enough that I could hear him a full floor down, but that complicated matters with my mom. *How could she possibly have fallen asleep next to that?* I listened for a second layer of waking noise in the background. Nothing. So for the second time in as many nights, I slipped out the back door while the rest of the house slept.

It took more effort to be brave when Ben wasn't there to impress. And apparently, adrenaline had affected the rest of the neighborhood too. Dotted along the street, porch lights still shone in houses that had sat dark the night before. I kept my eyes focused on 16 Olcott and tried to glide through the backyards until I reached Janie's. I even covered the screen of my phone while I texted her: *Here. Out back.*

I reached up and tried the back door. Locked. And then it suddenly swung open, almost smacking me in the face.

"You have got to be kidding me." Ben's voice rumbled low and furious. He switched on the flashlight on his phone, blinding me.

"Ben?" I shielded my eyes.

"You better hope so."

"Janie asked me to sneak out. Let's not act like you're unfamiliar with that concept."

"The two of you don't share a whole brain between you, do you?" He swung the light down. "It was kind of nuts of me to go see you last night, absolutely insane for you to come here now. What if my dad was staying up, keeping watch? What if he had a gun?"

"No offense, but with his temper your father should not own a firearm," I said. But I knew Ben was right. He wouldn't hear me admit that, but I understood. "Janie texted me. I felt like I had to." We stared at each other. "You know why."

His eyes darted away from me, right along with the beam of light. "I think she's asleep."

"Would you go check? Please? Maybe her phone's not getting reception?"

"She's asleep or she would be down here. I'll tell her you snuck out."

"Okay."

"And that you won't be doing it again."

"Okay."

"You should go—"

"You left your baseball glove. You know, on the lawn. That was you, right?"

"Yeah." He swallowed. "I guess I thought maybe we could talk. But that was before. Then tonight happened. Everyone's going to be watching more closely now."

"Okay." I knew other words. I just worried it would be too difficult to pronounce them.

"You'll see Janie tomorrow. I'll be around too. Okay, Livvie?" He didn't even wait for me to answer. He shut off the flashlight.

I stayed there for a minute or two with my back against the screen door, wondering if Ben still sat there leaning against the other side. When I felt the door give a little, I knew he had been and also that he had stood up and gone. It took everything to stop myself from calling out—but I wouldn't let myself plead pathetically. And I wouldn't let myself get caught. "Okay," I whispered, and made my way back, wondering whose eyes followed me home.

Ben must have kept his promise though, because my mom woke me up first thing in the morning. "Olivia, Janie's downstairs. Dad's left for work and I'm headed to town. Okay to send her on up?"

"Yeah, sure. She's here, like at the house? Right now?"

My mom smiled. "She said she got your message. She

seems fine." Mom took a step away and then came right back. "I'm all right with you girls spending time here, but if you go to Janie's, I need to know an adult's home. There, in the house, with you. No negotiations, okay?"

I nodded; it was reasonable, after all.

I almost tackled Janie when she came through the door, which probably doesn't count as the best way to handle trauma victims, but I was so glad to see her.

"What happened?" I asked. "Are you okay? Do they know anything yet?" She hugged me back, hard, so I just kept chattering on. "Did Ben tell you? I tried to sneak out. I mean, I actually did sneak out, but you must have fallen asleep already. When I finally got there, Ben gave me this whole lecture about safety and your father and guns."

Janie sniffled and laughed. "My father doesn't keep guns."

"I know, right? I think that's a really smart decision." We both giggled. Janie needed to wipe her eyes, either from laughing or crying.

"I don't know why I'm getting so emotional. It was just another letter. The police sergeant kept talking about escalating behavior, but it's the same kind of letter written on the same paper. They seemed to know us more this time around."

"What do you mean?"

Janie pulled out her phone to show me a picture. Black ink, creamy background.

Who are you, invader? I keep watch—I see the lights turn on, then off. I know when you are sleeping, when the children are not sleeping. Beneath the floorboards are bones. I hear them singing from the road. When you walk, know there are bones beneath your feet. Soon your bones will join them.

I felt cold all over again, the same way I couldn't get warm the night before, waiting for word that the Donahues were safe. I pulled my comforter off my bed and wrapped it around myself. "You don't think this is worse than the earlier letters?"

"Whoever wrote it wanted a reaction," Janie answered. "And they got one. The whole cavalry showed up." She looked past me, to my bed. "Is that my brother's baseball glove?"

I still felt cold, but my face went warm. "Is it? My dad found it on our front lawn. He thought maybe it was someone's from school." I handed it over to her as if I hadn't spent the night with my hand tucked inside like some kind of minor league creeper.

"He's been acting even more bizarre than usual lately," Janie said. I stayed still and blank. "Ben. Not your dad. It started when the police first interviewed us—you were there. And then last night he didn't even come home until after the police had come back. He walked in all casually like the cops usually swarm around our house."

"Really? Ben wasn't out with the rest of you?"

"No. We went to dinner. First he said he'd meet us and then he never showed. Can you imagine what my parents would say if Lucy or I did that? Just flaked without any explanation? We just sat there, for the longest time, waiting to order our food."

"Did he say what happened? Who he was with?"

"That's the thing: He wouldn't. He wouldn't answer any of us." Janie twisted her hair into a bun and leveled her gaze at me. "I'm going to ask you something and I need you to be completely honest."

Uh-oh, I thought. *She knows.* I closed my eyes. Opened them. Janie still sat there staring intently at me.

"You have to promise," she said.

"Of course I promise." I pulled the blanket more tightly and tried not to look at the baseball mitt in her hand. "Janie, what's going on?"

"I can't even say it."

"What, Janie?" *Just say it.*

"Do you think Ben's the Sentry?"

"No," I answered. Then more emphatically: "NO!" It took two and a half seconds to go from feeling completely guilty to feeling outraged. "Janie, you can't possibly think that's true."

"I could. I *do*. It's the kind of thing only Ben would dream up. You don't know him. When the first letter arrived, we all thought that right away—my whole family thought that. We've spent this whole time playing detective, making lists and interviewing neighbors. Sometimes the right answer is the simple one."

I shook my head. "It's not him, Janie."

"It fits. You don't how hard he fought to stay in Northampton. He asked to live with friends; he applied for boarding school. He set up a meeting with the school psychologist to try to convince my parents to rent him an apartment. After everything he put them through."

"That sounds like a kid who didn't want to leave his friends."

"One friend." Janie held eye contact with me, as if making sure her words landed every punch. "One friend in particular. She was really pretty and she preferred that we move away." Janie laid her case. "He's twisted enough to write the letters in the first place. He disappears all the time. Like last night— he stood us up for dinner, but he must have been here, in the neighborhood." She held up the baseball mitt and waved it— exhibit A. "He dropped this on your lawn."

"Think about what Miss Abbot told us. Those letters started arriving before you moved here."

"My parents made the offer on the house four months ago. Ben could have written the first one then." She leaned back on my bed and flung the glove across the room. The ball dislodged and rolled loudly on the wood floor. "Sorry." I shrugged, hoping she would leave it there. "I love my brother, Olivia. But this past year really messed him up. He's convinced himself that he loves this girl. And he wouldn't listen to anyone who tried to reason with him. I know he can be funny and charming and whatever. But he's just pretending that ending up stuck here doesn't matter to him."

Janie kept going and I kept listening, even though it felt disloyal. Somehow I had backed myself into a corner; every direction I turned meant betraying someone. "You think Ben is this sarcastic, hilarious guy, but he likes mocking people. Because he's angry. And you know who else is really angry?" She clicked on her phone and turned the screen toward me. "Whoever's writing these letters." In the pic, the white envelope of the Sentry's latest message seemed to glare at me. The writing looked larger—a voice rising to be heard.

"I think that's why my dad didn't want to go to the police— he believes it's Ben too." I decided not to mention to Janie that I thought Mr. Donahue's reluctance made him a front-runner in the Sentry sweepstakes. "Even last night—it was my mom who insisted on calling. But now the police are involved and they're going to figure it out. They took all these pictures, with real cameras. They dusted for prints. They'll arrest him all over again. For what? Some bratty prank because my parents decided we should move. So stupid."

I knew Janie meant Ben but wondered if I counted as stupid too.

Once I stopped making excuses for him and really listened to her, Janie's opinions sounded a lot like evidence.

CHAPTER FOURTEEN

Janie and I had just come home from the pool when another police car turned down Olcott Place.

"Seriously?" she said, hopping off her bike. The driveway sat empty, with neither of her parents' cars there.

"We should go to my house," I said, thinking of my agreement with my mom.

"Ben and Lucy are home."

"But they're not adults."

Janie leveled her gaze at me. "Lucy? Come on. She's pretty much geriatric." The police car slowed, but it didn't have its lights on. I braked but kept walking my bike toward my house.

"Liv." This time Janie's voice sounded urgent. "What if they question him alone?"

Just as my reluctance to disobey direct parental orders collided with my disinclination to write Ben letters in prison, the police pulled into a different driveway. Janie and I stared at each other. Officer Wycoff waved once he got to Miss Abbot's front porch.

"Wow," Janie muttered as she half-heartedly waved back. "Look what we did. Now the police are going to interrogate Miss Abbot."

"Nonsense," I deadpanned in my best Miss Abbot voice. "Miss Abbot is going to be interrogating *them*."

"What do you think she's telling them?"

"She's probably providing a detailed history of Glennon Heights. It'll keep the cops busy at least. I know she maintains a list of cars that drive by the park too much. Maybe she'll have them tracking down license plate numbers."

"How do you drive by the park too much?"

"She calls it cruising. She thinks the park functions as the epicenter of the Glennon Heights crime world."

I convinced Janie to come to the coffee shop with me, to meet up with Kaia, Mirabelle, and Brooke. First though, Janie ducked inside her house to let Ben and Lucy know the cops were across the street. She came stomping out. "I try to do the right thing, the sisterly thing. No one ever appreciates it."

"What did they say?" I asked.

"Lucy just answered in Latin and I don't take Latin. And Ben thanked me for the heads up and said he would put all the dead bodies back beneath the floorboards."

I burst out laughing. "Oh, come on, that's funny."

"It's like he has no idea he might be a suspect."

"Exactly. So he probably isn't. Right?"

I tried to sound confident. It didn't really work.

////////////

Wall-to-wall people packed the coffee shop. It looked like Glennon Heights High had just given up and decided to run our first day in the place we'd all feel most comfortable. Leather chairs, good lighting, and lots of caffeine: Those perks would have made the high school transition more tolerable. We had this whole awkward moment when Brooke waved us over to her table with Mirabelle and Kaia, but they had only saved one seat—for me, I guess. So Janie and I each sort of perched on half the stool. And then Brooke and Mirabelle exchanged this look, like it was such a big deal for us to share a seat.

I wished I could kick the stool from out from underneath Brooke and scream, "Then you should have saved two seats!" But you can't actually say those things out loud. Apparently high school, even more so than eighth grade, was about pretending not to notice the absolutely petty stunts other people pulled in an effort to make themselves feel important and other people feel smaller. Technically, we weren't even there yet but we already played by those rules.

A group of seniors occupied the table behind us and I recognized the redheaded guy from the pool, who always nodded at Janie and me as if he was personally approving our presence on the planet. Now he nodded toward us, toward Janie, and shoved an empty stool in our direction.

Brooke's eyes went wide. I dragged the stool closer to our table and nudged Janie but she'd already spun to face him. "Hey, thanks."

"No worries. It's good to see you here. I thought you lived in the water." Janie just shook her head. "You're Ben's little sister—the new guy." This time Janie nodded. The whole mute mermaid routine seemed to work for her. I always worried so much about talking to guys, but watching Janie, I realized that half of her allure was her restraint. She just kept smiling and the redheaded guy rushed to fill in the silence. "Your brother's cool. He was just here, with Thatcher. Do you know Thatcher?"

"We know Thatcher Langsom," Mirabelle called out.

I could have told Mirabelle that the redheaded guy was not about to look away from Janie, no matter what she contributed to the conversation.

"I'm Justin, by the way. You guys live in Thatcher's house, right? His old house?"

"I live in the water," Janie said lightly. It would have sounded creepy if I'd tried it.

Justin laughed. "Yeah. I hear that. But you all had some excitement over there, huh? I'm an EMT. Anytime there's police activity, we get a call." Janie looked suitably impressed. "But it turned out you didn't need us."

"Thanks, though," Janie replied. And then, without another word, she turned back to the rest of us.

Justin would not be deterred. He just talked to Janie's ponytail. "Yeah, anytime. It's cool that your brother and Thatcher are so tight."

Behind us, Justin's friends gave him a hard time. We heard a low whistle, then someone imitating the sound of a crash and burn.

"I'll see you around." Justin didn't sound dejected. His confidence impressed me as much as Janie's. It remained a mystery to me how people managed to speak to each other without ending up curled in a ball, doubting every word spoken and questioning every inflection.

Across the table, Brooke seethed. Mirabelle asked, "What did he mean? About the police?"

"It was nothing. We got some weird letters." Janie stayed nonchalant while I watched our friends carefully, searching for signs of recognition. We made a good team.

Brooke barely seemed interested. "What kind of letters?"

"Like crank calls, but letters." Janie's voice rose ever so slightly.

"Wait—seriously?" Brooke leaned forward in her seat. "How long has this been going on? Why didn't you guys say anything?"

"It just seemed like a dumb prank at first."

"And now?" Mirabelle asked.

"Now they're a little scary, honestly." Janie glanced around as she spoke, checking to see if anyone seemed to be eavesdropping.

"Do they look like ransom notes? Like with letters cut out from magazines?" Brooke giggled. "That's *nuts*." Suddenly more people around us were listening.

"Brooke, it's not funny."

She rolled her eyes. "Only in Glennon Heights would some loser send crank mail." She gazed across the table with a kinder look. "God, Janie. I'm so sorry. You haven't even started school yet and someone already hates you." Even Mirabelle cringed. She and I rushed to talk about other things—classes and cross-country—to fill the tense silence. *Why does Brooke always have to be such an issue?* I wondered.

Janie lasted about fifteen minutes before pulling out her phone and texting furiously. Soon after we heard a series of chimes. "Oh look," she said flatly without even a pretense of surprise. "My brother texted. He needs to pick me up immediately." I stared at her. "I mean, us. He needs to pick us up immediately. We can leave the bikes here, right?"

"Like overnight?" I stammered. But Janie fixed her steely eyes on me, so I said, "Of course."

"I thought your brother didn't drive." Brooke smiled sweetly. Only her voice sneered.

"Thatcher's driving." Janie shrugged, as if it didn't matter.

For a moment, I thought that had settled it. Brooke slumped a bit, anticipating, as we all were, the moment that Thatcher Langsom would pull up in his bright blue Jeep. We, two freshmen, would climb in and ride away, leaving most of Glennon Heights High to wonder how we'd managed to wrangle the captain of the lacrosse team as our driver.

But Brooke rallied. "At least he knows the address."

Janie swiveled to face me. "I'm going to wait outside. It's so hot in here—suffocating . . ."

When she distanced herself far enough from our table, I opened my mouth to speak, determined to finally shut down the petty factory that Brooke had operated for the past few weeks. But Brooke held up one hand and said, "No. Liv, before you start telling me how I need to be friendlier to your new next-door neighbor who barely tolerates us, why don't you ask me how my summer's going? Go on—don't you want to know if camp sucked? Maybe it didn't and I miss the people who stopped it from sucking but you don't know about those kids because I don't talk incessantly about the people I just met as if I'm the first and only person to ever discover true friendship. Or maybe you want to ask Mirabelle when her sister left for Syracuse and what that's like? Kaia landed an agent and is auditioning for commercials this fall—but you don't know about that, do you? And did you even notice that Allie isn't here? If you'd asked, I could have told you that she's grounded. Her homophobic parents wouldn't let her go to the Gay/Straight Alliance welcome picnic, so she had Ms. Evans call them and they were the opposite of supportive. I am so very sorry that none of us have gotten mean letters in the mail but we've been dealing with our own concerns. Maybe just once if you could pretend we matter to you, we might feel a little more ready to help plan a Welcome to Glennon Heights party for your new best friend."

I turned toward Mirabelle, but she only swallowed and looked away.

Maybe I'm the issue, I thought, remembering the times my mom had pressed me to reach out to more friends this summer. I was still looking for the right words to say when I heard Thatcher Langsom honk his horn.

"I'm sorry," I managed to mumble as I stood up. "I have to go." Brooke's glare traveled from my face to the door. "I'm really sorry." Mirabelle sort of smiled at me the way I saw my mom once smile at a lady in the grocery store who wheeled a cart over her foot. Kaia was hard to read.

I picked my way through the crowd, half expecting an

outstretched leg to trip me. Outside, Thatcher's car idled. He and Ben sat up front, with sunglasses on, looking as if they had just left an audition to play the villains in a John Hughes movie. Janie opened her door and scooted across the leather seat. "Jeez, Livvie. You couldn't tear yourself away?"

"Just trying to keep the peace."

"But that would ruin all Brooke's fun."

"She's just—" I searched for the right explanation.

"She's a terrorist."

"Who's a terrorist?" Thatcher leaned back and grinned at us, a thousand kilowatts of handsome surging through the car.

The last time we'd all sat in the coffee shop, Brooke had sat there snickering, mocking Thatcher's new job. *Maybe we all are*, I thought to myself.

"No one's a terrorist," I said.

"You girls, man—bunch of barracudas. Hey, I'm Thatcher."

"I-I know," I stammered. "We were neighbors."

"Oh yeah? On Olcott? Crazy. How's the old neighborhood?" He punched Ben's shoulder. "Now that this bad element has taken over?" If Thatcher was devastated by the change in address, he didn't show it. "Where we headed?"

Ben said, "Northampton?" and I gazed out the window and wished my name was Andi.

When Janie suggested, "Let's go to the VonHolt house," I wasn't paying attention. I was staring at Ben's hand, which clutched the strap of the seat belt in front of me. While the three of them argued, I noticed the fine hairs on his knuckles, how he had clipped his fingernails fairly recently. When we'd played catch the other night, Ben's hands looked pale, but now I noticed how tan they were—the hemp bracelet he always wore had slipped down and revealed a tan line glowing white in the dark car. I could squint and make it look like half a set of handcuffs, glinting.

"What can you possibly expect to find at that place?" Ben tugged at his seat belt strap. He turned to face Janie.

"I don't know. Something useful. There could be a link. Maybe whoever's crazy enough to live in a house where all those kids died feels comfortable sending death threats to another set of kids."

Thatcher braked hard at the stop sign and Ben's fist clenched. "Death threats? Are you kidding?"

"I told you about this," Ben muttered. "Another letter came—so that makes three total. Plus you said you guys got two."

"Yeah, but I wouldn't call them death threats. More like . . . house valentines."

"You're going to need to elaborate on that one," Janie said.

"It sounded like some guy obsessed with the house. You know those true-life stories of people who are in love with inanimate objects? Like that man who kept trying to marry a subway car?" Ben, Janie, and I all shook our heads. "Man, you guys just radiate ignorance. Anyway—that's what these notes sounded like." He dropped his voice and spoke with zombie flatness. "The house is mine. You trespass on my heart." He shrugged and smiled. "You know, that kind of thing."

"Nothing about blood in the walls?" Janie asked.

Ben chimed in. "Or something buried in the floorboards?"

"Sounds like our guy got pretty intense."

"He calls himself the Sentry," Janie said. "Did he use that name in your letters?"

"I guess so. That sounds familiar." Thatcher pulled the car over to the curb. Outside my window the VonHolt house sat sternly, its peaked roof scraping the sky.

"Yeah, you didn't take note of it?" Ben sounded incredulous. "It's kind of a creepy detail."

Thatcher killed the engine and stared out the windshield. "Guys, I get why they've rattled you. But in terms of crappy aspects of the past year, these letters don't even rank in the top five for my family." He spoke mostly to Ben. "Not the craziest. Not the scariest. They just seemed like another nail in the apocalyptic coffin lid that closed on my old life." He still didn't look at us. "I mean, you know about all that, right?" Thatcher turned his head to look out the window. "Pretty sure everyone knows about all that."

"Yeah, man. I'm sorry—I didn't mean—"

"It just didn't seem so important. It was mail."

"My sister Lucy? She thought maybe you wrote them," Janie blurted out. Both Ben and I stared daggers, trying to shut her down. It was too late. "That would make sense, right? She has this theory that the house represents everything about your old life and all the aspects of privilege that you've lost. So of course you're angry at us for taking over. You want to displace us the way you were displaced, punish us the way you might feel punished." I focused on the VonHolt house because staring at the home where three kids died felt less uncomfortable than observing the social carnage inside Thatcher Langsom's Jeep.

"Dude, what's wrong with your sister?" Thatcher slid his eyes to Ben.

Janie blundered on. "Lucy is really smart—"

"What's wrong with *both* of your sisters?"

Ben sank his face into his hands. I counted the steps on the VonHolt's front porch. I noted the shape of the silver mailbox affixed by the door.

"It's just a theory," Janie said.

"We also considered the theory that Ben wrote them." I tried to help. I did not help.

"Nice." Ben turned and looked at me as if he was trying to measure how much I'd reveal about him, how much I could hurt him. Then he shifted his gaze to Janie because apparently I stopped mattering. "Really nice, Jane. I thought we'd gotten past that."

"Well, sometimes you come up with stupid ideas. And you didn't want to move here."

"None of us wanted to move here."

"In retrospect, maybe it wasn't so awesome that you all moved here." Thatcher sighed. "Listen, let me give you guys a ride home. It's no problem, okay?"

"But we're right here," Janie said. "You don't want to get out and walk around?"

"Janie—" I whispered. But I didn't know what else to say.

"It's just a house. Something awful happened there."

"Right. But maybe whoever has latched on to our house also feels possessive over this house. That would make sense, right? They might attract the same type of crazy."

"It's a long shot," Ben said. But I saw his eyes flick to the front porch and settle on the black front door.

"Worse than a long shot." Thatcher stuck his keys back into the ignition. "For one thing, awful things happen in most houses. Maybe not VonHolt awful but I guarantee you I'm not the only kid in Glennon Heights to find out his dad was on pills. He's not the only doctor with a missing prescription pad. People hurt each other all the time. They cheat on each other." I looked down at my lap. "They suspect each other." I heard Janie's breath catch in her throat and Ben grunt as if Thatcher had landed a punch. "That happens in any house. You're going to do what—Nancy Drew around the yard and look for clues?"

I swung my head up. "Those people probably have enough to deal with. They don't need tourists."

"But we might find clues." I spoke up. "Listen, Thatcher, I get it and I'm really sorry if we"—I looked at Janie—"seemed insensitive. But Janie and I found a bunch of possible evidence in your old backyard. We found cigarette butts and soda cans, like someone needed to pass along the time while they . . . I don't know . . . watched the house. What if we just looked, real quick? We're here anyway."

Ben looked over. "No cars in the driveway, man. They won't even know we were here."

"Until we show up on a security camera," Thatcher pointed out. "Come on, there's no way they don't have this place wired."

"So Ben and I will go," Janie volunteered. "We just moved here. We'll just say we let our curiosity get the best of us."

"We'll be fast. I'll time us," Ben said.

"Yeah, sure. Whatever," Thatcher gave in. "But I'm keeping the car running."

"Two minutes," Ben told him, then faced Janie. "That's it. We do a quick tour of the backyard."

The Donahue siblings made a quick exit and I sat in Thatcher Langsom's car, feeling left behind and longing to disappear. The seconds dragged by. Finally I couldn't help myself. "Hey, Thatcher, thanks for the ride." His eyes flickered in my direction. "I'm really sorry about everything you've been through. I always thought of your family as sort of perfect. You know, seeing you guys in the neighborhood . . ." My voice faded out, without mentioning our wayward parents or wondering if Mrs. Langsom now regretted marrying the well-connected surgeon instead of my dad.

"You know it doesn't matter what they find," Thatcher said. "Someone smoking cigarettes and drinking soda—that doesn't necessarily count as illegal. It's a stretch to even call it trespassing. Honestly, you talking about my perfect family sounds a lot creepier. I mean, calm down."

That got me mad. At Janie, for darting out of the car without a look back. At Ben, for making me feel like I didn't count. And at Thatcher, who had seemed real for a second, but who suddenly felt the need to remind me of the distance between who he was and who I was.

"I'm sorry," I said, not sounding at all sorry. "I guess your family's been on my mind. I just found out about your mom and my dad. You know—together."

"Oh yeah? Was that a recent development?" His voice had gone surly; his look had gone sour.

"No!" I said, indignant. "It was like twenty years ago, when our moms were close. Apparently, my mom got over it."

"That's a relief. 'Cause it seems like your aunt has a more recent reason to be angry."

I heard myself gasp and that made me angrier, that

Thatcher knew his words hit their mark. It only made it worse that I didn't quite understand what he meant. My hand reached to open the door and nothing happened.

"My bad." Thatcher smirked. "Child locks."

I steadied my voice. "Can you let me out please?"

"Two minutes are up. We need to go." He nodded in the direction of the house and Ben and Janie came hurtling out of the dark space between the hedges. The locks clicked and the Donahues vaulted into the car like two bank robbers hauling cash.

"Go. Go. Go," Ben hollered, but he was laughing. Janie's breath heaved as she settled in beside me. She had stretched out the front of her sweatshirt like a hammock and held a collection of cigarette butts and wrappers there.

"What kind of garbage did you bring into my car?" Thatcher asked. He smiled though, his wide Langsom smile. The play-by-play of Ben and Janie's two-minute mission stretched for the duration of the ten-minute ride home.

"We found a spot," Janie started.

"Beneath a tree," Ben finished

"A big tree. Like an oak."

"You could hide behind it."

"If you wanted to."

"To spy."

"Well, yeah. To spy."

"Anyway, there was just a pile of cigarettes."

"Old, used."

"Basically an ashtray."

"Just like in our yard."

"Candy wrappers."

"Straight line of vision from the tree to the house."

"So we were right."

"Theory proven."

Thatcher looked impressed. "Theory proven indeed."

"Right?" Ben asked him.

"Will you turn it over to the cops?"

"Our collection of cigarette butts?"

"Maybe they can get DNA? Like on *CSI*." Thatcher whistled a low, impressed whistle. "I can't believe you guys were right. We didn't expect that at all. Right, Olivia?" It surprised me to hear Thatcher Langsom say my name. It seemed like everyone in the car turned to look at me. Even Thatcher, who should have kept his eyes on the road.

I didn't answer. I dug in my pocket and found a leftover plastic bag, the kind we used when we walked Toby, to pick up after him. I held the bag open so that Janie could shake in her collection.

"Score!" Janie said. "Livvie always thinks of everything."

"Listen, Olivia." Thatcher cleared his throat. "I'm sorry—I didn't mean to go on attack mode."

"What's going on?" Ben asked, on high alert. He twisted in his seat to see my face.

Thatcher looked toward Ben and then toward me. "Really. Sometimes when my family comes up in conversation . . . I just don't know what to say."

"Yeah, it's okay. I should never have said anything." I meant *I should never have attempted to hold a conversation with you, Handsome Lacrosse God.* Maybe I'd pounced the way Brooke or any number of other people might have, reminding Thatcher that his status had fallen in the past few months.

Thatcher parked the car exactly between his old house and mine. It occurred to me that he must have known where I lived. He had just pretended he'd never noticed we were neighbors. Now he turned to face me full on. "No. Of course you should have. I'm sorry."

"I get it," I told him. "Thank you. And thanks for the ride home."

"You want to come inside?" Ben asked Thatcher, but then looked back at me. "Everybody?"

"Liv, you have to. We need to compare specimens." Janie shook the green plastic bag in the air. "We can use Lucy's microscope. It's majorly impressive."

"Sure. Okay." Thatcher shrugged casually, but his eyes darted around the street. He saw us notice and smiled wryly. "Just a little strange."

"Yeah, man." Ben hopped down. "It doesn't have to be."

The four of us walked from the curb to 16 Olcott and it felt easy and familiar, as if these were the friends I'd known for years. Anyone watching us would have believed that. The setting sun glowed amber and dappled the leafy maples that arched across the road. Behind us stretched our four long shadows, linked at the arms, even though, in real life, none of us even brushed against each other, right then.

And just as suddenly, the connection broke. We had reached the front steps of the Donahue house or the Langsom house, depending on the moment in history. Across the street, Miss Abbot's sheer curtains fluttered.

"Look who's spying—" I started to say.

"Hey, you know what? I should actually head back." Thatcher stopped short at the bottom of the marble steps. He stared up at Ben, who had already reached for the door handle.

"What? No way. Come inside, man. It's fine." Ben looked at Janie, as if urging her to say something convincing. But Janie just swung her helpless gaze to me. Behind Thatcher, Miss Abbot stood fully framed in her front window, making no apologies for her surveillance.

"No, really. I have a whole lot to do for tomorrow. First day, right?" Thatcher backed down the walk, looking up at the three of us, who stood on steps of staggered height. "See you guys tomorrow. At school."

The three of us just stood there, facing the neighborhood, because we didn't want to turn our backs on Thatcher until he reached his car. Then Ben turned the doorknob and leaned back on the door. "This house," he said. "So much grief over a little architecture."

"You think he'll be okay?" Janie murmured.

Ben scoffed. "Of course he'll be okay. He probably just doesn't want to see Mom's miniature chair collection." I laughed in spite of my concern for Thatcher. Mrs. Donahue's collection was actually sort of odd—some of the chairs had creepy dolls perched on them. Some held figurines of animals. But Thatcher's sadness trailed into the house with us. It permeated our jokes. Janie and I shifted in our spots, feeling guilty. But Ben just nodded again, reassuring us. "Thatcher's fine. That kid's strong enough to deal with a lot more than we can even imagine."

"Look at you—showing empathy for another person," Janie said. "So you don't think our family counts as the worst-case scenario anymore?"

"Fifth worst, maybe."

We heard a cupboard thump closed and then Mrs. Donahue calling out, "Ben? Jane? Are you both there?"

"Yeah. Olivia's with us. We just went to the coffee shop. But we left our bikes there."

"What? Why?" Mrs. Donahue sounded exasperated. "Well, okay. But you're home for the night now?"

"Yeah, Mom." Ben wrinkled his brow. "I can't believe I'm the one pointing this out, but it's a school night. Thatcher Langsom just left. He gave us a lift home."

"Who?" Mr. Donahue came striding in. "What did you say?"

"Thatcher Langsom. The kid who used to live here. He drove us home from the coffee shop. He didn't want to come inside."

Mr. and Mrs. Donahue exchanged a look. If that look could have made a sound, it would have been the angry scrape of a chair against hardwood. Mrs. Donahue sighed and lowered herself into the sofa. "That's for the best. That's not a friendship I want any of you to pursue."

"Any of you," Mr. Donahue added with the hostile edge that occasionally sharpened his voice. He held up a hand to stave off Ben's objections and explained, "Your mother and I are filing suit against the Langsoms tomorrow morning."

CHAPTER FIFTEEN

For every first day of school that I can remember, my parents have taken photos of me in front of the azalea bush in our yard. Just me in front of fuchsia flowers. In the early photos, the blooms looked bigger than my head. In a few pictures, I'm reaching out awkwardly to touch one.

I couldn't say no to my mom, not on the first day of high school anyway. And Janie wouldn't let me opt out of carpooling. So that's how I ended up standing at the side of our house, in front of a botanical backdrop, urging my dad to take the photos already before the Donahues showed up and the whole scene forever imprinted on Ben Donahue's brain.

"Stand up a little straighter," Mom instructed while Dad's camera clicked away.

"We're done, right?" I craned my neck, checking for the minivan backing down the drive. "How many do we need?"

"Until we get a good one." The dew on the grass dampened my sneakers. "Look at the camera. Try to relax," Mom implored. "Janie and her mom will wait for a few photos."

"We've taken hundreds of photos."

"How about you turn, just slightly, and look back at Daddy? Peek over the backpack!"

As she said it, Janie's mom pulled into the driveway. Ben sat right up front, and even from my spot near the trellis, I could see his eyebrows arched in amusement. I almost sank into the ground. My dad kept clicking and probably caught the moment I realized that I would never achieve any semblance of coolness in the town of Glennon Heights.

"Mom?" I asked desperately. "Are we done now?"

Janie's mom killed the engine but I was the one who died, silently screaming in front of the azalea plant. Mrs. Donahue swung her door open. "You're so good! Every year I promise to take pictures. But then I count myself lucky just to get all three kids out the door."

My mom threw up her hands, "Well, get them out here!" She tapped her watch. "We have plenty of time!" A better friend might have waved her off, run for the car, and claimed a need to arrive early for registration or paperwork. But I stood with my hands folded across my chest and waited for Janie and the twins to suffer through it right along with me.

For the first few, just Janie and I stood with the plant between us like a science experiment we had cultivated together. "How did this happen?" Janie murmured out of the side of her mouth.

"Every year this happens," I said. Her mouth dropped open, just as my father's camera clicked. "In this same spot."

Our moms arranged Ben and Lucy on either side of us. Then the three Donahue kids stood together and I got to stand off to the side, smirking. Then Ben and Lucy, Ben and Janie, Janie and Lucy.

"Don't we need to get a shot of Ben and Olivia?" Lucy asked, her voice poisonous.

Janie's eyes moved from Lucy to Ben and finally to me. "Why would we need that?"

"We don't need that," Ben said. I concentrated hard on the azaleas.

Aware of Janie's eyes on me. I found my voice. "We should go." I spoke to the flowers. "We really can't be late on the first day."

In the car, I sat hunched as close to the window as possible without actually hanging out of it. As soon as we arrived, I sprang out of the car and grabbed my bag from the collection of bags in the trunk. "Thank you for driving me to school today, Mrs. Donahue," I sang out.

"Of course, honey. Look out for Janie today, okay? All of this has suddenly gotten so complicated."

Maybe it was different in bigger towns or boarding schools or other places where you didn't know by heart the people who surrounded you. But in Glennon Heights, the first day of school felt pretty anticlimactic. Maybe you felt different because your locker sat in an unfamiliar row or you were wearing new shoes. But most of the kids knew you too well. It was hard to start fresh in September even though you might have felt transformed. And if you actually were new, then the opposite happened. If you had recently moved to town like Ben, Lucy, and Janie, all eyes followed you everywhere. Heather Singer moved here from Seattle in the fifth grade and we still called her New Heather. Heather O'Leary, who grew up here, got to be Heather, unadorned and undescribed.

And then there was the Donahues' address. And the fact that Thatcher Langsom, previous occupant of said address, stepped out of the crowd to greet Ben as soon as we approached the school's domed awning.

"You have arrived," Thatcher announced, as if welcoming Ben to his kingdom.

Our classmates watched this scene intently because most of us were accustomed to watching Thatcher intently. I watched, wondering how Ben would react—his father's warning still scowling in my memory. But Ben just clapped one arm around Thatcher's shoulders and grinned. Lucy separated herself quickly, but Janie and I walked behind them as long as we could and I marveled at the way the crowd parted for Thatcher. The boy. The athlete. The recently rich kid. All this power he flexed without even realizing it. But then I remembered how quickly Thatcher had turned on me the night before, how easily he'd reminded me how insignificant I was. Maybe he understood exactly how much power he flexed.

Before, I had felt known in Glennon Heights. But now I felt noticed. In front of us, the boys' backs receded into the crowd and Ben didn't turn to pass along a reassuring look to his sister, let alone me. Janie's eyes darted and skidded around the corridor, and then I saw her take a deep breath and settle into the invisible spotlight. She smiled at the friends I pointed out and even waved to the coffee shop guys from the night before. I should never have doubted Janie.

She even handled Brooke. First period. World History. The three of us shared that class together, and I'd forgotten, along with so many other details that a good friend would know or remember. Brooke had been right about that. This time, Janie didn't wait for me to broker a connection.

"Listen," she told Brooke, "I'm sorry that we didn't get to know each other better this summer." She took the desk next to Brooke's, leaving me to claim one across the room, near the door. "Moving felt like the worst wrong turn of my life. And then just when things started feeling normal, those letters started arriving."

I wanted to shout at her to stop, to remind her that Brooke had achieved expert level in social manipulation. But the whole class had tuned in, listening. I bit my lip and waited. Brooke would deploy one of two options—she could go nuclear and unleash an onslaught of insults. Most of us, in that room, expected her to go that route.

But she had already done that—to me, the night before. Today was our first day of high school, after all. Maybe Brooke intended to transform herself a little bit too. "It sounds terrible—what you've gone through." The room held its collective breath. But she only went on to say, "You're pretty killer, taking on some crazy psychopathic letter writer. But at least your new place is amazing. I always thought it would make the best haunted house."

"Well, you should come over. We already found one hidden room." Janie spoke loudly enough to include the rest of the class in her conversation. "Liv found it, actually." Janie crowned me with the credit. "We'll keep looking and see what we uncover. We should have the Halloween party to end all Halloween parties."

"That would be incredible." Brooke sounded sincere, and when she looked up, her smile extended to me too. "I've really missed hanging out on Olcott Place."

Sometimes I got so wrapped up in wondering how I fit into the world, I forgot that there were people I fit with.

"Well," I offered, "Olcott Place misses you too."

"Yeah?"

"I miss you. I don't know about people like Miss Abbot. But she probably misses you."

Brooke and I smiled at each other, and Janie smiled, and for that moment and the rest of the class and even the rest of the school day, it seemed like maybe I could handle high school. I moved from class to class—sometimes with Janie, sometimes with Brooke. With Allie and Mirabelle and Kaia. With both Heathers and Sage and even an art class with Justin, who said to me, "You're Janie's friend, right?" as if that counted as my identity.

A couple of times throughout the day, I caught a glimpse of Ben. A sliver of jacket sleeve turning a corner. The back of his head bobbing down the steps a full crowd in front of me. I had thought that would make me nervous, but actually it reassured me. Unlike summer days, when Ben disappeared from his family for hours at a time, at least I knew he was in the same building, on the same patch of land.

My mom texted me a couple of times. First a heart. Then a question mark. I wrote back, *I'm handling it.* But that first day felt even better than that. All that worrying, but high school made sense to me. I had friends. I felt connected.

And then the dismissal bell rang. I stood up, swung my

bag over my shoulder. By the time I reached our locker, Janie already stood waiting. "Do you need to stay after?" she asked. "My dad's on his way." She looked down, texting Lucy and Ben. I couldn't get our combination on the first try, so I tried the numbers once more. Fumbled again—this time because Ben distracted me. He strode through the hallway, cutting a path through the rest of the freshmen milling around.

"Janie, we've got to go. Right now."

"Yeah. I'm just—"

"Lucy's already outside. We have to go to her."

"What's going on?" Janie looked at me. "Just give us a second, okay?"

"No time. Listen, Livvie. You should stay here, okay? Can you call your mom and grab a ride with her?"

"No, Ben. She cannot." Janie slammed on the locker. "Liv, don't pay any attention to him. There's plenty of room." She turned to her brother. "Seriously, what is your problem?"

"Guys, I'm serious. I can't explain it right now, but it would be better if Olivia found another ride."

"Stop it." Janie swung her backpack over her shoulder. "I guess things didn't go so decently for you today? I'm really sorry, Ben. We had a good first day of high school, right, Liv? Like surprisingly acceptable."

"Please just listen to me." Ben spoke quietly in the few spaces left in Janie's chatter. She kept going and I followed her. I'd already been following Janie for weeks by then. Why would I have chosen that exact moment to stop?

"Do you have a lot of homework? I don't. We have that summer reading essay thing, but she said it's due next Tuesday." Janie barely took a breath as we worked our way through the hallway.

"Jane." Ben's voice rang out in a warning. Janie and I swiveled to face him. People in the hall turned as well. He crossed quickly to us and spoke low and fast. "When we get outside, we stick together, okay?" He held up his hands: no questions. "You keep your head down. No matter what anyone says to you, you don't reply. You don't even look up." He glanced from Janie to me and then to her again. "I guess that goes for both of you."

Ben turned to walk backward, facing us, and bumped open the door with his backpack. We all stood for a second blinking up at the sun and then Ben took one of each of our shoulders, steering us firmly.

I kept my head down, like Ben had instructed, and that's when I saw the wires snaking around the sidewalk. Then I noticed the feet wore men's dress shoes, women's heels. Too fancy, even for the first day of high school. "Maurice! That's them. Three kids. The Donahues!" She lunged to block Ben's path and he tried steering us around her.

In a flash, I understood how I'd made the situation more difficult. The reporter lady thought I was Lucy, who'd probably been smart enough to walk out separately. They had been looking for three kids and there we were.

"Just a minute. Please. Hey, guys! Look over here for a second? Can we get a statement?" I felt Ben's fingers tightened on my shoulder. "How long have you felt unsafe in your home?"

Then another voice, "Your father has claimed your family is being hunted." Beside me, I heard Ben grunt softly. Heads down, we kept walking. There were only three of them, plus their cameramen, but they caused such a commotion, it felt like a full press conference.

"Who do you think is watching your family?"

Ben looked directly at the reporter asking that question. She stood the tallest and didn't seem so much older than us. Aunt Jillian would have described her as looking a little desperate, with all the makeup and her hair piled high on top of her head.

Encouraged by the eye contact, the woman repeated her question. "Who is watching your family?"

When Ben lifted his arm from my shoulder, I half expected him to hit the reporter. But he just gestured to the cameras. "You are, I guess." Ben spoke deliberately, like he knew they'd use that quote over and over. That night and the weeks after. "You're watching my family now."

CHAPTER SIXTEEN

As soon as we spotted Mr. Donahue's car, we hustled to it and found Lucy crouched in the front passenger seat. Ben opened the door and held it as Janie and I climbed inside. Behind us, we heard the reporters vie breathlessly for attention. "Mr. Donahue, sir, can we get a comment on the situation with your new home?"

I turned to see Ben shaking his head even as his dad rolled down his window. "No comment," Mr. Donahue declared. And then he pressed a button so the window rose up.

When I tried to buckle my seat belt, I noticed my hands shaking and looked up at Ben to see his jaw set rigid in anger.

When he spoke, his barely contained rage flared at his father. "Why not comment? I mean, you called them, right?"

"You don't know what you're talking about. And you're emotional."

"Yeah—I'm a little emotional. So is Janie. And Olivia, who is trembling and has absolutely nothing to do with this circus. Did you think about any of us, Dad? Lucy, how are you doing?"

"I'm fine. I'm certainly not overreacting." Lucy glanced up at her dad.

"Oh no. It's not overreacting—" Ben started.

But Lucy cut him off. "I would think you'd be used to scenes like that."

That jab landed. Ben grimaced and spat out, "Great job, sis. Now you get to be the favorite."

But Lucy only laughed. "Don't be silly. I've always been the favorite."

Next to me, Janie stared out the window.

"Just to be clear," Mr. Donahue said, "I have no idea how the press got ahold of our story. Your mother and I filed a lawsuit at the courthouse this morning. There must be some kind of case log reviewed by the local news." Mr. Donahue looked back at me. "Olivia, I apologize that you got caught up in that. I thought you might have cross-country practice after school."

"Not on the first day." My voice came out in a whisper. Even that embarrassed me.

Ben was not ready to let the matter go. "Well, they sure got people out to our school pretty fast. You know, for a local news story."

"It's compelling stuff. They're just doing their job— bringing news to the people." Mr. Donahue hit his blinker and we turned onto Olcott Place. Behind us, two vans turned too. "I will be honest; press doesn't hurt us. We're not the ones with anything to hide. And unfortunately, people sometimes need to be forced to do the right thing. Harrington's will settle faster if their reputation is on the line."

"And the Langsoms?"

"The Langsoms will take care of the Langsoms. They had every opportunity to disclose those letters. Don't ask me to feign sympathy for a family who willingly put my family in danger. My children."

Ben snorted.

"We understand, Dad," Lucy said, looking back at Ben as if she dared him to say different. "It's just that we were all nervous already about starting a new school."

"I hear that. As I said before, I have absolutely no idea how they knew to go up to the high school this afternoon. But you handled yourselves with maturity and grace. All of you. I could not be more proud. We have the police investigating these letters, and if the press wants to add to the pressure, I can only think that will lead to a break in the case." Mr. Donahue pulled the car into the drive. The vans behind us parked on the street in front of their house. "Who cares if we're on the local news? There's no reason to feel ashamed that people are paying attention to what happens in their community. We are not the criminals here."

"Really?" Lucy asked. "Ben doesn't count as a criminal anymore?"

"Lucybelle," Mr. Donahue admonished. "Let's remember that we're all on the same team." And then, as if he suddenly remembered that I didn't exactly qualify, Mr. Donahue met my eyes. "Olivia, if I had dropped you off, those vans would have just parked at your house. I didn't want to compromise your family's privacy."

Another snort from Ben, but I said "Thank you" in a politely firm way that would have made my mother proud.

"Here's how we'll handle this. Lucy, Ben, and Janie, when you get out of the car, I want you to go straight to the house. Have your keys out and ready. Olivia, I'm sure your parents are eager to hear about your first day. You should take the opportunity to walk directly and briskly to your home. Any reporters will have focused their attention on the kids and our house."

"Olivia can't come over?" Janie seemed to suddenly wake up.

"Why would Olivia want to come over?" Ben asked, and I thought that he possibly didn't understand me at all.

But it's not like I could sit there and argue. "Your dad's right. I mean, my mom wants me home. I'm sure she's dying to hear how everything went."

"Maybe she saw some of it on TV!" Ben spoke with fake cheer.

"Call me if you need me," I told Janie.

"Everyone ready? Let's give it a count of three. And don't worry—I'll step in, if needed, and make a short statement. That will buy us all enough time to get inside."

"Dad, that's really selfless of you." I could hear the disdain in Ben's voice.

But Mr. Donahue didn't take the bait. "Ready? One. Two. Three." He popped the trunk and the rest of us opened our doors. I slid out Janie's side, squeezed her shoulder, grabbed my backpack, and headed home.

Behind me, I heard the surge of cameras and questions. Not a tidal wave or anything, but still. I walked briskly, my head bent, ready to muscle my way past. But no one noticed me.

"We hope to resolve this situation quickly and fairly." Mr. Donahue carefully enunciated his words. "If any of you have kids, I'm sure you know that my only concern is for their safety. My wife feels the same. We love our new community. But we never imagined that purchasing our dream home would put the lives of our children in danger." From my own steps, I could see him preening. "Thank you. We will have no further comment at this time." And then Mr. Donahue stepped back into the house and the heavy black door of 16 Olcott seemed to swallow him up.

I waited on the steps while the camera guys wound up their cords and the reporters compared notes. No one appeared worried about being scooped. "You guys using this?" one of the women reporters asked the other.

That one shrugged. "We'll see how it reads."

"It's going to read as canned."

They chuckled. "You can't make this stuff up."

"Maybe you can." The two reporters laughed. But I still didn't understand the joke. It took my mom and Aunt Jillian to explain that some people believed that Mr. Donahue had concocted the whole thing.

"Adults don't always make the right choices," Jillian told me later after dinner. She'd rushed right over after we were on the local news. Or, rather, the Donahue family and a sliver of my shoulder and backpack were on the news.

"The whole thing baffles me, Jill," Mom said. "What's the point of the press at the school? Why not just hold court in his driveway?"

"It reinforces the idea that the kids are young and vulnerable." Aunt Jillian spoke with an unfamiliar authority. My eyes must have widened because she laughed. "If there's one thing I know well, Olivia, it is the bizarre and brainless behavior of man-children. I know you feel close to Janie and her brother, but their father definitely qualifies as a man-child." Another, darker look washed over her face. "Speak of the devil." She crossed over to stare out our window.

"Oh, for goodness' sake." My mother sighed. "As if we needed any more drama today."

The drama she spoke of had arrived in the form of Ned McGovern, who had started yelling at Janie's house even before he'd finished slamming his car door. "Donahue! Donahue! Gavin Donahue, get out here."

"Well, this promises to be a regular meeting of the minds," my dad said dryly.

"Oh no," Jillian murmured.

"This is not your circus, Jill."

"I know, I know. But there are kids involved. Are those two even supposed to be in contact? Isn't there a restraining order in place?"

"Not for Ned." I spoke up before realizing that none of them wanted to know I knew about that stuff. Three sets of concerned eyes narrowed at me at once. "That's just what I've overheard anyway."

The drama played on, right outside our window. Ned McGovern first stood on the Donahues' lawn and then he charged up the steps. "Come on out and face me like a man!" he yelled, pounding the door with his fist. "Donahue!"

My dad sighed. "Should I go out and talk to him?"

My mom bit her lip and peered out. "I think we should stay out of it for now." She raised her arms up, reached over, and shut the open windows, immediately muffling the sound of Ned's shouting. Mom's eyes flickered to my dad as if she expected him to argue. "It's a shame those reporters left. They're missing a story."

"Ned McGovern causing a scene on someone else's front yard doesn't exactly count as newsworthy," Dad replied. Aunt Jillian cringed but didn't argue. "Olivia, don't you have homework or something?"

"It's the first day," I answered, without peeling my eyes from the window.

"And that means?"

"No one gives homework the first day." While my dad focused on my scholastic endeavors, Aunt Jillian grabbed the opportunity to head out the front door. Presumably, she figured she'd try to calm Ned before the police made their now daily pilgrimage to Olcott Place.

"Jill! We just talked about this!" Mom called after her. "Honestly!" She looked at us helplessly.

Outside the scene unfolded like a movie with the sound turned off. I watched my aunt march toward Ned as he kept pounding on the Donahues' front door. When she reached him, Jillian grabbed Ned's wrist mid-swing and he spun around to face her.

I could tell my dad thought Ned might hit her. He tensed

up and headed to the door. Ned gestured to the Donahue house and I saw Jillian shake her head furiously. She tugged at his arm, pulling him toward his car. Just as she reached over and opened the driver's-side door, her head swung up and Mr. McGovern started struggling against her all over again. That's when Dad arrived, leaving our front door gaping open, with me and Mom right there to hear.

"Hey, Gavin, stay inside." Dad sounded nonchalant. "We've got everything under control here."

"It doesn't look that way," Mr. Donahue called out from behind his screen door.

"Please, just stay inside," implored Aunt Jillian. I moved to step outside but my mom placed a firm hand on my shoulder. I noticed she didn't shut the door, though. We both stood there watching and listening.

"You're going to name me in a lawsuit? Are you serious? If you wanted out of this sale you had every opportunity—the hours I put in," Mr. McGovern spat and sputtered.

"You neglected to mention the house came with its own stalker, McGovern. I'd call that nondisclosure."

"You don't know what you've done. This is my livelihood. You have a problem with the seller's disclosure, fine. Then we go back to negotiations. But to hold me personally liable—"

"Just business." And then, maybe because he heard how that came off as cold and unsympathetic, Janie's dad added, "Really, I'm trying to protect my family." That became the refrain we heard Mr. Donahue repeat to anyone who would listen. He said it again as Dad and Jillian loaded Mr. McGovern into his car. Later I'd read it in our local newspaper and then national magazines.

The *Detroit Tribune* came out with its headline: "Unreal Estate: Dream Home Becomes Family's Nightmare." *Buzzbot* ran a list: "10 Haunting Sentences from the Sentry's Letters." It took all of two days for the British tabloids to latch on to the story, with breathless accounts of death threats and a description of the Langsom house fit for a gothic novel. When *Entertainment America* picked up the story, it led with the image of Mr. Donahue standing on the front porch of 16 Olcott, his arms folded across his chest, with the familiar quote plastered below: *I'm trying to protect my family.*

But the more coverage the story garnered, the more vulnerable the Donahues became. Traffic suddenly choked our sleepy street, with cars slowing down in front of 16 Olcott to get a look. Whenever I spotted Ben—in town, in school—he wore a hoodie, his hands in his pockets, hunched over, exposing as little of himself as possible. Lucy wrote draft after draft of her college essay, but bristled when a tour guide recognized her while touring Wesleyan University.

Janie told me she'd overheard her parents fighting—that her mom had come home from the natural food market in tears because the checkout girl, who'd dated one of the older Langsom brothers, refused to ring her up. She avoided restaurants because she was convinced the waitstaff spat in her food. "They hate us, Gavin," Janie heard her say the afternoon Mrs. Donahue had walked out of a salon, her hair dripping wet, because the ladies there were so hostile.

As far as Janie, it turned out that nothing reverses the tide of ninth-grade opinion as quickly as a lawsuit against the Langsom family. Glennon Heights wasn't about to let outsiders knock them down.

You couldn't blame Thatcher. The definition of a Good Guy, you could not have even detected a hardening of his jaw when one of the Donahue kids walked by. His eyes matched his fixed smile even as he stared right through them. He left the casual cruelty of social consequences to the rest of the kids at school.

No one sat with us at lunch. The first day after the news stories broke, Mirabelle at least bothered to look apologetically in our direction, but Brooke and Kaia just wrinkled their noses in disgust. When we arrived at school and tried to make our way to the locker area, people moved aside for me the way you do when you are all rushing around to get to class before the first bell. But no one gave way for Janie. She stood there, in the school entrance, sealed off by a wall of cold shoulders.

Maybe because I grew up in Glennon Heights, it was harder to completely cast me aside. Or maybe I just functioned as a useful contrast. Treating me like I still mattered reminded Janie that she didn't.

The first day after the lawsuit went like that. Blank, frozen stares. Glowering faces. "Don't worry about it," I muttered to Janie under my breath. "The whole town's gone crazy."

Janie refused to acknowledge any of it. She threw her elbows around like a power forward driving to the basket. She reached our locker well before the first-period bell rang and spun our combination expertly. "Don't worry about what?"

All the Donahues steadied and steeled themselves to make it through the day.

But nothing could have prepared us for what happened when we got home from school.

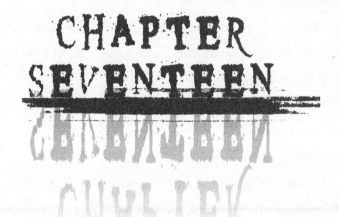

CHAPTER SEVENTEEN

By the time the three o'clock dismissal bell rang, the Donahues and I counted among the first students barreling through the exit doors. Maybe they felt the facades they'd constructed crumbling, but I doubt it. All three of them greeted their mom with carefully composed cheer, even Ben, which only confirmed how fake it all was.

"Hey, lady," he said heartily. "We expected the Dad-mobile." We moved quickly, keeping our backpacks on as we climbed into the minivan.

"Nope, you're stuck with me." Mrs. Donahue spoke rue-fully, as if already regretting the words that followed. "Your dad needed to meet with the attorneys this afternoon." Beside me, Janie stiffened slightly. From then on, we all sat silently with smiles plastered on our faces, pretending nothing—including lawsuits—mattered.

When we arrived on Olcott Place, Mrs. Donahue slowed the van by my house, but Janie piped up. "Livvie's coming over. We have homework."

"If that's okay," I rushed to add.

"Of course! I think that's great! Just let me know later if you'd like to stay for supper."

I nodded vigorously and texted my mom to let her know I'd be home before dark. We even slammed the car doors politely.

Inside the house, the atmosphere still felt stilted. At first, I assumed that was all that was off-kilter. When Mrs. Donahue asked, "Who moved the dining room chairs?" I thought she was just fussing. The air felt thick and heavy, like someone was waiting to speak. Janie surveyed the contents of the fridge and Ben lingered at the kitchen stairs, looking puzzled. Lucy grabbed a plum from the fruit bowl on the counter and bounded upstairs. "Gotta go. Need to start homework," she called down in her clipped tone of voice. It's not like any of us would try to stop her.

Moments later, we heard Lucy scream.

The sound wound down the stairs and ricocheted through-out the house until it felt like the walls themselves were screaming. In the kitchen, Janie, Ben, and I stood frozen in our spots. Mrs. Donahue sprinted past and pounded up the steps. We followed.

"Lucy!" Mrs. Donahue called out. "Lucy, honey—what's wrong?"

A white envelope, resting on her pillow—that's what was wrong. The same cream stationery, the same handwriting. The inky block letters stood out as the only glimpse of darkness on the white layers of Lucy's bed.

The Sentry had delivered another letter.

Not through the mail slot.

Hand-delivered to her bedroom.

With her name written across the envelope.

Mrs. Donahue and Lucy stood staring. Janie grabbed my hand and tugged me toward her room. We saw the second letter from the doorway, placed just so. Her full name written across the envelope: *Jane Louise Donahue.*

"He was in here too!" Janie shrieked. And then as the fact of it sunk in: "He was inside our house."

"Don't touch it—don't touch anything." Mrs. Donahue was all business, herding us together through the hall. "Ben? Where are you?" The three of us found him in his own room, glowering at the white note left on the tangle of blankets of his unmade bed. "Just leave it right where it is."

"I heard you." He held his hands up. His eyes didn't move, like he was watching a snake, expecting it to strike.

Mrs. Donahue whipped out her cell phone. "I'm calling your father."

"He was inside our house," Janie kept whimpering. Lucy reached out to squeeze her shoulders.

"Gavin, please come home right away." Mrs. Donahue leaned forward, examining Ben's envelope more closely. "Yes. Three of them. On the children's beds. I don't know! Somehow he got inside their rooms." She paused, looking incredulous. "Who do you think I mean? The Sentry. He was inside our house."

And then we heard a series of dull thuds, and maybe scraping against the wood floors. The noise broke Ben's spell and he sprang into action. He pulled all of us farther into his room and brought his finger to his lips, hushing us. We heard another scrape, more thumping.

Mrs. Donahue's eye widened. "Are you already home, Gavin?" She spoke low into the phone. "Is that you downstairs?" Her terrified face told us everything.

Lucy pushed us back with one arm and slammed the door closed with the other. She turned the flimsy lock and Ben set about moving the dresser in front of the door.

"Janie, call the police," Lucy said, tossing over her phone before helping Ben move more furniture in front of the door.

Janie spoke urgently. "I need to report an intruder. Sixteen Olcott Place. Glennon Heights. He's still inside our house. He's still here."

It felt like forever before the police arrived, but most likely it took minutes. They knew the route, after all. We spent every second braced against the dresser barricade, listening as thuds and thumps dragged along the house's corridors. I kept waiting to feel the Sentry push against the door. I half expected him to claw through the floorboards or plunge through the ceiling. But there was just the four of us in the room and our ragged breath—Mr. Donahue yelling from one phone and the 911 dispatcher soothing us from the other.

When the sirens closed in, we nodded at each other with relief. But then we heard a frenzy coming from downstairs—thunderous crashes and the silvery sound of breaking glass.

The Sentry had heard the sirens too.

"Stay where you are until the officers identify themselves," the operator instructed. "Wait for the police to give you the all clear."

When they did, when we shoved aside the dresser and unlocked the door, we still didn't feel safe emerging from Ben's room. At least I didn't. We banded together and took tiny steps forward, as Officer Wycoff guided us into the hallway and then down the steps. In the dining room, the chairs were lying on their sides. A hallway table had toppled over. Two kitchen windows had been shattered and shards of broken glass winked on the grass outside.

A female officer I didn't recognize introduced herself as Officer Nicolodi. She led us out to the deck and we sat around the table, as if attending the worst cookout ever. That's where we were when Mr. Donahue came home.

"Tell me you're all okay," he said, rushing out from the doorway.

"We're all great, Dad." Ben bounced his knee as he spoke—his adrenaline working its way out through movement and sarcasm. "Just a typical Thursday."

"When I think of what could have happened—" Mr. Donahue started to say.

"While you were with your lawyer."

"Ben, we're all upset." Mrs. Donahue stood up between her husband and her son. "Let's not conflate all the reasons."

But Ben spoke directly to his father. "You should have been here." I caught myself staring at Mr. Donahue's boat shoes. They didn't look weighty enough to cause the ruckus the Sentry had made moving through the house. But all the talk about how Mr. Donahue should have been home focused my attention on his claim that he wasn't.

I met Janie's eyes across the table and could have sworn she read my mind.

"Will the lawyer tell the police about your appointment?" She actually asked it out loud.

Lucy's mouth hung open and Ben let out a low whistle. "And what do you mean by that, young lady?" Mrs. Donahue demanded.

But Janie said, "Well the lawyer can't lie. He's not allowed to, right? People are saying all sorts of things . . . Maybe this will prove them wrong . . ." She trailed off and covered her face with her hands.

I felt ashamed sitting on their deck, evaluating alibis.

And yet. Mr. Donahue stood there, his arm around his wife. He spoke like he was at a news conference. "Listen—I understand that this has been hard for you, and that you disagree with the concept of the lawsuit. But that is a decision for your mother and me to make. Perhaps I should have been here to protect my family. But this lawsuit is another way to protect my family. That matter is not up for discussion."

I stood up then. I could see the roof of my house from the deck. My mom would be home from work soon and Toby needed a walk. Slowly, I started to edge toward the sliding glass door.

"Livvie, are you okay?" Ben asked.

"Please don't go home yet," Janie pleaded.

Officer Nicolodi poked her head outside. "We need you all to sit tight for a bit. We'll have a few questions, just as soon as we finish looking around."

"My mom—"

"Oh, honey," Mrs. Donahue rushed to say. "How thoughtless of me—of course we don't want her to come home and panic." She turned to the officer. "We need to call my neighbor."

The policewoman beckoned her inside. "Why don't you let

me give you some language to use? It's important that we don't broadcast what happened today too widely—hopefully that will shake loose some new information."

Right then Officer Wycoff came out to the deck as well. "We're ready to take your statements now. Individually."

So one by one we sat at the dining room table recounting the discovery of the letters, the commotion we heard. After that, we all gathered in the living room. Officer Wycoff held the letters in his hand, each sealed in its own plastic bag.

"Now we don't get to read our own mail?" Mr. Donahue asked.

"It's not exactly mail, Gavin." Mrs. Donahue smiled apologetically at the officers.

"Correct," Wycoff said. "They're evidence. And really, there's nothing particularly new here. Same basic content as the previous notes."

"Except these are addressed directly to my children," Mr. Donahue pointed out. "Would you characterize the language as threatening?"

"Yes. As threatening as previous communication—"

"And now we know he has a key. I'm sure you agree that changes things. You cannot simply dismiss this as some dumb prank."

Officer Nicolodi looked pained. "We've never dismissed this situation. But you are correct. Entry into the home does indicate intensifying behavior. That means we will respond accordingly. We've dusted throughout the house for prints. We'll increase patrols on the streets. Your family's safety is top priority."

Wycoff waved the sealed letters. "As soon as our tech processes these as evidence, I'll forward you copies of their content. Let's not read them aloud and add to the day's trauma."

Mr. and Mrs. Donahue both nodded—she enthusiastically and he grudgingly. There were forms to sign and follow-up appointments made at the station. After a while, they stood there awkwardly by the door, as if waiting for the last two guests to leave a party. Mrs. Donahue kept appraising the house's disarray and the black fingerprint dust left splotched everywhere. She absentmindedly traced the door's lock and then flinched.

Right when we thought the police were done for the night, when they finally headed out the same door they had burst through a couple of hours before, Officer Wycoff stopped and turned. "You know, come to think of it . . . There was something new in these recent letters. The suspect referenced the children sneaking around the neighborhood. *Lurking in the parks in the dead of night*: That was the phrase. It just struck me as odd. Given the previous letters, you're all probably hyperaware of safety. Right?" Wycoff's eyes traveled to each of us. "Nobody's been out past curfew recently, nothing like that? No loitering in the park?"

At first my heartbeat quickened at the possibility of being

discovered, the trouble I'd get into. Then I considered the rest—that the Sentry had been out there, in the dark, *witnessing* us. My heart stopped, as if I'd taken a line drive to the chest.

Eventually, Mrs. Donahue broke the thick silence. "Oh, we never have to worry about that. Gavin and I are lucky that way."

"Is that right?" Wycoff drummed his knuckles on the doorframe. Waiting. I looked at Ben. Ben looked everywhere but at me.

Finally he cleared his throat. "Yes. Of course that's right."

But of course that wasn't true.

CHAPTER EIGHTEEN

What was true was that everyone reacted to the new letters differently.

Ben stayed tense and guarded. His temper settled close to the surface and flared intermittently.

Lucy began to talk openly about moving in with her best friend's family back in Massachusetts.

Janie didn't say a word.

Mrs. Donahue had all the locks changed overnight and installed security cameras at both the front and back doors.

And Mr. Donahue decided there was one avenue we hadn't explored yet in searching for the Sentry.

"I don't want any of you to worry," he said a few days later from the front porch. "These people are professionals."

I sat on the curb diagonally across the street because that's as close as my mother would allow me to get. Toby sat beside me and occasionally wagged his tail as if reveling in his position close to the action. It seemed like the whole neighborhood had emerged from their houses. Mr. Donahue wore a faded tie-dyed T-shirt, the standard costume of a man who believed in hiring the services of paranormal experts. The van parked in their driveway was midnight blue, with lavender lettering across the side that read *GHOST ADJUSTERS*.

"It just doesn't have the same ring to it." My dad had the mower out, but he'd pushed it way past our property line. I glanced at it and then up at him. "Stop staring at me or I'll have to start the lawn mower."

"Mr. Leonardo, could you please explain your methods to my children? Just how do you intend to rid the home of evil spirits?" As Mr. Donahue spoke, he stared past Janie, Lucy, and Ben sitting listlessly on the steps of the front porch. Instead he looked intently at the Channel 5 Alive news station van, which idled in front of Miss Abbot's place. "What kind of evil spirits do you sense? Are we in danger at this very moment?"

Mr. Leonardo looked as if he could have been a few months older than Ben, but that's all. He'd frosted the tips of his black hair and sported a sparse goatee, which accentuated the sharp angle of his pronounced chin. He wore green cargo pants and had made good use of the pockets, with a professional-looking camera, a hammer, and what looked like a taser, each tucked into a separate compartment in the pants.

"Yeah, yeah. You know there is a tornado of passion and desperation swirling around here." That sounded about right. As Mr. Leonardo, the Ghost Adjuster, spoke, I stared at Ben, wondering what kind of emotional weather he was experiencing. Mr. Leonardo nodded sagely. "Real distress." He seemed to reach out his hands for Ben, Janie, and Lucy. Then his hands dropped down and sort of twitched by his sides.

"Daylight does us a great service, you know, keeping us safe. You all have absolutely nothing to worry about." Mr. Leonardo held up his hands again. "We are simply making ourselves known right now." He pointed what looked like a universal remote at the house and pressed a series of numbers. "Just trying to get a read on temperature of supernatural anger."

"That's probably just my mom," Ben offered, and I could swear he winked at me.

Mr. Donahue laughed nervously and clapped Mr. Leonardo on the back. "My wife remains unconvinced."

"None of you should be convinced yet. That's actually quite helpful," Mr. Leonardo said with the don't-worry-I'm-a-cool-guy tone of a substitute teacher encouraging us to call him by his first name. "The brain waves of skeptics tempt spirits to prove their own presence. That's when we witness and have the chance to document more paranormal activities." Mr. Leonardo nodded to himself. "This is an awesome dialogue to open up between our world and the spirit world. Kudos to you, Mr. Donahue."

It occurred to me that we all might have a calmer existence in Glennon Heights if someone like Mr. Leonardo could follow Mr. Donahue around all the time, praising him for his accidental achievements. Lucy leapt in, "We don't really want a dialogue, though." Her voice sounded as sour as usual. "We want it to stop."

"Ah, of course you do." Mr. Leonardo looked around and smiled indulgently. "But we don't rule the spirit world. We can only make modest requests." He dropped to his knees. Up and down the street, our neighbors craned their necks to see. We thought he might offer a prayer, but instead he opened a battered wooden box that looked as if it might contain treasure. Or ashes.

Mr. Leonardo pulled out a clump of feathery green leaves. He shook it toward Ben, Janie, and Lucy, but really toward the news van and the nosy neighbors. "Sage," he announced. Then he shook the bunch of leaves in the direction of the Donahues' front door. He crossed the yard and pointed the leaves at each window. He knelt down on the cobblestones on the front walk, chanting a song I could not decipher. Janie and Ben watched intently. I silently willed either of them to turn around, to grin or giggle or roll their eyes. But they faced forward. Apparently, Mr. Leonardo had jammed up all the psychic channels with his own efforts.

The guys standing against the news van appeared amused. One held up his camera sort of half-heartedly and I wondered where this latest episode would show up—nightly news, tabloid program, late-night bloopers? Mr. Leonardo spun around and declared, "This is the home of the Donahue family. All other essences must exit the premises!" Nothing moved on the breezeless street. Mr. Leonardo addressed Mr. Donahue: "Let's please enter the domestic structure."

I stood up to see the resolute back of Mr. Leonardo, the Ghost Adjuster, swallowed up by the darkened front hall of the house. Mr. Donahue frantically beckoned his children to follow. As they filed past him, he looked out toward the news van. The two guys shrugged and slouched forward too.

Janie's dad held the door open, nodding gravely to them as they passed. He looked out to the street like he might invite us all inside as well. But he didn't. He wanted to make sure we were all watching.

We were. Miss Abbot pretended to water her flowers with a limp hose. The Hurliheys had set out a blanket and were stretched out, enjoying coffee and pastries. My dad had already turned to start the trip home, pushing the toothless mower and nudging me to join him.

"Show's over, Olivia," he called. "Your mother and I would like you to steer clear of this mess." Dad whistled and Toby strained at the leash.

"Then I won't tell Mom on you either," I told him, following.

"Your mother is a smart woman. We'd do well to listen to her on this one."

I barely heard him, half listening for the sounds of breaking glass and slamming doors. When I turned back, the Donahue house looked ordinarily extraordinary—too big for the street but otherwise boring. The rest of the neighborhood had resumed its own business.

"How's school?" Dad asked me.

"Fine." The lawn mower squeaked a bit as he pushed it.

"Just fine? You're in high school now. Don't you feel empowered? Sophisticated?" I felt like my dad should have known that I had never, in the entirety of history, experienced those feelings. He cleared his throat and tried again. "You know, Liv, your mother and I have always encouraged you to stand up for what's right."

"I know that." The lawn mower squeaked in agreement.

"Right." We stood in front of our own house. "Sometimes it's not easy to figure out what the right thing is. Long-term. We think we know."

"We usually know," I said, unsure where he was headed but not expecting to like it.

Dad sighed. "You've been a good friend to Janie. But no one expects you to sacrifice your entire high school career in defense of a family who has been fairly"—he grimaced, searching for the right word—"disruptive."

"You mean their father?" My voice needled, like the lawn mower. "Their father is the disruptive one."

"Right. Of course. No one's blaming Janie—or any of the Donahue kids. But it might not hurt to just establish some distance. Do you understand what I'm saying?"

"I understand." The ball in my throat felt thorny. "But I don't think a kid should have to deal with the mistakes her father made." I rolled back my shoulders and directly met his gaze.

Dad nodded sadly, in such a way that made the thorny lump in my throat swell. "Right. I'm just asking you to take care, Olivia. It's not always okay to be selfish—you clearly know that. Sometimes though, it's not the end of the world either."

///////////

Whatever magic Mr. Leonardo made happen in the house, it didn't take long. Within an hour, Janie texted me a single word: *Dugout?*

"I'm going for a run." I went downstairs and told my dad.

"You want me to time you?"

"Not today. I just want to run until I stop thinking."

Dad sighed. "Yeah, yeah. Good luck with that."

I ran down Olcott and past the Donahues' because I knew

that otherwise I would have just wondered. Nothing looked any different, though. No ghostly vapors trailing out of the chimney. No black slime seeping out from under the heavy front door.

I refocused and kept running. I almost missed the little red car. Ned McGovern had parked it next to a hydrant and had some kind of song blaring—opera or something—and he pounded the steering wheel in time to the beat.

I picked up my pace and had almost cleared the corner when he swung open the driver's-side door. "You!" I pretended not to hear him. "You're Jillian's niece."

It made me mad that he didn't even remember my name. I stopped and turned to face him. "I'm Jillian's niece," I confirmed. His face looked red and sweaty and I reassured myself that at least I could outrun him. "My name is Olivia."

"Olivia, right. How are you doing, honey?" I looked past him, measuring how fast I could sprint to my dad. "Who was that man, Olivia?"

"What man?"

"You know what man." Ned nodded toward 16 Olcott. "He stood on the front lawn for a while. And then they let him in. The Donahues." He almost whispered the name.

"He's there to perform some ceremony. Like a séance or something. You know—to get rid of any bad spirits in the house."

I had expected the information to calm him down a little bit but Ned unleashed. "*What?* Unbelievable. They have no right." He kicked at his own tire and slammed his arm against the red car's roof. It seemed to me that Ned McGovern did not have a firm grasp on boundaries and the basic concept of possession. Of course the Donahues had a right. It was weird, but they had a right.

"He's not even supposed to be on our street," Janie said once I found her in the dugout at the baseball diamond and told her what had happened. We sat on the bench, both kicking at the holes in the chain-link fence. "It's not a restraining order, because the police said that would affect his livelihood, but they strongly advised him to stay away."

"I don't think you're fully appreciating how bizarre it was."

"He didn't chase you, right?"

"No, but he was blaring opera."

"Fair point."

"And speaking of bizarre . . . What did the Ghost Adjuster do anyway?" I asked Janie.

"He shook his plants all around. There was a lot of chanting. Candles. Pretty much what you'd expect if you researched ghost hunting on Wikipedia. Which is perhaps where he learned 'the ancient craft of his ancestors.'" Janie rolled her eyes. But then she cried out, "Oh! Sadly, the secret room no longer qualifies as secret."

"Why not?"

"That was the one kind of creepy moment—the last ritual or whatever. Mr. Leonardo said that we needed to open every door in the house. Like basement, attic, kitchen cupboards, the medicine cabinet—he said that the spirit world needed to flow through unobstructed."

"That's a lot of doors."

"I know, right?" Janie kicked at the chain link. "But that's why it freaked me out a little. Really it was the only time I felt actually scared. Because Mr. Leonardo wouldn't go forward with the ceremony. He kept repeating, *A door remains closed. A door remains closed.* Lucy ran around the whole house checking and then finally I opened up the bookshelf. Mostly because I just wanted the chanting to stop."

"What did he say? What did your parents say?"

Janie grimaced. "He just nodded. My parents said we'd talk about it later. But that was it. That was holding the whole ceremony up. Somehow Mr. Leonardo knew about the hidden room. Or else the spirits did."

"No way," I said firmly. "That guy earns his living with this routine. He must have noticed your eyes glancing at the bookshelf a bunch. Or he's spent so much time in these old houses that he knows just what to look for."

"The house feels kind of different. Tranquil, kind of."

"Power of suggestion. Besides if I were a trapped spirit, I'd hang out in your room."

Janie laughed. "Shut up!"

"I would. Or Lucy's room. Seriously, we're talking about ancient spirits. They deserve the best. If I were a poltergeist,

I would demand Pottery Barn furniture. I'd stretch out on one of Lucy's plush, white beanbags and pretend it was spirit spa day."

Janie's laughter trailed off into a sigh. "When is life going to get less bizarre?"

"I'm sorry your parents didn't tell you. This is just what Michigan is like." We stood up. "Let's go back to my relatively modest and happily unhaunted house."

But Janie said, "I need to check on Ben. Do you mind?"

"Of course not." But I had hesitated a little bit too long before answering. Janie didn't say anything but I saw her notice.

We walked for a full block before she said anything else. "Things are better between my parents."

"Uh-huh."

"They just go through these cycles. Like one minute they're falling all over each other and leaving for weekend getaways. And the next minute they're barely speaking."

"Yeah."

"They've been together for like twenty years. Clearly they've figured out something. I think my dad goes cold sometimes. He gets caught up in work. Then my mom acts up, like a little kid. She just wants attention."

"Right."

"That's all Ned McGovern offered her—a little attention. I don't think she actually went through with it. You know, cheating."

No question I considered Janie my best friend, but that didn't mean I felt comfortable speculating on her mom's love life. So we let the matter drop.

Once we reached the Donahue house, we heard incessant tapping. Inside, we found Ben kneeling in the not-so-secret room, with a screwdriver in one hand and small hammer in the other. Every book on the shelves had been removed and sat in stacks beside the opened doors.

"Hey, Ben," Janie said.

"Yup." He kept tapping, listening carefully as if he waited for someone to tap back.

"Morse code?" I asked.

"Trying to find hollow spots." Ben kept tapping.

Janie ventured as carefully as I had. "Well, Liv and I did that. We searched through the entire house. That's how we found the secret room." Ben looked up blankly. Janie spelled it out. "The secret room is the hollow spot."

"You're adorable." Ben smiled up at both of us. "The two of you, with your Nancy Drew ponytails—you think this is the only hidden room in this house of halfway horrors." Janie's look of shock mirrored my own. "I've found compartments all over—closets behind closets, passages down to the basement. Wait until I show you the wine cellar."

"How long have you known about all this?" Janie demanded.

"For a while," I answered for Ben. Because I understood

then why he let us keep the secret bookcase room to ourselves. He had plenty of other hidden places to explore. And besides, it kept us distracted. We wouldn't snoop around the rest of the house anymore. We'd found one passage and thought we found everything.

"Oh, come on. You cannot possibly be angry about this. You waited for the professional ghostbuster to demand access before you clued in the rest of the family about the trick bookcase."

Janie whirled her head around in disbelief. "But you didn't. You just said there are other secret doors but you didn't open them for Mr. Leonardo."

"I did not," Ben admitted. "Mr. Leonardo was a flake." He stood up and stashed the screwdriver and hammer in the pockets of his cargo shorts. "Let's go. I'll give you the tour the real estate agent should have given us. We'll start at the attic and work our way down."

We climbed the narrow back staircase. At first, Janie dismissed him. "I know about the passage from my bedroom to the attic. That's why I chose my bedroom."

"Well then, I regret to inform you that every single bedroom has access to the attic. But you just keep feeling special." Ben moved expertly through the attic, unfastening latches and turning rusted knobs. All in all, he showed us six different doorways. It was like one of those calendars at Christmastime—a surprise behind each wooden door.

Janie and I spent half the time grumbling at each other. We'd thought we'd searched the house so thoroughly.

"Why would anyone build a house like this?" I wondered aloud, honestly hesitant to hear the answer.

Ben shook his head. "I don't know. None of the scenarios are particularly reassuring, right? You wanted to check up on your sleeping family. Maybe everybody snuck upstairs to participate in secret attic rituals?"

Janie looked around the attic with new eyes. "Miss Abbot claims the Langsoms moved liquor during Prohibition, that they built the passages for smuggling. But I always thought bootlegging was more for mobsters than community pillars like the Langsoms. Maybe this was where they planned to hide when their covers were blown? Or when their enemies attacked the house?"

Ben snapped his fingers and pointed at his sister. "And Lucy thinks she's the smartest!" He crossed to a cupboard built into the northern wall. "Get a load of this." He unlatched the cupboard and twisted the handle clockwise. Violet satin fully lined the cupboard. Rows of leather bands dangled inside.

"It's empty?" Janie said.

"It's empty now, but look at the indentations." Janie and I peered inside but Ben didn't wait for us to identify them. "Guns. Knives. Someone kept his weapons cache here. We bought a house with a weapons cache."

Janie traced her finger along the gleaming satin. "We

bought a house with an empty cupboard. Someone took his weapons with him."

"Okay, yes," Ben conceded. "I just think it's worth noting that this person is heavily armed."

"With antiques."

"Antique weapons are still weapons. Provided they still function." Ben held up a finger. "There's more." He crouched down to show us a wooden box positioned beneath the round window at the back of the house. The box looked battered and scarred and was about the height of a small stool. You could rest your knee on it to peer out the window. Through the glass you could see the lush lawn of the Donahues' backyard, the bramble hedges separating their property from the Redmonds' behind it.

"Check it out." Ben swung open the chest's lid and started reeling out a strand of weathered board and heavy metal chains. They clanked on the floor.

"Shackles?" I felt queasy, imagining someone chained up in the attic, at the mercy of whoever owned those weapons.

"Nope." Ben spread out the wood and chains in order to display the full length of the ladder. It too was a built-in feature, bolted to the attic floor. "Escape plan!"

"Does it reach all the way down?" Janie asked.

"I guess it would get you near enough. I haven't tried it out yet," Ben admitted, like that counted as a failure on his part.

"Well, don't, okay? That's an old chain." Janie weighed one of the links in her hand. "Who were these people?"

"Mobsters makes sense. Maybe they just got so caught up in keeping the secret, the secret took over." He grinned ruefully. "I'd say we should ask Thatcher but, awkwardly enough, we're suing him." He folded the ladder neatly back into its chest. "That pretty much takes care of the attic. Now, ladies, if you will please accompany me downstairs to the wine cellar." Ben bowed with a flourish and led us down the worn stairs from the attic, then the carpeted stairs to the main floor. Finally he stopped outside a scarred, chestnut-colored door to the basement.

"We're not supposed to go down there," Janie muttered.

Ben grinned. "See? That's why you only discovered the bookshelf. You obey too much. Access your inner gangster." He leaned one shoulder against the door and explained to me, "This door sticks, so our mom is convinced we'll end up sealed in or something." Ben strained against the wood but it didn't budge. He stepped forward, threw his shoulder hard, and almost tumbled down the cement steps.

"Or broken at the bottom of the stairs," Janie added. She reached past me to flick on the light switch. The basement didn't necessarily look less spooky with the lights on—instead the creep factor was simply illuminated. Gray steps splattered with white drippings spiraled down and the wood paneling featured a collection of old brooms and mops hung from nails. As we descended, the air grew danker. It smelled like wet towels and vinegar. Some of the bricks in the walls had crumbled and some were missing altogether, leaving dark hollows punctuating the peeling paint.

White sheets shrouded several large pieces of furniture. I moved cautiously past them, in case they might spring to life.

"So it's mostly storage down here?" I said, my voice echoing through the underground chamber.

"Yes. Primarily dead bodies." Ben kept his tone matter-of-fact, chucking me lightly on the back as we walked. "Oh come on. It's just a basement. At least wait until I show you the best part before you go freaking out all over the place."

"When did you find all of this?" Janie asked him.

"On all those afternoons I spent by myself while you were out adjusting better to the move."

I pointed to a pile of metal apparatus in the corner. "What's that?"

"Farm implements? Possibly animal extermination tools. Interrogation devices."

"So something terrifying and possibly destructive?"

"Exactly."

"Could you imagine if you did get stuck down here?" My voice sounded as if I was shouting down a long tunnel.

"But that's the best part," Ben said. "We actually can't." With that, he crossed the room and yanked on the handle of an ancient-looking refrigerator. It was the white kind, with curved edges. It stood on metal legs so that there was a wide gap between the floor and the appliance.

Next to the fridge, someone had drilled a circular hook into the wall and a worn rope hung there, slightly fraying at the end. Expertly, Ben tied that rope to the handle of the open refrigerator door and then stepped back. "Ladies first," he insisted.

Janie and I leaned forward. Instead of an iced-over plastic interior, we saw a passageway. The refrigerator, while flush against the wall, had no back. "Holy smokes," I breathed and looked back at Ben. "How did you find this?"

"I wish I could claim it was more complicated than simply opening the door." He shrugged. "I'd been hoping for old beer." Then he nodded toward the fridge. "Go on."

For a short second, I remembered how barely a week before, Janie had half convinced me that Ben had written the Sentry's letters. How she had described him as disturbed and angry and hateful. If he was the Sentry, the passage could lead anywhere. Or, more likely, nowhere. Maybe Ben would untie the rope as quickly as he'd knotted it and slam the door. Janie and I would find ourselves locked in some musty cavity carved into the Donahues' basement.

I felt along the refrigerator's sides and pushed. "Oh no—it won't budge." Ben said it like that was a good thing. "Someone bolted it to the floor. It's a pretty solidly engineered situation, not unlike the passage built into the fireplace in the classic adventure film *The Goonies*." He stepped forward and held out his hand like he was a Victorian gentleman helping me into a carriage.

The notion that I might have risked being buried alive for the chance to place my hand in Ben Donahue's hand for a moment is not entirely unfounded. His hand was soft and warm and boosted me a bit as I stepped up. With his other hand, he grazed the top of my ponytail. "Watch your head." If I were a Victorian lady, I might have swooned.

Instead I coughed a little. While it wasn't turned on, the refrigerator still smelled like the inside of a Carvel ice cream parlor. "There's a little flashlight straight ahead of you. To your right." Ben sounded farther away than he could logically be. I reached forward and felt around in the darkness before me. The sides and floor of the burrow were covered in grit.

Janie murmured behind me, "You good, Liv?" And in response, I turned on the tiny flashlight. A thin column of light wavered in the dark.

"Keep going?" I asked her, half hoping that she would tell me to hold up.

Behind Janie, Ben said, "Be careful of the pipes above us. You don't want to smack your head. Don't worry! Just keep moving forward. I've done it a bunch of times."

"I'm sorry my brother is so weird," Janie muttered behind me. "I'm sorry my house is so haunted." Gradually, the cramped passage gave way to a wider tunnel with more room above us. I felt above my head before I slightly straightened up.

"Okay. Now point the flashlight down and you'll find a larger one right next to your foot," Ben directed. I kicked the metal Maglite almost immediately.

"Why not just start with the larger flashlight, Ben?" Janie asked. "You make everything so complicated."

"Don't question my system." As I closed my hands around the flashlight, it occurred to me that Ben had gone on this whole other adventure this summer, finding weapon trunks and rusty ladders and secret passages. I thought back to sneaking out and to playing catch in the dark, long past curfew. He was my best summer secret. But this was his.

I made sure my expression didn't look hurt before I flicked on the flashlight. It wouldn't have, though; as soon as the light hit the walls a look of wonder must have washed over my face. The room was a round dome, built from stones lined with wooden crates. A few pipes ran overhead and down into the entrance through which we had crawled.

"Welcome to the wine cellar!" Ben announced triumphantly.

"Where's the wine, though?" Janie asked, sort of hopefully.

"Gone." Ben held up a finger. "But . . . not for long." He reached out to run his index finger along one of the shelves and then showed it to us. "See? No dust. Someone's been in here pretty recently."

I nodded toward the passage exiting the round room. "Where does that lead?"

"It comes out right by the shed. Wooden trapdoor."

"Does it lock?" Janie's voice rose. "Can anyone just enter our house through the basement?"

"I don't think so. That fridge doesn't have a safety mechanism—it's too old. So you can't open it from the inside. You'd have to come down to the basement and set it up ahead of time, by tying the door open. We can go out if you want—" Janie and I both shook our heads. "It feels much farther than it actually is. We only crawled a few feet."

"Is this how you've been sneaking out?" Janie asked. I looked away.

"Not really," Ben non-answered. Apparently the secret-sharing portion of the afternoon had drawn to a close. Or maybe not. Because Ben said then, "Let's go back through to the main house and I'll show you the trapdoors in the bedrooms." We moved faster heading back, leaving behind the flashlights in their proper positions.

"How can there possibly be more?" Janie asked.

Ben grinned at us. "The passages go everywhere. There's a stairway behind the pantry that goes up to Mom's gift-wrapping room. That makes sense though, because that room is so small. It was probably the maid's quarters."

"Your mom has a room specifically devoted to gift-wrapping?"

Janie rolled her eyes. "She calls it the craft room."

"In her defense, there's no shortage of rooms," Ben pointed out. "And it's the tiniest one." He showed us the little door, which looked like a fireplace that had been filled in. You'd need to walk sideways through the stairwell and duck your head and tuck your shoulders to get inside.

I peered into the darkness. "We know the Langsoms are clearly not claustrophobic."

"I think most recently it was kids who made use of these little hiding places. There's another space under the window seat in the living room. But I keep finding Boy Scout stuff."

Janie and I looked at each other. "What do you mean?"

"I don't know. Like relics. Pamphlets and badges. A sketch-book. I found a couple of old flashlights and a bandanna."

"We found a book too—a scouting manual," Janie confessed.

"And a sleeping bag," I added. "A really old one."

"So same kid, right?" Ben asked excitedly. "Or kids. Maybe a little troop of creepy scouts. What did the book say?"

I exchanged another look with Janie and felt my cheeks burn. It sounded so obvious when he asked. Of course we should have read it.

"I can't believe you two. Go get it."

Janie jutted out her chin. "No way. Where's *your* stash of Boy Scout artifacts?"

"Hidden. And I will go get them as soon as you let me have a look at that manual."

I held up both hands. "You two make me relieved to be an only child. Janie, go get the book and the sleeping bag. Ben, go grab your stuff—all of it. We'll meet back here, in the gift-wrapping room." I gazed around. "It's neutral territory."

"It's really called the craft room," Janie mumbled as she headed out the door, with Ben smirking behind her.

When we reconvened in ten minutes, the siblings had relented. They unpacked their treasures sheepishly, sneaking peeks at each other's collections. The small room quickly transformed. It smelled musty. Dusty articles covered Mrs. Donahue's pristine table. It looked like a History of Scouting exhibit at a museum no one would ever choose to visit. Except maybe Ben, who gazed at each treasure almost lovingly. "You guys don't think this is so cool?"

I'd started to accept that I would never understand him. I could not think of a single other thing that Ben found particularly cool or compelling. Possibly the old transistor radio that the other girl carried around. His baseball glove. But he was totally enraptured by vintage Boy Scout memorabilia.

"It's interesting and all, but it doesn't tell us much." Janie examined all the pieces. She turned each item over in her hands and then passed it to me. I made a show of looking closely and then handed it to Ben, who caressed it, sniffed it. I half expected him to tear out a page of the manual and eat it.

"TM," he announced, pointing at two haphazardly drawn letters in the corner of the back cover. "That's our guy."

"No *L* for Langsom," I said and we all stared at the letters as if they might unlock some code.

"It's the same handwriting as in the sketchbook." Ben sounded more definite than I felt. "The drawings are sad." He flipped pages, explaining, "I don't mean unskilled—but they always just have this one figure—in a tent, in a house. Under a tree." Ben pointed out all the illustrations. "But there's only that one figure over and over—isn't that weird?"

"Well, he's documenting his own adventures," I offered, feeling defensive of TM and his singular figures.

"Yeah, but it's just him. No troop. No buddies. And look at the faces—half the faces don't even have a mouth. Most kids draw smiles. That's basic little kid technique." Ben ruffled Janie's hair. "You drew everyone: Mom, Dad, Lucy, me. I mean, even trees had smiley faces."

Janie studied the drawings. "Maybe TM didn't have many reasons to smile." Ben and I stared at her. Her voice was soft and a little spooky, as if she saw into a window invisible to us. "I mean, he obviously hid in the secret rooms. But I wonder why." She patted the sleeping bag and a cloud of dust rose up like a puff of smoke. "We need to know how many children the Langsoms had back then."

"Again. Not sure it's the best idea to contact the Langsoms right now," Ben reminded her.

"So we have to ask someone else who has long-established roots in the neighborhood."

Janie stared at me with an unspoken request. I floundered, "I mean, I can ask my parents, but it's doubtful—"

"Not your parents. No offense, Liv. But we need someone with a bit more expertise." She raised her eyebrows as if waiting for a name to dawn on me. "A local source of wisdom. A loyal customer of candy fund-raisers . . ."

"No, not Miss Abb—"

"Let's go pay a visit to Miss Abbot."

Janie talked Ben into staying home. "Better if it's just us girls," she said.

//////////

When we stood on the stoop of the little yellow house, I could feel the reassurance of his eyes on us. "We really have to do this?" I asked.

"Are you kidding?" Janie responded. "This is going to be so much fun." She punctuated her statement by reaching out and ringing the bell.

"Girls. Olivia and Jane Louise. My goodness. To what do I owe the honor?" Miss Abbot looked absolutely gleeful to see us, which didn't necessarily calm me. I was sure the witch had welcomed Hansel and Gretel enthusiastically too.

I held up a handful of packaged candy like I was

trick-or-treating in reverse. But before I could recite, *We won-dered if you might continue your support of the Glennon Heights Athletic Association,* Janie cut me off. "Oh, Livvie—let's not use the old selling candy door-to-door ruse." My mouth opened and closed, speechless. "Miss Abbot's too quick for that. I'm so sorry, Miss Abbot, but we could really use your help."

"Why, girls!" Miss Abbot exclaimed, looking as surprised as I at Janie's confession. She blocked Horatio, the cat, from escaping with one dainty, sandaled foot.

"You see, Olivia and I—we've been playing a fair bit of detective. You know—like in Nancy Drew?" I wished that Ben could see Janie work her magic. He would have been either proud or horrified. "We're really trying to get to the bottom of those letters."

Miss Abbot nodded her head thoughtfully and led us into her living room. "Yes. I see the efforts your whole family has been making—what with the publicity and the ghost chaser on a Saturday morning. It would be difficult not to notice, dear." Miss Abbot spoke with the sweetness of arsenic dust-ing her words.

"I really love this town." Janie covered her face with her hands. When she lowered them, her eyes were miraculously damp with tears. "But these letters are tearing my family apart. Olivia will tell you—my parents barely speak to each other these days. My sister just locks herself in her room with her homework. And my brother . . . Well, I worry about him most of all. He has a bit of a rebellious streak, you know."

"Most teenage boys do." Miss Abbot patted Janie's hand indulgently. "Maybe the move has turned out to be the wrong choice for your family." Miss Abbot smiled but her eyes narrowed, measuring Janie's reaction. "For more than one family, in fact."

Janie looked up with hard eyes. "Well, my family is here now. Not much anyone can do to rewrite history. It might help to know more of the local stories, though—specifically about the house itself. My father has behaved irrationally, but we all found those letters so disturbing . . ." She trailed off and then perked up, as if just remembering. "The last time Liv and I dropped by, you mentioned the magical Halloween celebrations the Langsoms once hosted. That must have been so wonderful for the children. How many sons and daughters did they have? Do you recall?"

Miss Abbot looked up, remembering. "Let's see—most recently there were three Langsom sons. I believe the youngest, Thatcher, attends school with you. According to the papers, he is quite an athlete."

"Yes." Janie practically bounced out of her chair with impatience. I nudged her knee with my own.

"That's right. I know the Langsom brothers. And Mrs. Langsom always made the best treats for us kids around holidays. Jane and I are more curious about maybe when Dr. Langsom was a boy—did he have siblings?"

"Yes. The Langsoms have always had large families. I was surprised when Hunter and Helena stopped at the three to speak completely out of turn. But sleuths like us cannot just go on minding our business can we? What fun is that?" Miss Abbot giggled. "I remember telling her, 'Helena, it seems to me you have more rooms to fill.' But you know how these modern women are. You just rarely see big families anymore. Such a shame. I love to see a full pew at church."

"Right. So Dr. Langsom had lots of brothers and sisters?" I prodded.

"Oh yes. There was he but also William and Thomas and Phillip and Matthew. The baby of the family—Margaret—was the only girl. Her brothers doted on her. That's probably why she was such a handful. But you know she was very close to the VonHolt girl. And when that terrible business happened, well, it was as if it just extinguished Margaret's inner light. It left us missing her troublemaking ways."

"Wow. You mean the murders."

Miss Abbot blinked. "Yes." She looked at the clock. I cringed—I was so clumsy with people. We were losing her.

Janie stepped in. "What about other kids? When we first saw the house, it was a dream come true. And I have to admit I imagined moving here would go differently. It's been harder than I expected to make friends." Janie's voice trembled ever so slightly. I recognized the theatrics but also knew there was a kernel of truth to what she said. "I don't get the sense it was ever like that for the Langsoms. Those kids had lots of friends, right? Kids over all the time? I bet the dad coached Little League or led a scout troop. And Mrs. Langsom was class mom every year. Was it like that back then too?"

"Even more so when Dr. Langsom was a boy. You know we used to value different forms of expertise. We wanted children to feel prepared for the world. I don't see those same skills—mostly you all navigate screens. Not forests." She stopped herself from speaking. "No offense."

"None taken." Janie smiled and I did too. "I've never even been camping," Janie confided.

"Well, back then the township youth camped right in your own backyard! I kid you not, girls. They pitched tents and built fires. Mostly boys."

"Anyone you remember in particular?" Janie pressed. I held my breath, waiting.

"Why would I remember anyone in particular?"

"Oh, it was a long shot. I just thought . . . We've already said what a wonderful family the Langsoms are—for generations. My dad says that the easiest explanation for the letters is that they wrote them, but I don't believe that. Thatcher has been so kind to us. I just thought maybe if you remember other people who spent a lot of time at the house . . ."

"Well, they were scouts of some kind. I remember one

year they did some yard work for me, to earn merit badges and such. Frankly they made a mess of my garden and I had to hire a man to come fix it, so I didn't allow them to come back. But I appreciated the spirit."

"Wow. I wonder if there are photos somewhere. Or a troop roster." Janie leaned forward. "I'd love to show that stuff to my brother, Ben; maybe it would inspire him to camp or learn other life skills like that. He's actually very good at yard work."

Across the street, Ben probably watched the yellow house, completely unaware that his sister was dangling him as a bribe in front of Miss Abbot and her geraniums.

Miss Abbot pondered the possibilities for a moment. "There must be photos. So many boys joined at some point or the other—it was a real source of town pride. Maybe the library?" She crossed her legs at the ankles and sat up straighter. "I would check there. Perhaps he will rekindle some interest in those endeavors. That would be lovely for the town—much more productive than video games and coffee. The amount of teenagers I see lining up at that coffee shop weekday afternoons . . . It will stunt your growth."

"Yes, ma'am," we answered automatically.

"I'm sorry I couldn't help more," Miss Abbot said as she stood up. "But I always appreciate a good mystery. Do stop by with updates. And you know, even if you're not raising funds, I am quite fond of chocolate."

"Of course," Janie answered, beaming. As we stepped outside, the door thudded shut behind us. Had Miss Abbot not said goodbye so sweetly, I might have thought she had slammed it.

"We should have brought M&M's," Janie muttered.

"You don't think that went well."

"She was holding back. She's protecting someone."

"Well, we know there was a troop and that they camped in the yard. We know about a link between Margaret Langsom and the VonHolt family."

"Do you think that's relevant?" Janie asked as we crossed the street.

"Maybe not relevant, but interesting. I think we got some good information." It wasn't that I didn't care about the letters. I just needed a break. "Why don't we go to Slave to the Grind?" I asked, almost afraid of how Janie would react. I tried joking, "We don't have to tell Miss Abbot."

"You want to question Thatcher? I don't think we should try that at his place of work."

"I don't think we should question Thatcher at all. Maybe we could just go grab some coffee, you know, remind people . . ." I searched for the right words.

"That I'm human? That I'm not some monster just because my parents aren't totally cool with imagining the blood of their children running down the walls? That this isn't our fault and, in any other town, people would probably be dropping off casseroles or organizing night watches?" Janie's voice kept rising.

"It's easy for people to blame you because you're new. If they have the chance to know you as a person, then they might feel differently."

"Well, that's messed up. Of course I'm a person. I'm not going to go sit in a coffee shop so that these idiots can discover that I am a person."

"It's just how small towns work," I said. But that sounded hollow even to me. I tried again. "It will only last until they move on to the next mystery."

"They won't move on to the next mystery until we solve this one." Janie reached out and grabbed my arm. "Also, you know what, Livvie? It's scary. It's scary to try to fall asleep there and remember those creepy notes. And no one has been able to stop them. Not my parents. Not the police. So actually I don't really want people to move on."

Her father would never let that happen anyway. I almost said it out loud. Glennon Heights might very well move on, but not until Mr. Donahue stopped calling news crews.

But then I thought about Margaret Langsom. She must have felt like the world went dark the morning they found her friend's body. All those bodies. Janie and I stood outside 16 Olcott and it looked more menacing now, with its secret passages and weapons cupboard and escape hatch.

"Okay," I said. "Then we should go to the library."

CHAPTER NINETEEN

"Saturday night at the library," Ben announced. "And I thought spending the morning with the ghostbuster might negatively affect my social credentials."

The Glennon Heights library looked larger than a town our size could possibly need. It functioned as a community hub, though. Only about a quarter of the square brick building held the books you'd expect to find. Otherwise, there was a computer center, where mostly old people browsed the internet and often loudly asked anyone nearby for help operating the mouse. You could take out DVDs and CDs. They even had a section of cookie cutters; you could sign out a particular shape you needed.

The library housed a couple of meeting rooms and a children's play area. In the very front, before the checkout desk, they'd set up a little café and the women's auxiliary sold drinks and snacks.

"You come in a building like this and you think, *This is adorable. We're so fortunate that our parents moved us to such a sweet little town.* And then some nut job writes a note claiming to have buried bones in your basement." Ben approached the reception desk and raised his voice slightly. "Excuse me, is there a special section for township history?"

"Glennon Heights history?"

"Yes, ma'am."

"That's so lovely that you want to learn more about your new hometown. Welcome to Glennon Heights."

"Wow." Ben looked surprised. Already this wasn't going the way we had expected. "Thanks. I know it's a small town, but I didn't realize we were such obvious transplants."

"Well, I've seen you on the local news."

"Right. That was crazy. I don't understand a lot of what's going on because I'm just a kid." Ben spoke first, trying and failing to sound casual. "I'm actually a special kid because I am an Eagle Scout. I am an Eagle Scout who is doing research on other scouts. Other scouts who live or have lived in Glennon

Heights. My scout leader in my old town asked me to do this research. So here I am."

Janie and I just looked wide-eyed at the librarian. I couldn't think of any way to make his terrible lying any better so I just echoed Ben. "Right. Here we are."

Janie added, "Helping."

"Okay, you three," the librarian said cheerfully, "you've come to the right place!" She didn't sound as if she found the request all that odd, but I guessed if she helped the elderly surf the web all day not much surprised her anymore.

"We actually have a local lore room—that's an ideal place to start." She came out from behind the desk. "Follow me." The librarian spoke softly as she walked briskly through the computer center. She passed under an arched doorway, into a cozy room with framed photos on the walls and a town flag on display in the corner. "You might be surprised that we have such a rich collection in a town this tiny, but we have several history buffs in Glennon Heights who have curated memorabilia from all corners of our community.

"Along those shelves are dozens of scrapbooks, with clippings from the *Glennon Heights Gazette*. Top shelf and to the right are yearbooks dating from last year all the way back to the 1950s. We also have VHS tapes of all school concerts and drama productions." The librarian lowered her voice even more, so that she barely whispered, "And in the back corner, we do have several scrapbooks devoted to the VonHolt murders. People often come to research those. It's perfectly natural to feel curious about such a dark chapter in our town's history."

"Oh no!" Janie's voice sounded so loud in the hushed room. "He really needs to know about other Boy Scouts."

The librarian smiled widely, clearly relieved. "Great. Your best bet is probably those volumes labeled *Youth Programs*. If you need to make copies, we charge ten cents apiece. But you can also take photos with your phone."

"Right," Ben said. "Thank you so much. I felt nervous asking for help but I'm glad I did."

"Of course! We love when kids spend their Saturday nights at the library!" She was so kind and helpful—she probably didn't fully understand that she had just twisted a dagger in Ben's hipster heart. The librarian backed her way out of the room and pointed back to reception. "I'm right out here if you need further assistance."

"Jackpot, right?" Ben burst out as soon as she'd left his field of vision. "We must have everything we need. What time does the library close?"

"I don't know."

"You don't know? You've lived here your whole life."

"I don't usually come on Saturday nights," I deadpanned.

"Oh. That surprises me," he answered, waiting a beat for the blow to land.

"Okay, you win that round."

"You're both losers," Janie muttered. "Let's each take a volume." We spread out—Janie and I on either side of a large reading table and Ben sitting in a wine-red armchair. "We're looking for anything involving scouts or camping or the house."

"Or the Langsoms?" Ben asked.

"Did you find something?" Janie got excited.

"No. I just wanted to contribute to the list."

"We need to work fast."

We flipped pages silently and carefully, painstakingly studying each blurry photograph and caption. Every once in a while someone sighed. At one point Ben took out his phone and snapped a picture.

"What did you find?" I asked.

"Nothing," he answered without offering explanation.

It was another fifteen minutes before I interrupted the silence.

"Guys, I've got tents here, I think." I tapped the pages excitedly.

"You think?" Janie said.

"Well, it's smudged but it looks like your yard," I said. Janie and Ben crowded around me. I read the type below the image. "'Troop three-one-one welcomes summer with their annual jubilee.'"

"Well, there you go! Good job, Liv!" Ben said.

But Janie pointed out, "It doesn't really tell us much, though. Other than what Miss Abbot already said."

"Yeah, but now we know we can trust Miss Abbot. At least a little." That earned a grudging nod from Janie. As I studied the photograph of the tents beneath the trees, a strange rush rippled through me. It may have been blurry, but it illustrated exactly what Miss Abbot had described. I felt like I held her memory in my hands. "Let's keep looking."

For a while longer, the room was quiet except for the turning of pages. And then Janie gasped. "This is it!" Even the figures in the framed photos on the walls seemed to lean in to look. I practically dove across the table and Ben rushed over too. "It's a group shot! Same troop number! And there's a Langsom!"

The boys had sat for the picture in a gymnasium. You could see a basketball hoop in the corner. They wore uniform shirts with the little kerchiefs tied around their necks. Shorts and sneakers, with striped socks pulled up to their knees. They looked about eleven years old. Some of them wore their hair shaggy. A few sported crew cuts. In the right upper corner of the page, a careful hand had written: *July 1983*. Below that was a yellowed slip of paper with a list of names: Robbie Franzmann, Elijah Kaufman, Vernon Loria, Kirk Gibbons, Nick Geltner. And then a second row: Steven Rizk, Billy Merrell, Hunter Langsom, Teddy McGovern.

"Dr. Langsom!" Janie breathed. "And right next to him— that must be our TM. Teddy McGovern."

"Maybe he's related to Ned McGovern," I said.

"The real estate guy?" Ben asked, looking troubled.

"Otherwise known as the guy who was obsessed with our mom."

"They're sitting close to each other—seems like they're friends." Hunter Langsom's dark hair feathered around his face. I could barely glimpse Dr. Langsom's features there, but the kid looked like a younger version of Thatcher. I studied the boy next to him with the shaved head and the slightly crooked kerchief. "Why so many hiding spots, Teddy?" I whispered.

"We should keep looking," Janie said. We returned to our respective stations with renewed energy. "Set aside anything that links the McGoverns to the Langsoms."

"Could they be family friends?" I asked. "Or cousins? Maybe look for engagement announcements." Ben nodded and reached for the volume labeled *Births and Weddings*.

Janie looked up. "Can't you just ask Thatcher? You guys are friends. He has to know Dad's gone crazy with this lawsuit. It doesn't involve you."

"I don't think he sees it that way."

"No one sees it that way. And it's not fair for the whole town to blame us for Dad's faults."

"Yeah. You think Thatcher Langsom doesn't realize that? After the year he's had? It just doesn't matter, Janie. He's not going to talk to me. I'm sorry. But we'll stick together. We'll be okay."

Janie sighed and picked up the last volume of *Youth Programs*. Ben was still studying announcements. I browsed through the rest of the stacks and stopped in front of the row of crimson yearbooks. Pulled out a few: 1987, 1988, 1989. I found the memorial page for Caroline VonHolt in 1988. I knew right away that was the year because the red leather was a little faded, probably from all the hands reaching for it to turn to that particular page. It was an eight-by-ten black-and-white portrait above the quote "There is a light that never goes out."

In the picture, Caroline smiled confidently and gazed somewhere beyond the camera. Her eyes crinkled at the corners as if she was about to break into laughter. She wore her hair long and straight and parted way over to the side, a little bit veiling the side of her face. I imagined that she usually hid a bit behind her hair, and eyed the world slyly from behind the curtain. But that day, maybe the photographer asked to see her whole face. And that was why she was almost laughing.

Caroline VonHolt didn't look like a girl who worried a lot. Who would feel nervous unlocking her front door one afternoon and calling out to see if anyone else was home. She looked like a girl like Janie. Someone who might sneak out to the baseball field and sit talking with us in the dugout.

"Olivia, what have you got there?"

Just as Janie asked, the overhead lights blinked on and off and my heart slammed into my chest at full speed. Mr. Leonardo would call that the spirit world stretching to communicate. But the librarian circulating through the building stopped in to tell us that it actually meant the library would close soon.

"I hope you found what you needed." She sounded like she meant it. But then her eyes skimmed over the yearbook open in front of me and settled on the familiar image of Caroline VonHolt's senior portrait. The librarian's smile faltered, as if she had expected more from me.

Ben said, "I think so—thank you. We might need to come back but we have a good start, right?" Janie and I nodded obediently. I slammed shut the yearbook and had clasped my hands on top of the whole pile.

"That's terrific. When you come back, bring an updated driver's license or your school ID so we can sign you up for library cards. And please put everything back where you found it." I fought the urge to announce that I had a library card, I hadn't just moved to Glennon Heights—and because of that, Caroline VonHolt was as much mine as anyone else's.

Instead I helped reshelve the scrapbooks, thinking about those earnest Boy Scouts who were all grown up now. And

Caroline, who wasn't. I asked Ben, "Nothing interesting in the wedding announcements?"

"Nah," he answered. "That stuff's probably easier to find online anyway. It's not classified information."

The overhead lights blinked again, so we scuttled off, along with some elderly folks and a bunch of middle-aged people who might have made up a support group. No one made eye contact with us on the way out.

We were just outside the door when Ben stopped short. My phone was out to text my mom that I was coming home.

"What?" Janie asked. "Did you leave something back there?"

"On your phone, Olivia. Look up nicknames for Theodore. For the name Theodore."

"Okay." I typed it in. "Nickname for Theodore: Theo, Ted, Teddy."

Ben shook his head. "Try nicknames for Edward."

"All right, sure." My fingers felt slow and clumsy. My phone's battery was at 9 percent. "Nicknames for Edward: Ed, Eddie, Ned, Neddie, Ted, Teddy." I looked up at Ben. "Oh God."

Ben nodded.

"What?" Janie looked from Ben to me and back to Ben again.

"It's not that Ned McGovern is related to Teddy. He *is* Teddy. He's that sad little kid all grown up."

CHAPTER TWENTY

"It doesn't necessarily mean he is the Sentry." Janie spoke in a breathless rush. "He has camping experience, that's all we know for sure. Our real estate agent, the guy who sold us our strange, sort of haunted house, used to be a Boy Scout. Right now, that's really all we know."

"We have to call Mom and Dad," Ben ordered.

"And say what?" Janie asked.

"We have to warn them."

"That's true. He was parked on our street just this morning."

Ben stared at me. "Who? McGovern?"

Janie scrolled through her phone.

"Are you calling Mom and Dad or not?"

Janie held up one finger. "Lucy. Hey, Lucy? Ben and I were just hanging out at the library. Liv too. What? I'm not joking. It just closed. Hey, are Mom and Dad home? No reason." Janie started pulling faces at me. I could hear Lucy's voice building to a high-pitched shriek. "Hey, Luce—can you put Dad on? Or maybe Mom? No reason." Janie shook her head at me. "Listen, Lucy. We found out some stuff today and we think we might know who's sending the letters. Just . . . I don't know . . . stay in the house, okay? You and Mom and Dad. Don't answer the door for anyone. We'll be right there. No, I'm not trying to be melodramatic. We'll be back in less than five minutes. I'm just asking that you not answer the door for the next five minutes. You can handle that, right?" The voice buzzing from Janie's phone blared more loudly. Ben made a motion with his hand as if to say, *Keep it going.* He wanted Janie to keep Lucy on the line as we got our bikes and started pedaling. "Okay now, there's no need to get crude. I love you, Lucy. And Mom and Dad too. Ben also loves you all . . . Liv doesn't but I bet she feels a certain fondness. Anyway, we'll be back soon."

We pedaled home as fast as we could. As he turned onto our street, Ben asked, "Do you want to go back to your place?"

"Are you kidding?"

"Your funeral." We cycled past and I saw the kitchen lights still on. I finally texted my mom, *Coming home from the library*, just as we parked our bikes into the drive a few doors down. We stood in the yard a second as Ben mostly spoke to Janie. "Let's be clear: We tell Mom and Dad everything we know."

"We don't actually know a whole lot."

Ben continued, "We're going to stay composed so that we speak clearly. Remember that we've been dealing with this whole thing for weeks. They're just catching up. Dad will probably freak out. We need to let him rant a bit. Deep down, he's a reasonable man. And if something really went on between her and McGovern, Mom might very well blame herself. But really that part is between them. We don't go near that. Understand?"

Janie and I nodded solemnly even as we understood that Ben's pep talk was mostly for his own benefit.

Just as we got to the steps, the porch light blinked on. Mr. Donahue stepped outside. "Do you three want to tell me what's going on? You've frightened Lucy half to death." Behind the screen door, Lucy hovered and glared.

Ben looked up and down the street. He leaned over to me. "Do you see his car?"

"No, but it's so dark." The street had seemed positively fluorescent back when we snuck off to the park, but now Olcott Place looked full of shadows.

Ben spoke up to his dad. "Let's all go inside, okay?" He even checked the trees and bushes as we made our way up the walk.

"You're acting paranoid. What is this?" Mr. Donahue called up the stairs. "Lindsay, the kids are back."

"How long have you all been home?" Ben asked him.

"Couple hours. Are you going to fill me in now? Because it's family meeting time and I want some answers." He called up again, "Lindsay, we need you down here."

Ben turned to Janie and murmured directions quietly. "Bring Liv with you and go upstairs to pack a bag. Ask Mom to do the same." Mr. Donahue looked bewildered to see Ben taking charge. As we climbed the steps, I heard Ben tell him, "A family meeting's a great idea, Dad, but I think we should hold it at a hotel. Let's just go stay somewhere else. Just one night to talk things through."

"What are you talking about—stay in a hotel? Do you have any idea what the mortgage on this place is? A hotel!" he scoffed.

Janie and I ducked into her room, right as Mrs. Donahue came out in the hallway. "Girls, what are you up to now?" She stood in the doorway with her hands on her hips, watching Janie dump a bunch of clothes into her duffel bag. "Jane Louise—what's gotten into you? It's the wrong night for a sleepover, I'll tell you that. You've stirred up your sister and she's got your dad all riled."

Janie faced her mom squarely and spoke clearly. This was the Janie I knew, the one her family didn't. "Mom, we have to get out of the house. Now."

"What's happened? Another letter?"

"Did we get one?"

"Yes? I don't know. Is that what you're saying?"

I wondered if my family sounded so much like crossed cell phone calls. I waded in, trying to translate. "Mrs. Donahue, we don't know about a new letter from the Sentry. But we might have an idea about who the Sentry is."

"Who?"

I stared past her at Janie, who stood frozen, with wide eyes and vigorously shaking head.

Mrs. Donahue whipped her head to Janie and then back to me. "For goodness' sake, girls, who?"

"We think it's Ned McGovern," I said. "I'm sorry if that's, ummm . . . awkward—"

"What do you mean? Why?"

"Well, we think he spent a lot of time in this house as a little boy. We think he had a hard childhood. That for some reason, he feels possessive of the house."

"Why would that be awkward? We've sought a restraining order against the man; he's acted absolutely bizarrely. It makes perfect sense . . ." Mrs. Donahue trailed off. "It's just that as the professional who handled the sale, it doesn't make much sense to drive us out. He loses his commission."

"Only if he's held responsible," I pointed out.

And Janie added, "If not, it gives him the chance to earn that commission all over again."

Mrs. Donahue stood up straight and looked at both Janie and me like she was suddenly seeing us clearly for the first time. "That's an astute point." She smiled wryly. "How long were you girls at the library anyway?"

Janie said quietly, "Do you worry Daddy will blame you?"

"Because I fell in love?" That was my cue to try to crawl into the carpet. But then Mrs. Donahue said, "It's true that this was my dream house, sweetheart. But moving here had other benefits. Lucy was driving herself mad with stress— just way too much pressure. And Ben"—Mrs. Donahue pursed her lips—"Ben needed a fresh start as well. And then there was your father's business." She sighed. "Across the board, the move made sense. And I loved the house."

Janie asked, "But didn't you and Mr. McGovern . . . ?"

"Me and Mr. McGovern what?" Mrs. Donahue appeared genuinely puzzled. And then I watched as she realized what Janie was really asking.

She breathed deeply. "Jane Louise." Mrs. Donahue narrowed her eyes at me too, but she didn't say my name in the same firm voice. "I am not in the habit of defending my marriage to my children." Janie and I stared at each other. She hadn't actually answered a question. "Girls, is that clear? I expect a certain amount of gossip in a small town but not in my own home." She glared at me as if I was fully to blame for this latest erosion of Donahue family bliss.

"Of course," I said quickly and desperately.

"Yes. Mom, I'm really sorry." Janie's eyes brimmed. "It just seemed like you were texting him a lot and Dad seemed mad and then Mr. McGovern kept showing up."

"Honey, it's okay." Mrs. Donahue swooped us both in for a hug. "You are growing up and you understand more than I give you credit for. But some things, some relationships, they are just really complex. Most marriages are like that."

She dropped her hands from around our shoulders and took both Janie's hands in her own. I pretty much ceased to exist in the room—and that was honestly preferable. "Nothing happened between Ned McGovern and me." Janie nodded. "And please tell your brother and sister that." She headed out to the hallway and we heard her calling for Mr. Donahue as she bounded down the stairs.

"Did you believe her?" Janie asked.

"Of course," I answered, as if it mattered what I believed about anyone really.

When we joined the rest of the family on the first floor, Ben was trying valiantly to explain how we'd come to suspect Ned McGovern, even as Mr. Donahue seemed more and more convinced he was out of his mind. "You're telling me that there's a maze of secret chambers behind almost every room of the house? You realize that when you purchase a house, especially a landmark property, it's customary to receive schematics of the property."

"I didn't know that," Ben admitted. "I've never purchased

a house. However, who would provide a home buyer with that?"

"Well, generally the realtor."

"Right." We all sat silently and waited for that to sink in.

"No." Mr. Donahue began pacing around the living room, with his hands clasped behind his head. "NO. Lindsay, are you hearing this?"

"Well, it does explain how he managed to get inside to leave those letters on our beds. McGovern might very well still have a key."

"No doubt, Mom. That's a good point but—" Ben looked at us for help.

"Some of the passages lead outside," Janie rushed to explain. "So, you know, you can access them from outside."

"So this guy could be coming and going freely, without any of us knowing?" Lucy demanded. "Could he be watching us?"

Janie quickly crossed over to the dining room and pulled at the leather copy of *Great Expectations*. The bookcase opened and revealed the tiny room behind the wall.

It was empty.

"We found an old sleeping bag in there, with books and even chocolate," she told her parents. "He used to sleep and watch from there, maybe while the family who lived here carried on their normal lives. Why would a kid do that? And why wouldn't anyone notice? Why wouldn't anyone miss him?"

Suddenly, there was a crash.

I checked to see who had left the room. I figured Lucy, but there she stood, with all the fireplace implements within reach. The Donahue family had all stepped closer to the dining room, to scrutinize the secret chamber behind the bookcase.

The crash sounded wooden and heavy and finished with a metal clanking. Ben met my eyes from across the room and instinctively we both stepped away from the walls. He said it before I could pronounce the words:

"He's here. He's in the house now."

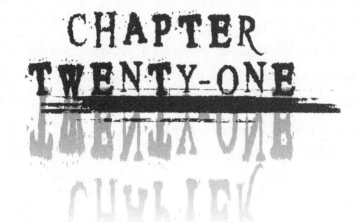

CHAPTER TWENTY-ONE

"How could he possibly have gotten inside? We've been here; we've been home." Mrs. Donahue seemed genuinely confused.

Ben tried to break it to her. "I think that's what he does, Mom." She recoiled and stood in the center of the living room, hugging her own body, as if through making herself as small as possible, she could avoid any contact with the Sentry.

"Let's just stay calm," I said. "Call the police. We'll wait for the cops at my house."

But when I checked my phone, it was useless. At the same time, Mr. Donahue shouted, "I don't have service!"

Ben waved his arms wildly. He raised his index finger against his lips and then whispered, "McGovern might be jamming service." He stepped lightly over to the landline and lifted the receiver to his ear. We all waited. Ben shook his head slowly.

Another crash echoed, definitely from upstairs. Mrs. Donahue jumped and then called out, "Ned. Stop this. This is crazy!" Mr. Donahue pointed to the front door and we moved en masse in that direction.

First we noticed the metal glider pushed in front of the door and realized he had been out there, moving stealthily, even as we stood around chatting. Then we smelled the smoke. Lucy craned her neck to see. "The porch is burning. He set the house on fire!" We backed away then, some of us clutching at one another, some of us fighting the urge to scream.

For the first few minutes, it had seemed like just another mystery. *Where was Ned McGovern? What would the Sentry shake up next?* But at that moment I saw a look pass between Mr. and Mrs. Donahue—terror.

Mr. Donahue led us back to the kitchen. We moved as one entity, facing different directions in case Ned broke through a wall and we needed to fight him off. We felt the heat against the back door even before we saw the flames. "Dad? Windows?" Ben asked in a quick, low voice.

Mr. Donahue clutched his head, trying to think. "Double

locks. We added all this extra security." He sounded apologetic.

Ben spoke directly to me. "We'll use one of the passages. All that racket, he won't expect us to go upstairs."

I shook my head. "It will take too much time for everyone to climb down. And that might have been the clanking sound. We could get up there and find that he somehow destroyed the whole ladder."

"Smart," Ben said. One word. And my chest felt warm not because the house was on fire but because I impressed a boy.

Together we shepherded everyone the few steps to the cellar. "Livvie and I have a plan," he whispered. "You have to trust us." Ben turned the knob and the door stuck. He furrowed his brow as he rammed his shoulder against the wood. It opened with a muffled thud. Ben met my eyes and glanced up. I knew what he was thinking—the sound was enough to have clued in the Sentry.

We hustled everyone down the steps. Ben led up front and I took the back, twisting my neck, half expecting McGovern to burst through the basement door. I heard the exact moment Ben opened up the refrigerator.

"You want me to do *what*?" his father asked.

"You have to trust us," I hissed. "Ben knows what he's doing. He'll go first and lead you through. I'll be behind you."

"Yeah?" Ben asked, over the heads of his family.

"Yeah." I motioned to the fridge. "Go." He hoisted himself up, crouched low, and crawled through.

I got to work tying back the refrigerator door. For a second, I debated it. If I tied the rope to the anchor hook, it would tip off the Sentry for sure. But if I let the door close behind me, we had no way back. We didn't know yet if the path was clear.

I knotted the rope. One by one, we all scrambled up and through. Mr. Donahue tried switching places with me, but I nudged him forward. I whispered, "I know what to do."

Crawling through the gritty tunnel, I felt hot and sweaty and tried not to let my imagination get away from me. I wondered if the house above us was already burning. In front of us, Ben called out a constant stream of reassurances. "Low here. Watch your head. Almost there. Keep moving." He kept his tone just as upbeat, just as steady when he said, "Hey, Ned. What's going on?"

Mr. Donahue and I hadn't reached the end of the crawl space. He stopped short in front of me. "Go back," he whispered.

"No way."

"Olivia, right now," Mr. Donahue ordered. Then he pushed forward to be with his family. If I crawled back, I'd be crouched down in the hot tunnel, listening to something terrible happen. I knew that. Stuck in that long coffin of darkness and dust, witnessing, with a fire behind me.

So I pushed forward. When I reached the wine cellar, I found that Ned had everyone sitting with their backs pressed to the stone wall. He stood over the group waving two long pieces of metal. One was a set of lawn shears. One was an ax. As Ned spoke, he gestured with the tools. They made the shadow he cast on the wall look like a monster with claws.

I stayed in the tunnel, hopefully unseen. Ned was already ranting.

"You have no idea what you have done. What you have trampled on. This was a sacred place. This was a place of joy. You came in here with your complaints and your petty disagreements and had the nerve to be ungrateful. I kept waiting. I thought maybe you just needed a reminder. How did you manage to live in this kind of splendor and still be so unworthy? Langsom property for generations. And I was no Langsom. I was never allowed to forget that. I was a visitor—a charity case. And then the mighty fell, didn't they? Suddenly there was a window of opportunity." I watched a vein in Ned's temple pulse with the rhythm of his anger. "I just needed a few more months to get together the down payment."

"So you did write the letters to drive us out?" Lucy piped up. Obviously, there was no one she was reluctant to antagonize.

"I wrote the letters to warn you."

"Don't be ridiculous!" Lucy cried out. With every word, she seemed just as undone as Ned. "Warn us about what?

Your hidden collection of scout badges? The commission you earned from the sale brought you closer to the down payment. That must have been so frustrating—like some sad real estate O. Henry story. But if you handled the resale, you'd double your commission. And who would want to buy the notorious Sentry house? You would do us a favor, taking the property off our hands. Except Dad got a little overzealous and added you to the lawsuit. That complicated the situation. Otherwise, everyone would be calling it the McGovern house, wouldn't they?"

Ned's grip tightened around the ax in his hand. I saw his knuckles whiten. "It will always be the Langsom house. And I was always looking in. Even from the inside, I was still looking in." He scoffed. "You're no different. Do you really think they call it the Donahue house? When they talk about it tomorrow, they'll say, 'Did you hear about the Langsom house? It burst into flames.'"

With that, he stretched his arm and went after the pipe above their heads with the ax. I didn't know what it was at first, but saw the look of horror wash over Mr. Donahue's face. And then, one by one, the rest of us seemed to realize the danger. Janie dove first. She clawed at his arm and bit his shoulder and even stomped on his knee. After Janie broke the spell, the whole mob of us tackled McGovern while he flailed with his sharp blades against the gas line.

A fire raged above us. And Ned McGovern raged too. He

was so strong. He kept tossing Mr. Donahue off him like he was a dog shaking off drops of water. And then he would swing his arm and the shears would arc through the air, the blades almost whistling. Every time the head of the ax clanged against the pipe, we expected the air to explode. "Get out!" Mr. Donahue screamed to the rest of us.

Ben bent toward his dad and pointed at the passage to the yard. Mr. Donahue shook his head.

Ben pointed and yelled, "The gas valve. By the shed." He dove for Ned's waist and held him back. "Now!" Ben screamed. But Ned wasn't chasing us anymore. His blank stare had focused completely on the pipe as he swung and swung at it.

Mr. Donahue crouched with his arms over his head and ran forward as if the ceiling was already on fire. Mrs. Donahue guided Janie and Lucy out and yelled at me to follow. I couldn't hear outside myself. I might have only screamed Ben's name inside my head.

But probably not. Because for a split second right before Mrs. Donahue yanked me forward, Ben looked at me and said calmly, "I know what to do." And then he let go of Ned McGovern and stepped backward into the opposite tunnel, the one leading back to 16 Olcott.

Mrs. Donahue was boosting me up when we heard the explosion. It sounded like the noise when they launch fireworks, right before the sky lights up. That deep thunderous sound of igniting. We felt a fierce gust at our back. It pitched Mrs. Donahue forward, smacking her head against the hinges of the trapdoor. Sprawled on the ground, I felt myself trembling everywhere but then realized it was the earth shaking beneath me. Janie and Lucy knelt down and together we hauled Mrs. Donahue out of the hole.

"Gavin?" Mrs. Donahue asked desperately.

"I got it." Mr. Donahue had reached the valve and almost tore off the handle in his panic. We collapsed in a pile—all of us—entwined and weeping beside the old wood shed. We shielded our eyes against the thick smoke and stared at 16 Olcott, expecting it to fall. And then the night filled with sirens and the red lights of fire trucks.

In the middle of all that chaos, Mrs. Donahue asked, "Where is Ben?"

In answer, Mr. Donahue scrambled to his feet, trying to run back inside. We all screamed then. He didn't get far before needing to turn around. Thick plumes of smoke streamed from the passage, blocking any entry.

When the firemen found us, they moved us farther back, to the edges of the property. They examined Janie's arm and Mrs. Donahue's forehead. They kept shining a penlight into Lucy's eyes and she kept swatting it away, staring at the scorched ground like she expected someone to crawl out. One of the firefighters spoke into his radio. "Various degrees of shock. One case requiring stitches." My parents were with us too. With me. Asking me questions. But I could only look at the house.

Then I saw him walking toward us, a firefighter on either side.

Ben was covered in dark soot, except for light streaks around his face where he'd wiped away sweat or tears. His hair stuck out wildly and his clothes were frayed. "Hey, guys," he called out as if it were any ordinary Saturday night and he'd shown up late for dinner again. "There goes the neighborhood."

I know for certain that I didn't shriek his name out loud that time. I left that to Lucy and Janie, who knocked him to the ground with their hugs, quickly followed by their parents. The firemen looked over and grinned. One of the firemen stepped forward. "Mr. and Mrs. Donahue, I don't know who taught this young man to shut off the internal gas valve in an emergency, but that was time well spent. Your boy's actions saved your home, possibly lives up and down the street." Their dad reached down to squeeze Ben's shoulder and their mom wiped away tears.

The fireman nodded and gave a moment before he continued. "Now we've resolved the small fires at the front and back of the main domicile, with minimal damage to the building. Obviously there are structural issues that will take weeks and months to address. I would recommend that you spend tonight in a neighbor's home or a hotel." He cleared his throat. "Because of the history of the property and your most recent conversations with law enforcement, we do have some questions. We would like to conduct interviews tonight."

"Absolutely." Mr. Donahue nodded. "As soon as my family checks out medically, you understand."

"Of course." The firemen looked at each other. "Your son did indicate this was a deliberate act. Of course this is a small town in terms of news. We're familiar with the letters you've been receiving."

"A sick man, Ned McGovern." Mr. Donahue looked away. "Particularly shocking because he was a friend of the Langsom family."

"Well, I'm sorry to say the team hasn't found anyone else inside. That root cellar in your backyard is, for all intents and purposes, incinerated. We'll get down there as soon as we can. Heck of a shame."

My father spoke up then. "Ned McGovern. Someone should inform his wife."

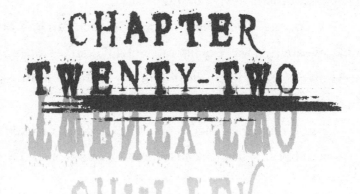

CHAPTER
TWENTY-TWO

If the firemen were shocked at the unveiling of the Sentry, they didn't show it. In the weeks and months that followed, nobody showed it. That's the thing about towns like Glennon Heights—we circle up around our own. Mrs. McGovern had fled often enough to her parents' house in Delaware that no one blinked when she up and left for good as soon as his body was found. No one blinked and no one blamed her.

People talked more after the Donahues moved. Probably because they felt guilty. They hadn't believed them. They had judged too harshly. In the weeks after the explosion, Mr. Donahue turned down all interview requests. He asked

Officer Wycoff to escort one of the more persistent news magazines off our street. He even nailed a sign to the front door: *Please respect my family's need for privacy.*

At first I made a game of giving the press something to work with. I sat in old Halloween costumes on our front steps. Mostly I was bored, but also it entertained Miss Abbot. She tried to talk the *New York News* into interviewing Horatio, the cat.

For months, the media didn't seem to understand that the Donahues didn't live on Olcott anymore. They lived at an extended-stay hotel and then left right before winter break. At first they said they couldn't live in the house because it was structurally unsound. But Janie told me it was easier to fall asleep in a hotel room. She said, "At least there's supposed to be other people in a hotel."

I've spent a lot of time thinking about Ned McGovern and ways that people can be structurally unsound. And then how other people somehow possess a surprising strength, as if they've got solid wooden beams braced above their hearts. Sometimes Jillian and I sit quietly together in the dugout and I know we're both wondering what happened to little Teddy to cause so much damage at his core.

And sometimes I go to the baseball field alone. Sometimes I run. Sometime I sneak out at night and bring along the mitt that I tried to give back to Ben, the one he made me keep. I knew when they moved, the Donahues were gone for me too.

Janie and I lied. We said we would text, but I remembered what she'd said about her old friends and how pointless it seemed to hang on. I knew there would be a girl in the next town on whom Janie would come crashing down. I would keep floating along in Glennon Heights, where everyone seemed to know me.

//////////

Ben showed up on my front stoop his last night in town. I was dressed for a run and my dad must have seen him on his way in from work. But he didn't stop me from going out. He let me walk out there and find Ben sitting with the baseball glove beside him.

"The thing is," he said, "I believe in goodbyes."

"You barely believe in anything, but you believe in good-byes?" I asked.

"I believe in lots of things."

"Name one thing that's not an eighties movie or pop culture phenomenon." I was jogging by then but he refused to run, so I just had to awkwardly jog circles around him as we made our way up the street. It helped to have a distraction.

"I believe in the power of a good game of catch."

"Yeah," I said. "Okay."

"But it's got to be a well-matched game of catch."

"I know what you mean." I slowed to a walk. I felt the cotton of the sleeve of my T-shirt brush up against the sleeve of his T-shirt. I didn't always know what to make of people but I heard how Ben said my name differently from anyone else's name. I hadn't merely invented the way his eyes slid to me every time he made a joke, each moment he had a reason to feel proud. I knew Ben liked me. But I also knew he wouldn't let that matter.

"The thing is, Livvie, you're really good at catch. I want you to keep that mitt and make sure when you throw, it's to a person who deserves—"

"Okay." I cut him off then and picked up my pace. I held up the glove and clutched it to my heart, recognizing it for the treasure that it was. "I get it." I nodded to him.

"That's it?" Ben asked. "Okay?" At first his face wrinkled with worry and then it broke open in wonder. In that moment I was the coolest girl he'd ever met.

"That's it." I took a deep breath, the kind I always did right before sprinting on the last block home. "Goodbye, Ben Donahue," I said and ran fast enough that he could not see me cry.

////////////

In my bedroom closet, I keep a wooden crate. Just inside my ordinary closet—it's not a closet behind a closet or anything. That's where I store Ben's baseball mitt. I have some newspaper clippings too both from that summer and after that summer. And at the very bottom, I have Teddy McGovern's artifacts wrapped in the old Boy Scout kerchief.

I still sometimes need to spread the crate's contents out

on my bedspread. I arrange those fragments in a way that makes some kind of sense. I convince myself that it all actually happened. Eventually though, I'll bring the collection to the library and see if that librarian wants any of it for the local lore room. There are plenty of people who have heard of Glennon Heights, who stop by to look at a yearbook photo or old newspaper clippings.

I used to mind that, but now it seems right that in a town like ours, there should be a place we might go to visit the past.

 ACKNOWLEDGMENTS

Love and gratitude to the Corrigan, McKay, and Ryden families, as well as Anne Glennon, Steve Loy, and Pat Neary. I have been writing for most of my life now and feel profoundly lucky for so many years of their encouragement and steadfast support.

Thank you to Cormac and Maeve, who I hope will one day understand why their mom sometimes focuses so ferociously on her laptop. And to Rose Abondio, Rob Franzmann, and Ella Nowak, who have shown us that families grow in all kinds of ways.

I am grateful for my friends, especially those who helped talk through this book and all its sinister possibilities: Joe Chodl, Hannah Garrow, Elijah Kaufman, Stacy McMillen, Billy Merrell, Mark Nastus, Sara Nardulli, Sherry Riggi, Denise Ryan, Meredith Santowasso, and Nina Stotler.

Every day and every page, I count myself lucky to work with David Levithan and his team of wizards at Scholastic.

Finally, I spend my days at Rutgers Preparatory School, surrounded by remarkable characters. While no aspect of this book is based on individuals or events on campus, our exceptional community inspires me every day.

ABOUT THE AUTHOR

Eireann Corrigan's novels for YA readers include *Accomplice*, *The Believing Game*, *Ordinary Ghosts*, and *Splintering*. She is also the author of the acclaimed YA memoir *You Remind Me of You*. She lives in New Jersey in a house that she hopes remains unhaunted.